MIDDLE SCHOOL MAGIC

# THE
# KINDLING

# PRAISE FOR *THE KINDLING*

"*The Kindling* is fun and well-written. I enjoyed reading it."
—J. SCOTT SAVAGE, *author of*
*the Case File 13 series and Farworld series*

"*The Kindling* is an exciting blend of imaginative magic and intrigue. . . . The different powers the children possess and how they are applied [are] fascinating and the characters have broad appeal. The story clips along at a lightning pace, and the conclusion left me hoping for the next installment."
—MICHAEL YOUNG, *author of*
The Canticle Kingdom *and* The Last Archangel

"*The Kindling—(kin-dling) n. 1. Easily ignited material 2. Courageous students who recognize the magic within and fight the forces of evil.*

Every middle school student needs to experience *The Kindling*! Page-turning adventure, wit, humor, love, evil stalkers, inner magic, spontaneously combusting gym shorts, and most important HEROES—*The Kindling* is sure to inspire and entertain."
—STEVE WESTOVER, *author of*
Crater Lake: Battle for Wizard Island

"The battle between light and dark, good and evil, has never been told like Braden Bell tells it, for his narrative sparkles with inventive images. The mental picture of dark forces running amok in Disney's Small World ride is priceless, and that's only one of the exciting situations that Conner, Lexa, and Melanie find themselves in after kindling."

—LIZ ADAIR, *author of*
Cold River *and* The Mist of Quarry Harbor

"I adore Braden's storytelling style! Smart, funny, and inventive, *The Kindling* will draw in even the most reluctant of young readers with inspiring characters and a story packed full of action and intrigue. Loved this one!"

—RACHEL RENEE ANDERSON,
*author of* Minor Adjustments

MIDDLE SCHOOL MAGIC

THE
KINDLING

BRADEN BELL

SWEETWATER BOOKS,
AN IMPRINT OF CEDAR FORT, INC.
SPRINGVILLE, UTAH

ISBN 13: 978-1-4621-1027-8

Published by Sweetwater Books, an imprint of Cedar Fort, Inc.
2373 W. 700 S., Springville, UT 84663
Distributed by Cedar Fort, Inc., www.cedarfort.com

LIBRARY OF CONGRESS CATALOGING-IN-PUBLICATION DATA

Bell, Braden, author.
The kindling / Braden Bell.
pages cm
Summary: When unusual powers kindle inside them, Conner, Lexa, and Melanie discover that their teachers are powerful magi too and the students are exhilarated to add fighting evil to their daily classes--until the dark forces of the Umbra kidnap Melanie's young sister as part of a grotesque experiment.
ISBN 978-1-4621-1027-8 (alk. paper)
[1. Magic--Fiction 2. Kidnapping--Fiction. 3. Middle schools--Fiction.] I. Title.


PZ7.B3889145Kin 2012
[Fic]--dc23

2012011285

Cover design by Angela D. Olsen
Cover design © 2012 by Lyle Mortimer
Edited and typeset by Melissa J. Caldwell

Printed in the United States of America

10  9  8  7  6  5  4  3  2  1

Printed on acid-free paper

To Vickle, with gratitude and love.

And to my students and colleagues at Harding Academy. Thank you for the laughter, love, and learning.

# CONTENTS

# Author's Note

WRITERS WRITE WHAT THEY KNOW. SINCE I spend my days teaching middle school in a wonderful school, it is inevitable that some of what I have experienced over the years will seep into my writing. But the characters in this book are unique. Some of their mannerisms or personality traits may have been inspired early on by people I've known, but they look, talk, and act differently than any real students or teachers at my school. They are creatures of my imagination, and this is particularly true for Dr. Timberi. While I'll admit to some similarities in appearance, he is not me. Although, I would love to be him.

# CHAPTER 1

# STRANGE THINGS

CONNER DELL DIDN'T MEAN TO SET ANYone's gym shorts on fire.

He didn't know it would happen—he didn't know it *could* happen. And if he had known, he never would have—well, that might be going too far. It started in seventh period science.

✳ ✳ ✳

"All right, people, careful getting those Bunsen burners lit," Mr. Keller said. "Nothing ruins my day like a seventh grader on fire. Requires all kinds of paperwork, which will make me the grumpiest teacher in Nashville."

Conner flicked the lighter and watched the spark jump into the stream of gas.

The spark stretched into a flame, swaying on the Bunsen burner like a dizzy hula dancer. Conner's friend Pilaf plugged his nose. "I hate that smell—ouch!" Pilaf jumped out of his seat, knocking his textbook to the floor with a thud.

"What's wrong?" Conner asked.

"Nothing," Pilaf muttered.

"Look up here, people." Mr. Keller used giant tweezers to stick a chunk of rock in the flame of his Bunsen burner. "The color of the flame tells us—"

"Ouch!" Pilaf jumped again and rubbed the back of his skinny pencil neck.

"Mr. Larson, is something wrong?" Mr. Keller's red mustache magnified his frown.

"No, sir," Pilaf said in his squeaky voice.

Mr. Keller shifted his frown to Conner. "Mr. Dell, are you causing problems?"

"No, sir." *Why do teachers always think I'm causing the trouble?*

"Glad to hear it. As I was saying, the color of the smoke tells us this mineral is calcite . . ." Mr. Keller returned to his burning rock, and Conner focused on the experiment. But when Pilaf jumped again, Conner got curious and glanced backward.

What he saw sparked a bonfire of anger in his gut. Geoffrey Anderson sat at the table behind them. Geoffrey always managed to look like a black-haired, blow-dried weasel trying to sneer while inhaling raw sewage. At the moment, he was smirking while barbecuing a paper clip in the flame of his Bunsen burner. After a few seconds, when the metal glowed red hot, he threw it at Pilaf's neck. Pilaf jumped, and Geoffrey and his friends laughed.

*Jerk!* Conner turned around to confront him, but Pilaf grabbed his arm and shook his head. He didn't say anything, but Conner understood. In seventh grade, some things are more important than first-degree burns.

"Mr. Anderson, stop messing around with the Bunsen burner." Mr. Keller's voice ended Geoffrey's bring-your-own-bully barbecue, and Pilaf didn't jump or wince again.

Still, Conner's anger simmered for the rest of the class, crackling just below the surface. When he got to PE, he tapped into the rage, letting it drive his laps around the gym. Lacrosse try-outs were coming up and he needed Coach to see how fast he could go. Faster and faster, his legs pounded the floor as he flew past the rest of the class. Past Pilaf. Past his twin sister, Lexa. Past her friend Melanie—he swallowed as his heart did a backflip. Past Geoffrey—something tugged at his feet. Conner caught a blurry glimpse of Geoffrey's retreating shoe, then cannon-balled into the floor, and rolled across the gym.

"You okay, Dell?" Coach Jackson jog-waddled over.

"Yes, sir," he gasped.

"All right, catch your breath, then return to your laps." Coach Jackson shuffled back to the middle of the room. Across the gym, Conner noticed Pilaf, gasping and flailing through his laps. As Pilaf staggered forward, Geoffrey slowed down and let Pilaf pass him. He shot his elbow out, launching Pilaf into a tangled roll of knobby elbows and skinny, white, chicken legs. As Pilaf rolled, Geoffrey laughed until he couldn't run anymore. He stopped and leaned against the wall by an old heater.

*Freaking jerk!* Conner's pulse pounded. Picking on a helpless, harmless thing like Pilaf was mean, even by the low standards of middle school. Conner wanted something bad to happen to Geoffrey. Something specially and memorably bad. Something humiliating and possibly painful. He saw the heater behind Geoffrey and remembered an old cartoon where a character's pants caught on fire. *How awesome would that be?* He laughed at the thought, walked over to Pilaf, and held out his arm.

"You okay?"

Pilaf ignored Conner's hand. He pulled himself to his feet and squinted up through strands of stringy, blond hair. "Yeah, thanks."

Loud shrieks sliced the air, followed by the smell of burning cloth. Conner looked over in time to see Geoffrey jumping up and down, yelling and shrieking. Smoke poured from the seat of his shorts while blue and yellow sparks snapped, crackled, and popped all around the heater.

Coach Jackson ran over and covered him with the contents of a fire extinguisher. "You okay, Anderson? You're seriously lucky these shorts are fire retardant. No burns. Anderson? Anderson? You look like you're going into shock, son. I'm taking him to the nurse's office. The rest of you get back to your laps—and stay away from this heating unit. Let's go!"

Everyone went back to running laps, but, deep down, something nagged at Conner.

*Okay, that was really weird. Did I—no way! That's crazy. Total coincidence. Freak accident.*

*Right?*

Later that night, in the Dells' dining room, Conner's sister, Lexa, stared at her history book and tugged on her ponytail. She looked up at Conner and Melanie and tried to focus, but March was throwing a temper tantrum of a storm. The lightning flashed so often that the night sky seemed light with a few flickers of occasional darkness instead of the other way around, and it looked as though heaven were blasting the street with her dad's pressure washer.

A huge crash of thunder shook the house, and a flash of lightning seemed to set the whole room on fire.

Lexa dropped her book. "Okay, that was giantly huge!"

"Giantly isn't a word, Lexa," Melanie said. "Plus, huge means giant, so you're just repeating yourself."

"I like *giantly*." Lexa shrugged. "It's what I'm thinking."

"You and your weird adverbs." Melanie looked back at her book and scrunched her nose. "So, the Ninth Amendment says—"

Another blinding flash of light struck nearby, almost in the dining room.

Melanie's phone chirped and she picked it up. "Hello?" She listened. "Yes, ma'am." She put the phone down. "My mom's almost here, and she wants me waiting for her." She closed her book, pulled her stuff into a neat pile, and squirted hand sanitizer all over her hands. "See you tomorrow, Lexa. Bye, Conner."

Conner didn't look up, but his skin flushed a shade darker. "See you, Melanie."

"I'll wait with you, Mel." Lexa stood, and they walked to the porch. The storm was fierce enough that no one else was out, and there were no cars on the road.

A flash of lightning blinded them and thunder punched their ears. A humming noise filled the air and every outside light on the street exploded one after another: boom, boom, boom! Sparks sizzled and fizzled, and shards of shattered glass from the porch light shot at the girls. Lexa threw her hands up to protect her face and yelled, "No!"

From behind her hands, Lexa saw another flash. She winced and waited for the glass to hit her, but nothing ever came. She peeked through her fingers and saw the sharp pieces on the ground, several feet away.

*Weird*, Lexa thought. *Did the wind change?*

The inside lights went out now, house by house, smothering the neighborhood in complete darkness.

A loud tearing noise ripped through the air followed by another explosion of thunder.

"Okay, this is not a normal storm." Lexa shivered in the darkness. "It's like it's angry or something. How long's it been going on, anyway?"

"Um, I don't think storms can be angry," Melanie said. "But this is a really bad one."

A pair of headlights drove around the corner, piercing the darkness. "Okay, there's my mom," Melanie said.

As the car turned the corner, the lights caught a man standing in the middle of the street halfway down the block. His immense black coat flapped while the wind whipped, blowing his long hair.

"Mel—look at that guy!" Lexa grabbed Melanie's arm.

The darkness seemed thicker and heavier near him, as if the light from the car was scared to get too close.

"Creepy! Where did he come from?" Melanie asked as her mother pulled into the driveway. "Glad we don't have to wait out here anymore. Bye, Lexa!"

Melanie ran to the minivan, and a moment later, she and her mother drove away.

Lexa turned to go inside her house, but she couldn't. Some kind of power radiated out from the man, drawing her to him, even though she wanted to look away. He made her feel queasy and nauseated inside, but she was frozen.

"Lexa!" Mrs. Dell opened the door, and her voice broke Lexa's connection with the man. "Come in before you blow away!"

"Yes, ma'am." Lexa walked in, and her mom pushed the door shut behind them.

Mrs. Dell had covered every flat surface with candles, so the house flickered and glowed. It smelled like a street fight between the rose and cinnamon gangs.

"Lexa, can you please take some candles upstairs? To your room, Conner's, and maybe the bathroom?"

"Yeah, Mom."

"Thanks, Lexa. Hey, remind me to talk to Dr. Timberi tomorrow about starting some singing and acting lessons. I keep forgetting." She gave Lexa three candles and a small box of matches, and Lexa started upstairs, walking as fast as she could. She shuddered. The darkness seemed heavy and hungry . . . alive.

She put the candle in her bedroom window, striking the match and watching the candle flicker to life.

Framed by the window, the flame looked brave somehow—a tiny, lonely light dancing against the darkness.

Outside, the man still stood on the street looking up and down the block. He strode to the curb and then walked across the front lawns, pausing to stare at each house. The dogs in the neighborhood barked and howled over the noise of the storm. They sounded scared, mad, and then scared again.

When he faced Lexa's house, her room grew cold. The candle choked and sputtered.

*Please don't go out,* Lexa thought, but it died anyway. For some reason, she wanted the light to stay between her and the man. *Stay lit!*

The flame sparked and flashed back to life, pushing against the darkness.

The man jerked his head up and stared at her window. She squealed and turned around to call her mom, but something stopped her. An urgent thought and a powerful feeling shouted inside of her at the same time. *Don't say anything! Do NOT tell her! Something bad will happen.*

The dogs howled even louder, more urgent and fearful.

The man made a chopping motion in the air, and waves of darkness rippled through the night.

All the dogs stopped barking.

Lexa's candle went out.

# CHAPTER 2

# WEIRDER AND WEIRDER

THE NEXT MORNING, LEXA WOKE UP AND smiled at the sun streaming through her window. *Much better*, she thought. She showered and went downstairs, where her mom was watching the morning news.

"Mom—"

"Shhh!" Mrs. Dell waved her hand and turned the volume up.

". . . autopsies carried out this morning suggest the dogs all died at the same time and from natural causes. Both inside and outside dogs were affected. Veterinarians are unable to explain the simultaneous death of such large numbers—"

"What happened?" Lexa asked.

Mrs. Dell turned the TV off. "It's the strangest thing. They don't know why, but last night, every dog in this part of Nashville died."

Lexa froze—hot nausea simmered inside her. *Was it that man?* "Every dog? Are you serious?"

Mrs. Dell shook her head. "It's just disgusting that someone would do that."

Lexa almost said something but again felt an overwhelming feeling telling her she shouldn't.

Several short, precise honks interrupted her.

"Gotta go, Mom." Lexa grabbed her backpack and dashed into the hallway, where Conner thundered down the stairs. Together, they ran out to the driveway.

Inside the minivan, Melanie watched Conner and Lexa run out.

"Three honks—I think that's a world record for Lexa," Mrs. Stephens said as the car door opened. "Good morning, Lexa."

"Hi, Mrs. Stephens." Lexa dropped her backpack in the aisle and threw herself in the seat next to Melanie. Conner stowed his lacrosse gear in the back, then scaled Lexa's backpack and dropped down next to her. "Hi, Melanie. Hey, Madi." He smiled at Melanie's little sister in the middle row. "What's that?" His dimple winked as he pointed to the shoebox buckled in the seat belt next to Madi.

"It's my endangered species diorama. It's a very important project," Madi replied in solemn tones.

"Oh, yeah, I remember doing that when I was in first grade. Mine wasn't that good."

*He's so good with kids*, Melanie thought.

In the front seat, Mrs. Stephens turned the radio on.

"Investigators are still baffled by the unprecedented death of so many dogs . . ."

"What'd they say? What happened?" Conner asked.

"Every dog in this part of Nashville died mysteriously last night," Lexa said. She dropped her voice to a whisper. "Mel, remember that guy we saw last night? I bet he did it."

Melanie shivered, remembering how the man had made her feel dirty icicles in her spirit. "I don't know, Lexa. My mom said there wasn't any poison or injuries. How could he have killed them?"

Lexa shrugged. "Just a feeling. I watched him after you left, and he was just really—I don't know—weird, evil, something. The dogs were going crazy while he walked across the lawns. Then they got quiet. He was a stalker or something."

"You watched him, Lexa?" Conner asked.

"Yeah. From my window."

"Awesome. So you, like, stalked the stalker!" He gave her a high five, and they all laughed, pushing away some of the weirdness of dead dogs and stalkers.

Mrs. Stephens pulled up into the long driveway that circled several red brick buildings. Large letters on an ivy-covered wall said, "Marion Academy." She pulled toward the back of a double line of cars and stopped.

A tall man with a whistle presided at the top of the line. His hair was a mixture of black and gray, a duet with the gray singing louder. His perfectly pressed tan slacks, brown sweater vest, and white shirt erupted into a red and gold bow tie around his neck.

"That's weird." Melanie sat up straighter in her seat. "Has Dr. Timberi been in charge of drop-off before?"

Lexa tugged on her ponytail and shrugged. "I've never seen him out here before—maybe he's just filling in or something."

In the front seat, Melanie's mother rolled her window down as Dr. Timberi walked past the car. Melanie, Conner, and Lexa each sat straighter and stopped talking.

"Good morning, Morgan," she said.

"And a good morning to you, Elise," he said in a milk chocolate voice.

"Have you recovered from the play yet?" Mrs. Stephens asked. "Melanie's still going to bed early."

"I believe I'm almost there. Another week and I shall be back at full strength—just in time to hold auditions for the next one."

"Well, thanks for all your work. We enjoyed the performance so much. Melanie had a wonderful experience, and Cathy Dell told me that Conner and Lexa haven't stopped talking about it."

"That's very kind, Elise. They certainly did very good work—" Someone in the line of cars honked. Dr. Timberi's eyebrows flirted with a furrow, and he glared toward the noise. "Excuse me, I need to make sure everyone has stopped before I blow the whistle. Good morning, Elise." He walked with brisk, king-like strides back up the line of cars.

"I don't know why you're all are so scared of Dr. Timberi," Mrs. Stephens said. "He's always very nice when I talk to him."

"He's just so strict and scary," Melanie said.

"He's so—I don't know—cold. Like, no feelings at all," Lexa added.

"Yeah," Conner said. "He could totally slit your throat with his conductor's stick and not even blink."

Dr. Timberi blew the whistle a few seconds later, and students flooded out of their cars. Lexa and Melanie were immersed in a conversation by the time they got to the curb, so Melanie didn't notice Zach McDowell sneak up behind her. He made a buzzing noise and jabbed each side of her waist with pointy fingers. She screamed and jumped—like she always did.

"Taser!" Zach laughed.

"Zach! Stop it, that's—" She turned to glare at him, but as she turned, something across the street hijacked her attention. She froze.

"What's wrong, Mel?" Lexa asked.

"Across the street," she whispered. Instead of a pulse, it felt like wounded butterflies fluttered in her veins.

Lexa strangled a loud squeal and grabbed her ponytail. "Is that—ohmigosh, it is!"

"Why are you squeaking like a chew toy, Lex?" Conner stepped beside them.

"Remember the freakily scary guy I told you about on the street last night?" Lexa squealed again. "Look over there."

Melanie watched as a slow frown rolled across Conner's face. She looked again too.

A man stood in the park across from the school, shrouded in a long, black coat. Long, wild strands of dark hair made his head look like it was unraveling. He stared at them, beetle-black eyes boring into their souls.

"Whoa. He is pretty scary looking," Conner said.

"What are you guys looking at?" Zach poked his head between them.

"Look how creepy that guy is." Melanie jerked her head toward the man.

"What guy?" Zach squinted.

Melanie rolled her eyes. "Hello, Zach! That guy across the street. By the tree."

Zach squinted, then shrugged. "Okay, okay, you got me. I almost believed you for a minute." He walked away.

The man's stare grew fiercer and more intense, as if he were trying to yank the spirits from their bodies. Melanie felt a tug deep inside. She pulled back mentally, but he pulled harder, and soon their souls locked in a tug-of-war.

Unfortunately, he was stronger, and she felt her right foot step forward, moving toward him. She fought it, but her left leg took a step too. Her brain screamed at her feet to stop, but each leg took another step. Next to her, Conner's face burned bright red. He grunted and his body shook, trying to resist. He took half a step. Lexa twitched and jerked, trying to fight the pull, but the stalker had wrapped them with invisible chains. They struggled and groaned but stepped forward again.

"What're you doing?" Pilaf walked up to them. The invisible chains broke, and the pull disappeared.

"Look away!" Melanie gasped, and they all turned around.

"What are you guys doing?" Pilaf repeated.

"We thought we saw something in the park," Conner said. "Do you see anything?"

"Yeah." Pilaf squinted through his glasses. Then he shook his head. "Wait. Nope, sorry. I thought I did but—oh snap! I've got to see Mr. Duffy before school. Bye, guys." He scuttled away, crablike under the shell of his massive backpack.

"Pilaf wouldn't lie." Conner raised his eyebrows. "Are we the only ones who can see him?"

Melanie took a deep breath and pushed her anxiety back inside its normal boundaries. "This is like the beginning of one of those stalker horror movies. We need to tell someone."

"What would we say?" Conner asked. "That there's a weird guy no one can see?"

"He's right, Mel—there's nothing we can say." Lexa remembered her feeling about not telling anyone.

"Is anything wrong?" Dr. Timberi's deep voice rolled over them, and they turned to face him.

Melanie opened her mouth, but Conner and Lexa shook their heads. She hesitated, then turned on a sunny smile. "No, sir."

The bell rang.

"First bell—gotta go! Bye, Dr. Timberi." Lexa pushed Melanie inside, and they went to their lockers, where Lexa unzipped her backpack and dumped the contents inside. She then paced the hall while Melanie placed each book in her locker organizer.

"Hurry, Mel, we'll be late to English."

"Just a minute—you know I like them in a certain order."

Lexa tugged her ponytail and rolled her eyes. "You are so OCD!"

Melanie shut her locker, squeezed a generous blob of hand sanitizer onto her hands, and grabbed a three-ring binder. They sprinted into the classroom across the hall and dropped into their seats as the second bell rang.

Mrs. Grant marched to the front of the classroom, sensible shoes tapping a brisk march on the carpet. Her short, mouse-brown hair hung a respectable distance above her white sweater and the stiff, tweed skirt formed a shield against middle school silliness. She looked grim, like an early Christian preparing to face the lions. She sighed and waved a thick stack of papers in the air.

"Now, ya'll." Her southern accent fought a constant battle with her proper English teacher voice. "I've got your *poim* analyses here, and I'm so disappointed. Seventh graders ought to be doing much better work than this, especially by the spring.

"For example"—she squeezed her lips into a single, thin line and brandished a paper decorated with red ink— "Mr. Dell, you said Frost's poem *Stopping in the Woods on a Snowy Evening* was about a serial killer hiding from the police." She grimaced, and everyone laughed, which made her grimace more.

"I'm returning these, and I want you to spend the next twenty minutes revising them. Ask for help if you must, but don't just make it into a joke." Mrs. Grant started returning the papers but was interrupted as a sobbing, wispy, blonde girl flitted in.

"Sorry I'm late." Laura Dalton's shoulders shook, and her lips trembled. "My d-d-dog!" She gasped for breath. "My d-d-d-dog d-d-died last n-n-n-n-n-night!" Torrential tears flooded her words away.

Mrs. Grant patted Laura's shoulder with stiff, awkward fingers. "Yes, I saw the *nyews*. I'm sorry, Miss Dalton. Why don't you go to the ladies' room and wash your face." She steered Laura to the doorway and continued returning papers.

"Laura's such a drama queen," Lexa whispered to Melanie. "But today I actually feel bad for her. I still think that guy on the street had something to do with it. And why was he here today—is he following us? And who dresses like that? I mean, hello! All that black? Is he six months late for a Halloween party?" Lexa's voice rose louder than she realized.

Conner, who was behind Lexa, cleared his throat and jerked his head backward. Melanie noticed it and looked over her shoulder. Mrs. Grant stood there, peering down over her glasses. "Miss Dell, did I hear something about a strange man following you?"

Melanie froze. She felt grateful Mrs. Grant asked Lexa, not her. She would have stammered and burst into tears before telling everything.

Lexa, on the other hand, didn't skip a beat. "No, ma'am," she replied. "We were just kidding."

"Are you sure, Lexa? This could be important."

"Yes, ma'am." She smiled at Mrs. Grant and looked her straight in the eye.

Mrs. Grant stared at Lexa for several seconds. Lexa met her stare without blinking.

"I see." Mrs. Grant finally walked away and finished handing out the papers. "Now, ya'll, I want some serious thought for the next twenty minutes." She walked back to her desk and tapped something on her keyboard.

"I'm glad that was you," Melanie said. "I'm so bad at lying."

"Why would she care?" Lexa asked. "And it's acting, not lying."

"It's lying, and I don't know," Melanie replied, "maybe

she's upset about the dogs. I mean, she's way into recycling and birds and stuff—"

"Miss Stephens! People are trying to work." Mrs. Grant's voice shot through the classroom.

About two minutes later, Dr. Timberi stepped into the room. "Mrs. Grant? I apologize for disturbing you, but I received your email."

"Yes, Dr. Timberi. Thank you for coming so quickly." He walked to her desk, where they began to whisper.

Melanie tried to focus on the assignment, but her analysis paper made her brain feel fluffy. She took a break and stared at the pictures and posters on the wall. As her eyes sauntered from Harper Lee to Robert Frost, she noticed Mrs. Grant and Dr. Timberi staring in her direction. At least, she thought they were.

*Calm down, Melanie,* she thought. *Why would they be looking at you? Relax. You're just being paranoid.*

She looked away, counted to ten, and then looked back.

*They really* are *looking at me!* She took a deep breath, then dropped her pen on the floor by Lexa's foot. She bent over to pick it up and tapped Lexa's shoe.

Lexa dropped her pen too and bent down to pick it up as well.

"Dr. Timberi and Mrs. Grant are staring at me," Melanie whispered when their heads were nearly touching. "They're talking about me."

"Are you sure you're not just doing your paranoid thing?"

"No! I swear they're talking about me."

"Okay." Lexa grinned. "Sneaky skills to the rescue. I'll see what I can find out."

Lexa sat up, tapped her pen on her desk, and frowned. She sunk her chin in her hand, sighed loudly, and looked into space. After a minute of this, she stood up and walked to Mrs. Grant's desk, where she managed to eavesdrop for six seconds before Mrs. Grant looked up.

"Yes, Miss Dell?"

"I don't get what this line means."

"I'll be with you in a few minutes, Miss Dell. Return to your seat."

"Yes, ma'am." Lexa walked back to her desk and knocked Melanie's textbook over. They both bent down to pick it up.

"They're talking about us. And the dogs," Lexa whispered. "They're way interested in the dogs. Mrs. Grant said, 'Measures must be taken immediately.' And Dr. Timberi said something about a sodality. What's a sodality?"

"I don't know. What did she mean by 'measures must be taken?' Do you think they're trying to hurt us—"

"Miss Stephens! Miss Dell! People are trying to work." Melanie took a deep breath and tried to focus on her poem.

Fifteen minutes passed. Then twenty. Thirty. Dr. Timberi and Mrs. Grant talked for the rest of the class period. When the bell rang, Mrs. Grant looked up long enough to say, "Please put your revised assignments on the desk closest to the door. Neatly!"

When everyone else walked out, Melanie stayed behind and gathered her books for as long as she could, hoping to hear more of the discussion.

"Very well, Carol," Dr. Timberi said. "You let the others know. I will keep watch for now." He marched out of the room.

Mrs. Grant's fingers clicked as she typed another email. Melanie sneaked up behind her and saw the subject line: "URGENT—DELL TWINS AND STEPHENS."

Backing away, she ran out of the room. Her pulse was racing as her stomach churned with seasick butterflies.

# CHAPTER 3

# ꓥWKWARD ꓢILEꓠCES

**N**OTHING ELSE STRANGE HAPPENED FOR the next two periods. The three of them met up outside the choir room, followed their classmates inside, and took their places.

Dr. Timberi raised his eyebrows, and the room grew silent. "Good morning, little cherubs." One corner of his mouth twisted up, and his voice was as dry as last year's Christmas tree. "Just a reminder—your composer research papers are due today."

Conner gulped and raised his hand.

"Yes, Mr. Dell?"

"Uh, sorry, I left mine in my locker. Can I go get it?"

"Very well." Conner wilted a bit under Dr. Timberi's famous glare. "But please be quick," Dr. Timberi said.

Conner walked out of the room and bumped into Madame Cumberland, the French teacher. Her silvery hair was swept up in a wavy bun with several strands trying to escape. Her jewelry clanked softly, and her perfume shouted something about purple flowers.

"Bonjour, Conner!" Everything she said sounded like a hug. "What are you doing?"

"Oh, hi, Madame Cumberland. I'm going to my locker to get an assignment for Dr. Timberi."

"Well, isn't that nice? I'm going that way too. Is this the research paper Dr. Timberi assigned you all?"

"Yes, ma'am."

"Which composer did you study?"

"Irving Berlin."

"Oh, isn't that wonderful! You know, I'd love to hear more. May I walk with you?" She beamed as if Conner were a litter of cute puppies.

*Madame Cumberland is way nice, but is she really interested in my report on Irving Berlin?*

"Uh, sure." Conner felt a little claustrophobic as she followed him to his locker and back to the choir room. She chatted the whole time in a bright voice and didn't leave until the door closed behind him.

He turned his paper in and sat through the rest of choir, unable to get rid of the feeling that the walls seemed a little closer.

When the bell finally ended choir, Conner waited for Melanie and Lexa, and they started walking to the lunchroom.

"Excuse me, Mr. Dell?" Dr. Timberi popped up out of nowhere.

"Uh, yes, sir?"

"Keep walking. I would not want you to be late to lunch," he said, matching Conner's stride. "I spoke with Coach Jackson yesterday. We agreed that you may audition for the next play and still be on the lacrosse team. There will be only a few weeks of overlap, and we can be flexible during that time. The benefit of a small, private school, I suppose."

"Thanks," Conner said as the noise of the lunchroom devoured the conversation.

Dr. Timberi left, and the three of them got their food and went to their regular table. Conner frowned.

"What's wrong?" Lexa asked.

"I don't know," he said. "But I feel like the teachers are sort of everywhere—I mean, like they're following me."

Melanie frowned and scrunched her nose. "I know I'm always being paranoid, but I kind of thought the same thing. No matter where I've gone today, there was a teacher right there. Really awkward."

Conner nodded. "I left history to get a drink. There was Coach Jackson. Back to my locker during choir and Madame Cumberland wants to discuss Irving Berlin, and you just heard that whole thing with Dr. Timberi."

Lexa waved her hands. "When I left art to use the bathroom, Dr. Timberi was in the hallway, and in pre-algebra I had to go get a band-aid from the office, and Mrs. Grant was going the exact same way—and then back again."

"Should we tell someone?" Melanie looked at Conner with brown eyes that sparkled like root beer.

"Well . . ." His train of thought ran off the track. He looked away for a minute, and it came back. "What would we say? 'Hey, Mom, last night there was a guy in our neighborhood no one can see, and today at school there were teachers all over the place.' Yeah, things are a little weird, but what would we say?"

Silence dropped over the table.

"Awk-ward," Conner said.

"Guys." Lexa's voice was quiet and almost shy, which got everyone's attention. "Last night I was going to tell Mom about the stalker guy. But I had a thought—no, it was more like a thought and a feeling at the same time. I *thought* something in my mind and *felt* it in my heart. Anyways—"

"Hey, guys?" Pilaf's head popped out from behind one of the pillars by the table.

Seeing him sparked Conner's memory of Pilaf's first day at Marion Academy. Pilaf had moved to the school in second grade. Their teacher, Mrs. Buchanan, started every day by leading the Pledge and reading the lunch menu. One day, she looked down over her pointy-edged glasses and said, "Boys and girls, today we'll be having meatloaf, mixed vegetables, and rice pilaf."

The class had never heard the word *pilaf* before, and it seemed hysterically funny. They repeated "pilaf" every time they could, dissolving in overwhelming, paralyzing fits of little-kid laughter whenever someone said it.

Pilaf—who's real name was Olaf—moved in the next day. "Class, this is Olaf," Mrs. Buchanan said.

"What?" Geoffrey stifled a smirk and forced his face into a fake puzzled expression. "Did you say his name is"—he paused for dramatic effect—"Pilaf?"

The whole class erupted in laughter, and the name "Pilaf" stuck. By seventh grade, it wasn't funny any-more—it was just his name.

Pilaf blinked twice and squinted again. "Can I sit by you guys?"

"Sure," Conner said.

"Hey, Pilaf." Melanie stared at him. "Are your glasses broken?"

"I, uh, slipped." He looked down at his fried catfish.

"Pilaf," Conner growled. "Did you maybe slip on Geoffrey's foot or something?"

"It might have been an accident." Pilaf sounded a lot like Piglet from *Winnie the Pooh.*

Suspicious, Conner looked across the cafeteria. Geoffrey and his buddies sat at their table, laughing. Geoffrey made circles with his fingers and held them up in front of his eyes like glasses. He blinked and squinted while one of his friends pretended to shove him in the face.

Bubbles of white-hot anger popped in Conner's head. He growled and pounded the table with his fist. The lights flashed, and across the cafeteria, Geoffrey's food exploded all over his face, as if an invisible fist had smashed into his food.

"Conner . . ." Melanie's voice quivered. "Did you—?"

"Did I what?" Conner's tone was sharp. He felt jittery and jumpy, disoriented and hot all over. *Did I do that? Seriously? No way. No freaking way. What's going on?* He swallowed, pushing back against the panic that was boiling up in the back of his throat.

"Nothing." Melanie shook her head. "Nothing."

There was another awkward silence that Lexa finally broke with a squeal.

"Oh no! It's Tuesday! I've got science next, and I forgot my homework. Again. Keller's going to kill me. And then Mom will kill me all over again for getting a bad grade."

She groaned. "I wish Mr. Keller would go home sick or something!"

"Lexa!" Melanie's brown eyes got big. "That's mean."

"Well," Lexa muttered, "not very sick. Just enough to make him go home and sleep it off."

The lights flickered again.

They finished their lunch and went to science, which they all had together.

They walked in and sat down just before the bell rang. They waited for two or three minutes. Finally, Dr. Timberi walked in. "Good afternoon. Mr. Keller became quite ill suddenly . . ."

Lexa choked on a squeal.

". . . and since I do not have a class this period, Mr. Gregory asked me to step in. Mr. Keller wanted me to remind you that science fair projects are due on Friday, for those who are participating. Today, he wants you to read chapter twenty-three. Should you finish before the end of the period, you may start any other homework you have."

Conner looked at Lexa and Melanie. They stared back at him.

As soon as everyone else was busy studying, Lexa dropped her voice and whispered, "You guys, something seriously, freakily weird is going on, and if we can't tell anyone else, we at least need to talk to each other. The thing at lunch when you got mad at Geoffrey and Mr. Keller getting sick—ohmigosh!" She stared at Conner.

"What?" He didn't like where Lexa was going. This was not something he wanted to talk about.

"When Geoffrey's pants caught on fire the other day—"

"I didn't do anything!" he snapped, feeling defensive and tense.

"Yeah, but did you *think* something?"

"I *think* I really need to do my science homework." Conner hid behind his science book. *What if someone figures out that was me? Can you be arrested for making bad things happen to people?*

"Fine, but after school we're meeting to talk about this. We have got to figure out what's going on."

"I've got lacrosse clinic after school," Conner grumbled. "Tryouts are Monday. I'm not missing the clinic today."

"Fine. We'll wait for you, and we'll talk after lacrosse. But we have *got* to talk before we split up and go to our house and Melanie goes to hers."

Conner stared at his science book, but he couldn't concentrate.

*Did I really do those things? Seriously? What's happening? What if someone finds out and I get arrested or expelled?* Uncertainty and fear gnawed at him.

*It's one thing to make bad things happen to Geoffrey, but what if it was someone else, someone I liked . . . ?*

Conner tried to slap those thoughts away, but they buzzed back like annoying mosquitoes. He pretended to study for the rest of the period and went through the motions in PE. When the bell rang, he grabbed his lacrosse gear and ran across the street to the park.

Coach Jackson was waiting. "Okay, men, let's start with some stretches. Down to the right, now down to the left . . ."

When Conner stretched down to the left, something

caught his eye. He turned around and felt ice form in his gut. The stalker was back—pale skin, long black hair, black cape, and cold black eyes staring at him.

Conner felt like someone had emptied a Gatorade cooler of ice water all over him. He shivered and felt a tug inside. Clenching his teeth, he tried to look away. His legs fought him, pushing to walk to the man. The muscles in his calves and thighs shook and burned from the tension.

A whistle shrieked and broke the spell. Conner turned and saw Coach Jackson winding up to pitch the lacrosse ball. He swung his stick, and the ball screamed through the air toward the boys, about six hundred miles an hour. It shot way over Zach McDowell's head—not even close to any of them. But it went so fast and so hard they all ducked anyway, out of instinct.

Once the ball had landed, Coach Jackson said, "Okay, men, let's get back to stretches and then we'll run shuttles."

"That was random," Zach muttered to Conner. "It wasn't even close. No way Coach missed by that much. It's like he was trying to hit something else. Hey, Conner, what are you staring at?"

The stalker was gone, but there were scorch marks in the grass where the ball had hit. Which was exactly where the stalker had stood.

Conner looked at his coach, who didn't look back at him—not for the rest of practice.

*This is getting really weird.*

While Conner was at lacrosse, Lexa dragged Melanie

to study hall, where Mrs. Grant sat tapping her red pen on the desk.

"Mrs. Grant's never done after-school study hall before," Lexa whispered as they sat down.

"Miss Dell, please! People are trying to study." Mrs. Grant's voice shot through the room.

Lexa opened her pre-algebra book and tried to work, but the math problems kickboxed her brain. She tugged on her ponytail and tried to focus, but the kickboxing continued, so she decided to ask Melanie for help.

The second that thought appeared in her head, Mrs. Grant looked up and frowned. "Miss Dell, please! People are trying to work."

*Sheesh! It's like she can read my mind or something*, Lexa thought. She battled her pre-algebra until five o'clock, when Conner came in, dragging his lacrosse gear. It looked like someone had cleaned the park with his shirt. Sweat had twisted his hair into hundreds of small curls. The second his foot poked through the door, Mrs. Grant shot him a laser-beam stare. "Mr. Dell, please don't talk! People are trying to study!"

He stepped back out of the room and gestured for them, so Lexa and Melanie grabbed their books and followed him out, dodging lethal stares from Mrs. Grant. Melanie's books were all neatly organized in her backpack, while Lexa's were crammed into her arms, and she struggled not to drop them.

"Sheesh, Conner, how can one player smell like the whole team's locker room?" Lexa asked.

He ignored her, and no one said anything while they walked outside to the driveway. When they got there,

Conner whispered, "Okay, now I'm as freaked out as you two."

"What happened?" Melanie's voice got really fast. "Are you okay?"

"Yeah, fine. But that stalker-goth guy was at our practice."

"Did anyone else see him?" Lexa shivered.

"No. At least, I don't think so. No one said any-thing—and he's so weird looking I guarantee someone would have said something if they'd seen him. Coach Jackson threw a ball where the stalker was. He said it was for us to catch, but it was nowhere close, and Coach couldn't have missed by that much. I almost think Coach was aiming at him on purpose. When I looked back, the stalker was gone."

"Good afternoon." Dr. Timberi appeared next to them, startling Lexa.

She jumped, and her pre-algebra book flew out of her arms, crash-landing on Dr. Timberi's foot.

He picked it up and handed it back. "Are you three waiting for a ride?" Even after a full day, his clothes and voice were like one big, starched crease.

"Yes, sir," Lexa answered. "My mom will be here in a few minutes."

"Very good." He closed his eyes and took a deep breath. "What a glorious time of year: the smell of the hyacinths, the blooms on Bradford Pear trees. Spring break cannot come soon enough." The wrinkles on his face relaxed and disappeared. "Do you have plans for the break?"

"We're going to Disney World," Conner said.

"All of you?"

"Yeah," Lexa replied. "Since our moms are best friends, our families do a lot of stuff together."

"How delightful. And how did the day go for you all today?"

"Fine." Lexa smiled back.

"Good," Conner muttered.

"Interesting." Melanie blushed a ripe tomato red.

"Yes, Miss Stephens. 'Interesting' certainly describes recent events. Mr. Anderson's gym shorts catching on fire, his lunch exploding, and Mr. Keller getting sick suddenly. Interesting, indeed. I shouldn't wonder if you were all a bit confused." He stared at them, and Lexa felt as if something sharp was poking through her heart and soul.

They all looked away, trying to avoid his stare.

He continued. "Sometimes a teacher can help in times of trouble or confusion. Often a teacher has life experience that might benefit his students." Lexa felt his eyes carve into them again.

No one knew what to say, and another awkward silence dropped on them.

Lexa was grateful to see her mother pull up.

"Well, I must get home and get my spinach seedlings planted. Have a good evening." Dr. Timberi walked away, whistling, "Oh, What a Beautiful Morning."

As they drove out of the parking lot, Lexa noticed Dr. Timberi standing by his car, staring across the street at the park, looking sick. And sad.

Then she noticed one more thing.

The stalker was back.

# CHAPTER 4

# THE PIZZA GUY

MELANIE LOOKED OVER AS LEXA STIFLED A gasp. "Guys!" Lexa dropped her voice. "There's the stalker again," she hissed.

"Mom, do you see that guy over there?" Conner asked.

"What guy?"

"Right there, in the park. By the tree."

"Very funny, Conner."

The fluttery feeling in Melanie's pulse rushed back. Lexa whispered, "We *so* need to talk about this. You cannot go home, Mel." She looked toward her mother and sneaked her face into an innocent expression. "Mom, can Mel spend the night? We have a hugely major project to work on."

"Lexa, that's a lie," Melanie whispered.

"We do have a project," Lexa whispered back. "Just not a school project."

It took only a few minutes and two phone calls to arrange everything. Melanie felt bad lying to her mother, but in the end, it was comforting to be with Conner—with Lexa and Conner, that is.

The setting sun outside Conner's car window painted gold highlights on the curls in his hair, and Melanie turned to get a better look. When she did, something flashed in the corner of her eye. She turned around to see what it was and nearly died.

A scream rushed out of her mouth, and Mrs. Dell slammed on the brakes. "What's wrong, Melanie?"

Fear grabbed Melanie's throat and squeezed. "Nothing," she gasped, then took a deep breath and tried to push the fear away. She thought of the only thing she could. "Conner tasered me, and I'm really ticklish. Sorry."

Mrs. Dell started driving again.

Conner and Lexa both stared questions at her. She dropped her voice as low as she could. "Look out the back window."

Lexa turned around and let out a bloodcurdling scream.

"Conner!" Mrs. Dell yelled, hitting the brakes again. "Do *not* make them scream again."

"Uh, sorry, Mom."

Conner looked back. He bit his lip and started to shake.

The stalker was four yards behind them. He didn't run or even walk fast. He took long, regular strides and stayed exactly the same distance behind them, no matter how fast Lexa's mom went. His stare started the tug-of-war inside of Melanie again. She tried to look away but couldn't break the emotional grip.

Just then Conner laughed a big, gulping belly-laugh,

which broke the stalker's grip on Melanie's mind. She looked out Conner's window to see what was so funny and started laughing too, followed by Lexa.

Dr. Timberi drove in the next lane. His windows were down, his CD player blasting Broadway show tunes. He sang along at full voice, bobbing and dancing as if he were at a concert.

"He's rocking out to *South Pacific*!" Conner gasped between laughs.

They watched and laughed until Mrs. Dell turned on the street leading to their subdivision. Her phone rang, and she started talking.

"Guys, the stalker's gone," Lexa whispered. "What are they up to? The stalker and the teachers?"

Mrs. Dell pulled into the Stephenses' driveway, so Melanie got out, ran upstairs, grabbed her pillow, and placed a few things in a bag, then ran back out to the Dells' car.

"Okay, so, why are they doing this?" Melanie asked. "I think they're taking turns. The stalker follows us when the teachers can't. It's a tag-team."

Lexa sat still and silent, as if she was listening to something. "I don't know, guys. This morning in English I agreed with you. But now—it just doesn't feel right to me. I can't explain it. But I just *know*. I have a—well, it's a thought and a feeling at the same time—a theeling." Mrs. Dell pulled into the driveway and turned around, looking at the twins. "That was your dad," she said. "His plane got delayed, so I'll order pizza for you three to eat while you work on your project. I'll fix something for him and me later. Remember, it's a school night, and I

34

promised Melanie's mom that I wouldn't let you stay up late, so don't waste your time."

The three of them jumped out of the car and ran upstairs to Lexa's room.

"Okay, let's get organized." Melanie opened her notebook. "Let's list all our questions and figure out the biggest problem first, and then we'll decide what to do."

"The biggest problem is the stalker."

"And if the teachers are helping him." Melanie tried to make a note, but the bed was too soft. "Hey, Lexa, give me your pre-algebra book. I need something hard to write on." Lexa tossed it over. "Okay, so first priority is the stalker/teacher relationship. I think the next thing is the weird coincidences."

Downstairs, the doorbell rang.

"Hey, kids!" Mrs. Dell yelled up the stairs. "Can you get that? I'm on the phone with your dad. The money for the pizza's on the table by the door."

They ran down the stairs and opened the door.

It was the stalker.

He wore a pizza guy's clothes and carried a pizza box, but it was the stalker.

Melanie—and the others—froze, unable to move or scream.

The stalker laughed, harsh and wheezy, and his face suddenly seemed much younger. "If you come with me now, no one else will get hurt. Like your parents." He stared at Conner and Lexa. Then he looked at Melanie. "Or your little sister. Let's see—is it Madi?" A cruel laugh twisted his mouth, and he suddenly looked older again.

Something reached deep inside Melanie and started

pulling again. This time, there was no battle. Maybe because he was so close, or maybe because she could hear his voice, she couldn't resist. All of them took a step, and then another. They stepped out of the house and onto the front porch. One more step.

Lightning flashed, blinding and bright, breaking the stalker's spell.

"Good afternoon!" Dr. Timberi's voice rang out like the metal of cold church bells in winter. He stood just behind the stalker—who turned to face him. The stalker snarled, and they circled each other, never breaking eye contact. When Dr. Timberi had put himself between the stalker and students, he said, "Lexa, hand me that money. I shall pay this gentleman, and he will *leave*." Lightning crackled in his words, and Melanie shivered. The stalker was scary, but Dr. Timberi made her nervous too.

Lexa put the money in Dr. Timberi's outstretched arm. He held it out toward the stalker, who scowled and snarled again like a rabid wolf.

Dr. Timberi stood still, a rock in the raging river of the stalker's fury. As he stared the stalker down, he looked angry, but Melanie also thought she saw deep, heavy sadness flicker in his eyes.

The stalker lost the staring contest. He grabbed the money and shoved the pizza toward Dr. Timberi. His pale lips curled back over sharp teeth as he snarled again—and then he vanished.

Dr. Timberi's shoulders relaxed and fell several inches. He handed the pizza to Conner. "There you are. I am sorry to disturb you at home, but Lexa, you left this book at school." He handed Lexa her pre-algebra book.

*What? How did he get that?* Melanie shouted in her thoughts.

"I thought you might need it to study with tonight," Dr. Timberi continued. "I know what a stickler Mr. Duffy is about homework." He looked up at the sky. "There will be a storm tonight, I think." His eyes stayed focused on the sky. "Stay inside. No telling what nasty things may happen out here. But I imagine you'll be quite safe inside."

He turned and walked away.

"Wait, Dr. Timberi! What's going on?" Lexa yelled. He didn't stop or turn back, so she ran after him, darting around the corner of the garage. She came right back just a few seconds later. "He's gone. It's like he just disappeared."

Melanie looked up at the sky. "Did you all see lightning when he told the stalker to leave?"

"Yeah," Lexa said.

Melanie shivered. "But the sky's clear. There're no clouds or anything. Let's go back inside, you guys."

Back in Lexa's room, Conner opened the pizza box and Melanie winced. "Oooh! I don't think I want to eat that if the stalker had it." She shuddered. "It could have really bad germs."

"Good point." Conner dropped the piece he'd grabbed. "Or be poisoned."

"Dr. Timberi's not on his side." Lexa's voice was firm. "He's trying to help us."

"Maybe," Melanie replied. "But how did he have your pre-algebra book? You just gave it to me a minute ago so I could write on it! Was he up here somehow? That's really creepy. Anyway, how can we trust him? He knows something, but he's not telling us anything! If he's really on our side, wouldn't he tell us everything we need to know?"

"Good point." Conner frowned and nodded.

"What if he can't?" Lexa stared at the pizza box.

"What do you mean?" Conner asked.

Lexa shrugged. "Maybe there's a reason he can't. Anyway, if he's with the stalker, then so is Madame Cumberland, and I *cannot* believe that. She's way too nice."

"Wait, that reminds me of something," Melanie said. "I heard the teachers mention something about contacting a sodality. I wonder what that means—I've never heard of it before. Do you have a dictionary?"

"On the desk," Lexa said. Melanie walked over and thumbed through the "s" section.

"Here it is. 'Sodality: an organized society or fellowship.' That proves it! There's some kind of conspiracy to kill us."

"I don't know." Lexa frowned. "Just because they have a club doesn't mean they're trying to kill us."

They talked and debated, debated and talked for three hours. The longer they talked, the more convinced Lexa and Melanie became of their positions—and the more heated the discussion grew.

"Melanie, just because you're the smartest person in the whole school doesn't mean you know everything!" Lexa snapped.

"I never said I did!" Melanie snapped back.

"Then why won't you listen to me?" Lexa yelled. "I'm telling you Dr. Timberi and the teachers are doing something to help us."

"But it doesn't make sense." Melanie took a deep breath and spoke in a patient voice that infuriated Lexa. "You can't just say you know it and expect us to believe it, right, Conner?"

Both of them shot glares at Conner.

"Uh . . ." Conner squirmed, looking away—and was interrupted by a car pulling into the driveway. "Dad's home!" Conner jumped up and ran downstairs, happy for an excuse not to take sides.

Mr. Dell walked in, and Conner ran over for a big hug. "Dad!"

"Dad!" Lexa ran down and hugged him too.

*That's so sweet. Some boys would be all weird about that.* Melanie watched Conner from the hallway.

"Good to be back! I missed you guys!" Mr. Dell smiled. "Hey, sweetie!" His smile grew when Mrs. Dell walked in from the kitchen.

"I've got supper ready." Lexa's mom gave him a big, long kiss. They grabbed hands and walked back into the kitchen.

"So gross!" Lexa shivered and cringed. "Old people should not kiss like that."

"Pretty disturbing," Conner agreed.

"I think they want to be alone," Melanie said. "Let's go back upstairs."

"So you can tell me how stupid I am again?" Lexa muttered.

"No, so we can discuss this like adults." Melanie's voice dropped to subzero temperatures.

An hour later, Conner yawned. "Lexa, Melanie's right. If they were on our side, they'd tell us what's going on."

"No, no, no!" Lexa's voice crescendoed on each word. "Dr. Timberi's trying to help us. I know it."

"But what if you're wrong?" Conner's voice rose to match Lexa's. "We can't risk our lives just 'cause you have a feeling or theeling, or whatever."

Melanie took a deep breath and tried to make her voice soft. "Lexa, we're just saying that we need to tell someone. Let the police figure it out."

"No!"

"Lexa, come on," Conner said. "We've at least got to tell Mom and Dad. That guy has followed us all over the place. He almost kidnapped us a few hours ago!" He stood up. "I'm going to tell them right now."

"NO!" Lexa grabbed his arm. "Conner, I'm serious. If you tell them, something really bad will happen. I know it." She stomped her foot, then held her fists up. "I'll fight you, I swear I will."

"Hey, gang." Mr. Dell poked his head in the door. "Time to finish up for the night. You've got school tomorrow. Everything okay? Lexa, you look upset."

"Everything's great, Dad." Lexa turned on a smile and a bright voice.

"Are you sure? Conner, are you being rude?"

"No, Dad."

"He's not. Everything's fine."

"Okay, well, good night." Mr. Dell left.

Lexa looked at Conner. "Conner, don't—"

Conner pushed past her. "Whatever. I don't want to fight. I'm going to bed."

"Fine!" Lexa yelled.

After Conner left, Lexa and Melanie got ready for

bed, then lay in frosty silence until Melanie fell asleep.

When Lexa finally dropped off, her sleep was inter-rupted by strange dreams. In one dream she stood on a table in the cafeteria, waving a big wire whisk. Dr. Timberi lay on the floor, singing something from *South Pacific* in a croaky voice. Whenever Lexa waved the whisk, flaming pizzas flew through the air and smashed into Geoffrey, who cowered under a table across the cafeteria.

## · CHAPTER 5 ·

# DEMERITS

WHEN MELANIE WOKE UP THE NEXT morning, Lexa was still mad at her—which made Melanie mad. They managed to get ready and eat breakfast without saying a word to each other. They were almost out the door when Mrs. Dell said, "Conner, where's your belt? I don't want you getting any more dress code demerits."

"Yes, ma'am." He ran up to his room and came back down shoving a belt through the loops of his pants. "Stupid belts," he muttered. "Stupid dress code. My friends in public school don't have to—"

"Come on, Con," Mr. Dell said. "Your mom and I make some big sacrifices to send you to private school. If that's the worst thing in your life, then life is pretty good. All right, everyone ready?" Mr. Dell walked out to the car smiling, whistling, and embarrassing his children.

He backed out of the driveway. "You three are quiet

this morning," he said. "Tired? Hey, there's Mrs. Grant." He waved as she pulled up next to them at the stop sign.

Seeing Mrs. Grant reminded Melanie of all the questions they'd wrestled with the night before. That stress and her fight with Lexa made her feel nervous and tense, and a heavy feeling pushed down on her.

At school, it got worse. On the way from the car to her locker, Melanie passed Mrs. Grant, Madame Cumberland, and Dr. Timberi. It looked like they were patrolling, and today they were joined by Coach Jackson, Mr. Duffy, Mrs. Davis, and Mrs. Sharpe. All of the teachers had circles under their eyes and seemed edgy and tense—which made Melanie even more tense.

After English, she walked to history. While making sure to stay several steps away from Lexa, she felt familiar jabs in each side.

"Taser!" Zach laughed.

Melanie screamed, and something deep inside of her snapped. All the tension and fear of the past twenty-four hours exploded in an firestorm.

"ZACH! Stop. Doing. That!" She turned around and shoved him. The lights in the hall flickered, and Zach flew back fifteen yards through the air, slamming into the top row of lockers. He slid down onto the floor and crumpled in a heap, like the dirty clothes on Lexa's floor.

Melanie froze. As one of the smallest girls in the grade, she was surprised. So was everyone else, and the noise in the crowded hall froze into tense, brittle silence. Her eyes get warm and moist as a hallway full of curious stares devoured her.

"I'm sorry!" Melanie burst into tears and ran over to

him. "Zach, I'm so sorry! Are you okay?" He nodded and stared at her, stunned.

"Whoa, Melanie." Conner's voice was loud and strong. "Those kung fu lessons you started must be pretty hard-core."

*Thank you, Conner! I could kiss you! I mean—not literally.* Gratitude for his quick thinking surged through her. Now, when the middle school rumor mill started, everyone would talk about her doing some kung fu moves on Zach, not about her doing some freaky, unexplainable thing.

"Yeah, pretty intense." She tried a kick and karate chop combination. "Hi-yaahhh!" *I hope that looked real.*

"All right, guys, head to your classes." Madame Cumberland's warm maple syrup voice poured through the crowd. "Zach, are you okay?"

"Yes, ma'am." Zach pulled himself up. "Sorry, Melanie." He scurried off on wobbly feet.

"Melanie, are you okay?" Madame Cumberland's smile felt like a warm bubble bath.

"Yes, ma'am. Zach just startled me."

"Is anything wrong, Mona?" Dr. Timberi came down the hall.

"No, Morgan, just a little accident. Zach startled Melanie."

Madame Cumberland looked back at her, and Melanie realized that Madame Cumberland's warm smile provided camouflage for a shrewd, searching stare.

"Ah, Mr. McDowell's tasering finally caught up with him." Dr. Timberi chuckled. "Miss Stephens, why don't you move along to class now?"

"Yes, sir." As she walked away, she heard them whispering. *What are they saying? I know they're talking about me.* Melanie strained her ears to hear even though she knew it was impossible. She wanted to know so badly she could hardly stand it. She wanted it like she wanted Christmas morning to come when she was five. She wanted it like . . .

"You know, Morgan—"

Melanie jumped. She heard Madame Cumberland with perfect clarity. She looked over her shoulder. The teachers still stood at the other end of the hall. But Melanie heard them perfectly, as if someone had turned up the volume on their conversation. She ducked around the corner and pressed herself against the wall.

"—we can't let this go on much longer," Madame Cumberland continued. "We need to take care of those three once and for all."

"I agree, Mona. It is sooner than we had planned, but we really must stop this for good."

*Once and for all? Stop this for good?*

"If we keep them here today after school, we can finish it off."

"I think you're right, Morgan. I'll tell the Sodality."

Melanie felt like her heart had been replaced by frantic, fluttering hummingbirds. A flood of adrenaline coursed through her veins, and she wanted to run and run and not stop.

*Be calm, Melanie! I need to warn Conner and Lexa! We've got to figure something out. I can't let the teachers know I know anything. Calm. Calm. Calm.*

She pushed her tears away and walked into history class. Mrs. Sharpe's yardstick froze in front of a map of

Nazi-occupied Europe. "Melanie, you're late. That will be a demerit. Please take your seat."

"Sorry, ma'am. Dr. Timberi and Madame Cumberland were talking to me." She topped her meekest voice with the sweetest smile she could manufacture.

"That may be. But you are still late, and now you have disrupted class as well. Two demerits. Please take your seat."

Melanie sat down in the back row and brooded. *My teachers want to kill me, Lexa's mad at me, and I have two demerits. Great. Really great. I've got to talk to Conner. I mean Conner and Lexa.*

But Lexa was at the front, ignoring Melanie in an obvious way, and there were no seats nearby. Conner was in a different class. She would have to wait.

On the way to his next class, Conner passed Mr. Duffy, the pre-algebra teacher, moseying through the crowded hall, singing and tapping his hand with the big wooden compass he used for geometry.

"Oh, m'darlin', oh, m'darlin', Clementine . . . Mornin', Conner," he drawled. "Got that homework done?"

"Oh, well, uh, I'm still behind from the play." Conner paused and blinked. He thought he saw a flash of light, but it disappeared.

"You've been saying that for a week, now. Hey, sonny, where's your belt?" Mr. Duffy shook his head. "You know better than that. Out of dress code—one demerit."

Conner laughed. "You scared me, Mr. Duffy. I

thought you were serious." He grabbed for his belt, but it wasn't there! "What the—no way! My belt's gone!"

"One demerit." Mr. Duffy shuffled back to his room, still singing.

Melanie walked past Conner and pulled her locker open. Conner blinked, thinking he saw another flash of light. But he forgot about the light as Melanie opened her obsessively organized locker. The contents poured out, nearly burying her in an avalanche of books, binders, and notebooks. When the binders hit the floor, the rings opened, and papers flew everywhere.

"No!" Melanie threw herself over her notes, determined to protect them even at the cost of being trampled.

Conner tried to help her gather them, but it was impossible to get them all with people rushing through the halls going to their classes.

"Now, Melanie." Mrs. Grant stood above her, tapping her hand with a red pen. She looked tired and persecuted. "You're creating a traffic jam while you clean that up. I'll have to give you a littering demerit for this mess."

"But, Mrs. Grant, I didn't—"

"One demerit for littering." Mrs. Grant shook her head and walked off.

"That's three demerits," Melanie groaned. "Four more and I have detention."

"Open up!" Conner looked across the hall where Lexa yanked on her locker door with both hands. "Open up!" She grunted. "I'm going to be late!" She slapped it.

"Do you need some help?" Conner walked over to her.

"Stupid thing's stuck." She backed up and gave the locker a sharp kick.

"Knock that off!" Mr. Miller, the gruff mountain of a custodian, stood behind Lexa, waving a mop. "You don't kick lockers like that!"

"Sorry." Lexa put on her polite smile. "It's jammed."

"No wonder, when you kick it like that. Three demerits. Destruction of school property."

"But, Mr. Miller—"

"Don't let me see you kick it like that again." He glared and walked off, shoving angry breaths in and out of his nose.

"Oh. My. Gosh!" Lexa said as she watched Mr. Miller walk away. "That's *so* unfair. I can't believe he gave me demerits!"

It took ten minutes to get Melanie's papers picked up and Lexa's locker open. By the time they were ready to go to class, the halls had emptied. "Guys," Melanie whispered. "I need to talk to you."

Melanie stopped as Laura Dalton came out of a classroom and walked to the bathroom.

"Can't talk now," she grumbled. "Meet me back here in fifteen minutes. It's important!"

Conner meandered off to art while Lexa and Melanie darted into French. Madame Cumberland stood at the front of the class, tapping the Smart Board with a long pointer. "Parlez-vous—Lexa, Melanie, you're late." She smiled and sounded like she was presenting an award. "That will be a demerit each, girls. Please take your seats."

"But—"

"Page 143. Merci."

When Conner walked into art, Mrs. Davis greeted him with a glare that hung in the air like an angry abstract painting. "You're late. One demerit."

Her frown told him arguing was pointless. "Yes, ma'am."

Conner grabbed his pastels and paper and started shading underneath the eyes on his self-portrait. The pastel just barely brushed the paper, leaving a tiny excuse of a smudge before snapping in half. He grabbed another pastel and tried again. It snapped too. And a third one. And the fourth.

Conner made a mental note to have his mom get him a doctor appointment because he saw another flash of light. *Did I get a concussion from football last season? Like a delayed reaction?*

"Conner Dell! What are you doing to my pastels?" Mrs. Davis's eyes flared with anger. "Destruction of school property. Three demerits."

"But I didn't—"

"You want another one for arguing, buddy?"

He dropped his head and tried to imitate Melanie's meek-and-humble voice. "No, ma'am."

"I want the left side of that project finished by the end of the period, and you're way behind. Pick up the pace, and no bathroom breaks or drinks or anything."

When art finally ended what seemed like ten hours later, Conner fled from Mrs. Davis's evil stare and went to choir.

"Hello, little chipmunks." There was something comforting and normal about the dry sarcasm in Dr. Timberi's voice. "Get your music quickly, and please sit down."

BRADEN BELL

Everyone walked to the music cabinets. Conner bent over, grabbed his choral folder from its slot, and stood up. He paused to stare out the big windows into the court-yard. *Weird day. Fights, demerits, lockers . . .*

His eyes wandered down to the big, eight-point com-pass star carved into the courtyard concrete. Did it flash with light? He shook his head. Something had to be wrong with his eyes.

"Quickly, now, jackrabbits," Dr. Timberi said. "I left my music at my desk, and I want you seated when I return."

The students sat down on chairs along the risers at the back of the room. On their right, opposite the windows, was a long wall covered with framed posters of the plays the school had produced. Conner noticed a new one that had just been hung up and smiled. It was for *Beauty and the Beast*, and he, Melanie, and Lexa were all featured in the picture. At the far end of that wall was the door to Dr. Timberi's office. Dr. Timberi walked out of his office with music in his hand. He looked in his office window and straightened his bow tie. He buttoned his sweater vest over his rounded stomach, then strode back to where everyone sat.

"Zach and Bennett, I believe I made it very clear last week that there were no conditions under which the two of you were ever allowed to sit anywhere near each other for the remainder of your natural lives. Please move very far away from each other.

"Very well. Kindly fix all your beady little eyes on me. We will warm up with a five-note descending scale on 'ah.'" Dr. Timberi hit a chord on the piano. "On that note, please." Everyone sang, but Dr. Timberi cut them off. "Someone is

50

flat. Again please." Dr. Timberi moved his head to find the culprit, and Conner turned around to Melanie and Lexa. They were assigned to sit next to each other, but Lexa had pulled her chair as far away as she could.

"Sorry," Conner whispered. "Davis wouldn't let me out of class."

"It's okay. Madame Cumberland wouldn't let us out, either," Melanie whispered back.

"Very well." Dr. Timberi cut them off with a crisp flick of his white baton. "Nice, round, open vowels—mi-may-mah-moh-moo."

"Perfect." Conner grinned. A few months earlier, Melanie had figured out how to talk during this particular warm-up. The trick was to sing an entire word each time Dr. Timberi cued the class to sing a new vowel. It took a while, but with patience, it could be useful.

Dr. Timberi cued the class to sing. They all sang "mi," while Melanie sang "They."

Dr. Timberi flicked his baton and cued the next note. "Are."

Flick.

"Going."

Flick.

"To."

The class all hit "Moo," and Melanie sang, "Killooooos."

"What?" Conner whispered over his shoulder.

"One more time, please." Dr. Timberi started the sequence again on a higher note.

Melanie sang, "Kill." Then she took a breath and then sang the last word of her message: "Us."

Conner choked.

# ESCAPE

"**M**ISS STEPHENS, MISS DELL, MR. DELL? IS something wrong? Once again, please."

Dr. Timberi's baton signaled them to start again, but this time he watched Melanie too closely for her to talk.

"Very well." He cut them off and looked at the boys. "Gentlemen, today we shall conquer the bass part in 'The Star-Spangled Banner,' or you will die trying. Now, on this note." He hit a note, then cringed as ten boys all sang different wrong notes at the same time. "No, no, no! Gentlemen, you are to music what the Detroit Lions used to be to football. Again." He pounded the note on the piano.

Lexa summoned up a sudden coughing fit. She coughed like she had pneumonia until Dr. Timberi said, "Go get a drink, Miss Dell."

As she walked past Conner, she coughed the word, "Bathroom."

Lexa signed her name on the legal pad Dr. Timberi

kept on the piano and ran out of the room. Conner counted to twenty, then went down and signed out as well. He left the room and waited with Lexa in the hall. A few seconds later, Melanie joined them.

"Okay," Conner said, "so what—?"

"I think you're right, Carol, that would be the most efficient way." Mrs. Sharpe was just around the corner and coming closer.

"Thank you, Norma." So was Mrs. Grant.

"Come on!" Conner pushed the door to the boys' bathroom open.

"No way!" Melanie screeched.

"Hurry!" Lexa shoved Melanie in. "They won't come in here. Just close your eyes."

Conner checked to make sure no one was in the middle of anything important.

"It's safe. You can open your eyes," he said. "Stop staring at the funny toilets and tell us what's going on."

Melanie's dark eyes flashed, which Conner thought looked cool with her red hair. "They're going to kill us."

"What?" Conner yelled.

"Oh yeah, right." Lexa rolled her eyes.

"I'm serious!" Melanie stomped her foot. "I heard Madame Cumberland and Dr. Timberi talking. They said they needed to take care of us once and for all, and they'd finish everything off after school today."

"Kill us?" Lexa smirked. "You're not being paranoid at all, Melanie."

"Shut up, Lexa!" Conner said. "You're the one who always wants to talk about everything—so let Melanie talk. It sort of makes sense that they're going to kill us. I mean, it doesn't make sense, but it explains my day. I've gotten more demerits in two hours than I've had all year. One more, and I've got detention."

"Hey, me too," Lexa said. "That *is* kind of weird." She didn't seem so sarcastic all of a sudden.

"I got six too," Melanie said. "I guess they're planning on killing us in detention hall. Should we just run away now?"

"Seriously? Kill us?" Now Lexa seemed uncertain, not sarcastic at all. "Shh!"

"Yes, it will be nice to get this over," Mrs. Grant said from the hall. "Those three have been causing all kinds of trouble lately. I'll be glad to be done with it."

Lexa turned white. No one said anything for a few seconds.

"I can't believe it," Lexa said. "I mean, like—this is really strange. Sorry, Mel. I guess you were right. I just can't believe it. So do we run away?"

"No." Conner shook his head. "They've been all over us lately. They've gotta be watching. If we try to get away and they catch us, we're dead. We need to take them by surprise. Like after school—when the bell rings, and the halls are really crowded, they won't be able to keep track of us, and we can get away."

"Good idea," Melanie jumped in. "We can run down to Walgreens. That's a really public place, and we can call the police or our parents. Hey, why don't we just call them now? My phone's in my locker."

"Too risky," Conner said. "If they catch us in the hall, they might do something or at least take away our phones. We can try calling at lunch next period. But

I still think we need a Plan B in case something goes wrong. If calling doesn't work, we make a break for it at three. Go team!" Conner put his hand in the middle of their little huddle. Melanie put her hand on top of his. *Her skin is so soft . . .*

Lexa put her hand in too.

"Go team," they repeated.

"Okay, guys." Lexa pulled her hand off. "We better get back to class. I'll go first."

She walked out of the bathroom.

Melanie's hand was still on Conner's.

Their eyes connected, and Melanie's face burned red. She pulled her hand away and ran out of the bathroom.

Conner got a drink and then went back into the choir room, his heart pounding.

When he walked in, Dr. Timberi frowned. "Miss Dell, Miss Stephens, and Mr. Dell, for the convenience and comfort of my students, I have a liberal restroom policy. However, you three have stretched it to the outer limits. One demerit for each of you."

*Detention*, Conner thought. *Or death. Great.*

Melanie poked at her lunch. Her stomach did gymnastics while her heart pounded in her brain.

"I almost hope they *do* kill us!" She smacked the table with her hand as the words burst out of her mouth.

"What?" Lexa squealed.

Half a smile crept up on Melanie's face. "If they don't, my mom will kill me when she finds out I earned detention in one day."

Mrs. Lehman, the middle school secretary, walked up to the table, waving three red slips of paper.

"Oh good, you're all together. You've each earned seven demerits today."

Her words murdered Melanie's half-smile.

Mrs. Lehman continued, "I called your parents and told them not to pick you up until five o'clock." She handed everyone a slip of paper.

*Front-row tickets to our own murder*, Melanie thought.

She read her slip of paper:

## Detention Hall Notice

**Name:** Melanie Stephens
**Date of Offenses:** March 15 (all offenses)
**Date of Detention:** March 15
**Supervising Teacher:** Timberi

"Okay," Lexa whispered. "It's time to call. I got my phone out of my locker on the way to lunch. I'll go to the bathroom and call Mom." She walked out of the lunchroom on shaky legs. A few minutes later she came back. Her face was pale and her legs wobbled.

"What's wrong?" Melanie asked.

"My phone won't work. No signal. Nothing." Lexa yanked her ponytail.

"Let me try." Panic propelled Melanie out of her seat. She ran to the bathroom and pulled out her phone. It was dead too.

When she returned, Conner tried to send a text. "Dead," he muttered.

"Bonjour!" Madame Cumberland appeared at their

table. "The teacher's table is full today. May I join you?" Normally her warm smile cured frostbite, but today it froze Melanie's heart. *They're everywhere. We'll never get away. I'm going to die. In seventh grade.*

Nothing else happened for the rest of the day, but Melanie felt like she was in the eye of a hurricane. They went to their classes after lunch, stuck together, and tried to concentrate. Companions in a dangerous situation, their earlier fights were forgotten. When PE ended, they ran down to the locker rooms.

"I hope Conner's ready," Melanie whispered.

"He will be. He always gets ready way faster than me," Lexa replied.

"Boys!" Coach Jackson's shouting spilled through the walls of the boys' locker room next door. "If you're coming to lacrosse clinic, I want you on that field no later than 3:02!"

The bell rang, and a flood of adolescent bodies poured out of the locker rooms. Melanie, Conner, and Lexa threw themselves into the current and ran out of the first door they found. Walgreens was a hundred yards away on a busy street, and cars were everywhere since parents were pulling in for the after-school pick-up.

*We might make it after all*, Melanie thought, feeling safer by the minute.

"You go first. I'll make sure no one's coming," Conner said. They ran across the courtyard: first Melanie, then Lexa, followed by Conner, who ran backward.

Melanie heard Dr. Timberi shout but didn't look back.

"Hurry! Timberi's coming. So's Grant!" Conner yelled.

They paused at the street to let a car pass—and then the lacrosse boys galloped out of the gym like a crazed herd of buffalo.

Thirty bodies ran between Conner and Lexa, slicing Conner away, then surrounding him. Before he disappeared in the crush, he gestured for the girls to keep running. They paused, not wanting to leave him—but then Mrs. Grant hurried down the steps from the middle school, waving her red pen and yelling. Mrs. Sharpe ran right behind her, brandishing a yardstick in the air.

Conner managed to surface long enough to yell, "RUN!" Then the stampede swallowed him up, like Simba's dad in *The Lion King*, and Melanie and Lexa ran to the street in front of the school and turned left toward Walgreens.

When Conner extricated himself from the pack of lacrosse players, he found himself in the park across the street.

"Hey, why aren't you dressed out?" Zach asked.

"CONNER DELL! You are supposed to be in detention!" Coach Jackson barreled toward Conner, waving his lacrosse stick and looking mad. Madame Cumberland followed a few steps behind him, waving her pointer stick in the air. She looked worried.

Conner took a deep breath and tensed his leg muscles to run. Getting away from Madame Cumberland wouldn't be a problem, but Coach was fast. He launched himself, feet pounding the grass beneath him. The park flew past, and he aimed for the houses ahead.

*Maybe I can use someone's phone . . .*

Four men in black appeared just outside the border of the park, each wearing a black hood and holding twisted black clubs with shiny silver blades. Conner looked back and saw that Coach Jackson had gained on him. And, somehow, Madame Cumberland was right there too.

He was trapped.

Melanie ran behind Lexa as fast as she could since getting to Walgreens for help was the best chance to save Conner. They heard teachers yelling but didn't look back. The afternoon traffic was thick and slow, so they dodged between cars and ran across the street. Melanie looked over her shoulder and saw Mrs. Grant and Mrs. Sharpe on the curb across the street, yelling and motioning for them to stop.

"Keep running!" she shouted to Lexa.

With only fifty yards to get to the drugstore, Melanie started to feel safe. She allowed a breath out of her clenched lungs and . . . A flash of black in the corner of her eye caught her attention, and she peeked over her shoulder. A man in a black hood jumped out of nowhere, waving a strange club with a long metal blade. She screamed and grabbed Lexa's hand.

*Just thirty yards to the drugstore.* The man chased them, but they were faster.

*Thank heavens for PE.* Melanie thought between gasps and palpitations of her heart.

Twenty yards.

Ten yards.

A big tree stood next to the sidewalk a few feet in front of them. Someone stepped out from behind the tree. It was the stalker.

"Conner!" Coach shouted from about twenty yards back. "Stop! Do not proceed any farther!"

Conner froze. *What should I do?*

Coach Jackson turned and yelled at the team behind him. "Three laps around the neighborhood. NOW!" His whistle screamed, and they took off.

*Great. He's getting rid of the witnesses.*

Somehow, Coach appeared right next to Conner.

*How did he close the gap so fast? What the . . . ?*

A bright, silver comet shot past them and smashed into two of the men in black. The silver light flashed and crackled, and the men fell over. The other two men ran toward Conner.

"Dell, if you don't run to Timberi this second, you ain't gonna live long enough for me to kick your butt to China and back. Now MOVE!" Coach Jackson twirled his lacrosse stick above his head and flipped his arm. A bright ball of purple light flew out of the stick, slammed into one of the men, and knocked him down.

"DELL!" Coach Jackson yelled so hard that he was hoarse by the end of the name.

Conner turned and ran back to the school as fast as he could.

When Lexa saw the stalker, she and Melanie screamed and darted out into the middle of the street.

For a second they froze, sandwiched between the stalker on one sidewalk and the teachers on the other. Oncoming cars honked and brakes squealed. Perfect clarity flashed in Lexa's mind, and she knew what to do. "Follow me," she yelled. "I have a theeling."

They sprinted toward the school, dodging the cars. When they got to the sidewalk, Mrs. Sharpe ran up to them. "Go to Dr. Timberi's room!" She ran after the guys in black, and Lexa didn't look back, even when she heard explosions and saw flashes like lightning.

They ran into the courtyard at the same time Conner arrived. "You'll never believe what Coach Jackson just did," he panted.

"Ah, my little detention buddies." Dr. Timberi stood in the doorway of the fine arts building. "If you want to live for more than a few moments, I suggest you come with me. Quickly."

"Do it," Lexa said. *Oh gosh, I hope my theeling is right.*

Inside the choir room, the afternoon sun poured through the big windows, making it warm and calm. Above the windows, the clock said it was 3:10.

A baby earthquake shook the ground, and the sky grew dark, killing the peaceful sunlight. Dr. Timberi walked to the window, and his frown sunk down almost to the ground. "Why would he choose . . ." His voice faded, and he pushed his hands inside the pockets of his sweater vest.

"Who chose what?" Lexa asked. "What's happening—"

"Miss Dell!" Dr. Timberi's voice sliced through Lexa's

sentence. "Must you always find the worst possible occasions to talk, or could you, just once, hold your tongue? I must think!" He looked at their shocked faces, and his expression softened. "Please listen and follow my directions *exactly*. Your lives depend on it. I shall explain everything in due course, but we haven't time now. You are in very real danger."

He grabbed his conductor's baton and waved it in the air. It glowed bright gold and left a gleaming line in the air. He traced a glowing circle, in which the air shimmered and sparkled. The sparkles grew bigger and bigger until they formed one glowing window of light.

"Daniel, Mona, Carol!"

The circle flashed, and three faces appeared, floating in the air, like they were on TV: Mr. Miller, Madame Cumberland, and Mrs. Grant. Dr. Timberi pointed to the students. "They're here. But I think he's coming after them."

"'Fraid you're right, Morgan." Mr. Miller growled and looked down at his watch, which made a weird beeping noise. "Looks like they're trying to get on campus."

"Here or through the Otherwhere?" The muscles on Dr. Timberi's neck bulged.

"Son of a gun! They're trying to come through the Otherwhere." Mr. Miller's voice was grim. "They're blasting away at the courtyard gate. You should have a few minutes, though. I'd better get down there and help Norma and Thomas." Mr. Miller's face blinked out of the light-picture-TV-thing, and a green comet flashed past the windows.

"We're on our way too," Mrs. Grant said.

A graceful silver comet shot into the room, slowed down, and turned into Madame Cumberland, holding her pointer stick. She was followed by a blue flash that became Mrs. Grant, clutching her red pen in a death grip.

Mr. Miller appeared in a flash of green light, waving his mop as if it was a light saber. "They're all over—here and in the Otherwhere. We're gonna have to fight it out. They're pretty strong, and the wards won't hold much longer."

The three teachers looked at each other.

"Sound battle stations, Daniel," Madame Cumberland said. "We'll keep the children safe."

"All righty." Mr. Miller's nod was curt.

"Farewell, Daniel." Dr. Timberi's voice was soft. "Be careful."

Mr. Miller snorted. "Any Darkhand who steps on my campus is the one who needs to be careful." He slammed his mop down, and streaks of bright green light spread across the floor like a spider web. Then Mr. Miller disappeared in another flash of green light.

In the courtyard below, the compass star carved into the concrete flashed, then burned with blazing green light that filled each line. Lexa noticed it looked different than before—inside the compass was the shape of a moon surrounding a star.

"What about everyone else?" Madame Cumberland asked. "The other students. The teachers. This is such a bad time!"

Mrs. Grant stepped forward. "You know, pick-up is over, so most of the kids are gone. If everyone else were simply asleep. . . ." She flirted with a smile, then pushed it away, as if she was proud of herself but didn't want to seem arrogant. She waved her red pen and muttered something about gerunds and participles. A glimmering galaxy of blue stars swirled around the end of her pen and grew into a miniature tornado, which broke free and spun in perfect circles out the door.

Lexa and the others watched through the window as the star-cyclone twirled into the commons area and split into two cyclones, then four, then eight, and—they finally lost track. A group of sixth graders ran out of the gym in track uniforms followed by Coach Thompson, the cross-country coach. One of the cyclones whooshed past, leaving them asleep on the sidewalk.

"They'll be safe now." Madame Cumberland cooed in her soothing voice. "We don't have time to explain anything right now. You need to trust us. You'll see some strange and maybe scary things. But Dr. Timberi is your Guide, and Mrs. Grant and I are your Guardians. We'll keep you all safe."

An old-fashioned alarm pierced the air, and Mr. Miller's voice thundered everywhere. "Breach at the Courtyard Gate! Breach at the Courtyard Gate!"

"We don't have gates on campus," Melanie whispered. "What's he talking about?"

Mr. Miller's voice continued booming. "Darkhands on campus. Repeat. Darkhands on campus. This is not a drill. Report to your posts."

Colored comets blasted out of buildings everywhere and exploded into the compass courtyard. Mrs. Sharpe, Coach Jackson, Mr. Duffy, Mrs. Davis, and even two of the lunch ladies appeared, wearing flowing robes and glowing like ghosts in front of bonfires. The second their comets faded, they ran across the courtyard toward the steps that led to the street below.

As he ran, Coach Jackson swung his lacrosse stick back and forth, pitching balls of purple light through the air while Mrs. Sharpe slashed the air with her yardstick and shot jagged blasts of green lightning. Mr. Duffy rotated his big wooden compass back and forth, and precise orange lines of light burst out from each end. Mrs. Davis flipped her paintbrush, sending multi-colored squiggles of light through the air, while the lunch ladies swirled ladles over their heads, serving up steaming blobs of maroon and dark blue light.

While the teachers shot and ran, they moved clockwise into a circle pattern, running faster and faster until all Conner could see was a big blur of colored light with blobs and blasts and dots and balls shooting out.

"We go to a seriously weird school," Conner whispered.

"It is best you not see anything." Dr. Timberi's voice was soft but firm. "Your lack of understanding might still protect you. Go into my office and shut the door. Don't open it, no matter what! Quickly! There is little time. Lexa—do not peek!"

# THE CLASH

BEFORE THE DOOR SLAMMED SHUT, LEXA heard Dr. Timberi say, "Please, if there is any way, do not harm him—"

Right then golden light filled the cracks around the door, welding it shut, so she didn't hear anything at all for maybe two minutes.

Then she heard—and felt—a massive crash.

Lexa looked at Conner.

"Should we . . . ?" he asked.

"No way I'm missing this!" Lexa ran to the window.

"He said not to look." Melanie's voice dripped with worry.

"He said not to open the door," Lexa said. Conner joined her at the window as a huge tearing sound split the air.

"I've heard that sound before!" Lexa yelled. "The night of the storm—"

Lexa and Conner gasped.

"What's happening?" Melanie stood in the corner with her hands over her eyes.

It looked like someone had ripped the air open in the middle of the choir room. A big, black gash of emptiness appeared, framed by torn, silver curtains fluttering in the air. The stalker ran out of the gash, pointed at the three teachers, and yelled. A black cloud burst out of his hands and swam through the air at the teachers like a feral stingray. Dr. Timberi sang something from *The Music Man*, while Madame Cumberland belted out "La Marseilles," and Mrs. Grant shouted poetry. They started to glow, and their regular clothes morphed into flowing robes, each a different color—gold, silver, and blue—with a silver symbol sparkling on the front.

As the black cloud flapped toward them, Mrs. Grant stabbed the air with her pen, and a wispy blue light danced around the cloud. Madame Cumberland waved her pointer, and strands of silver light shot out and wrapped it up. The dark cloud quivered and quaked, then turned into a fluffy silver and blue cloud.

Dr. Timberi's baton flashed bright gold, and the doors of the cabinets flew open. The sheets of music inside lit up like they were on fire, then shot out into the air, opened up, and flapped like birds.

The glowing music-birds zipped through the air, flying circles around the stalker until they surrounded him with a blur of gold light.

The circle seemed to have him trapped, and the stalker shrank down into a tiny huddle on the floor. As the circle tightened, he jumped up and threw his arms wide open.

Jagged clouds of darkness exploded outward, scattering the music-birds across the room.

Dr. Timberi's hands flew faster, and the music-birds regrouped, zooming back at the stalker. But this time the stalker was ready, and he made a ripping motion, tearing another black gash in the air. It swallowed the music-birds whole, and they vanished.

When Dr. Timberi sent another flock, the stalker smiled a creepy, evil smile that gave Lexa chills. He made another ripping motion with his hands, and each page of music was torn in half and fell to the ground, fluttering and flapping like wounded birds. The stalker swung his club, and a storm of shadowy black arrows shot out, piercing each piece of music. As the arrows stabbed them, their lights faded, and the faint flutters stopped.

Two men in black ran in through the gash and stood on each side of the stalker. Madame Cumberland ran a few steps, grew blurry, and turned into a silver comet, shooting at one of the men. He dodged her, but while he wasn't looking, Mrs. Grant turned into a blue comet and hit him from behind, knocking him down. Then both comets hit the second man, and he went down too.

The stalker snarled and whirled his club faster, sending out burst after burst of angry, black blobs. Dr. Timberi flicked his baton, and flickers of flame appeared in the air, eating the stalker's blasts. One blob got past and crashed into a play poster, which steamed and smoked as a big hole grew in the middle, as if some kind of living, carnivorous nothingness ate it away.

Dr. Timberi changed his song to something in a

strange language. Lexa couldn't understand the words, but she felt what he was singing about.

She saw the glow of a sunrise on the ocean and the color of the mountains at sunset. Lexa imagined a full moon shining on new snow and the golden light of an autumn afternoon. She felt the pale light of the first morning in spring and the glow of the embers from a fire in December—somehow, his song created these things in the room, which got brighter and brighter.

As the song grew stronger, the stalker's movements slowed down, until he moved in slow motion and the darkness around him had faded away.

While Dr. Timberi sang about fireflies in summer and candles at a romantic dinner, Madame Cumberland and Mrs. Grant reappeared and sent a blast of rainbow-colored light at the stalker. He ducked and rolled a few feet away, dodging the light by centimeters. The stalker jumped up and screamed like a furious, wounded animal. He made wild gestures with his hands, and small spurts of black clouds puffed out from his fingers, but they faded away.

The stalker looked light gray instead of black, and he seemed almost blurry. Bits of light clung to him, causing him to thrash around, screaming and yelling. While he thrashed, his head turned toward the office window, and his eyes met Lexa's. As soon as their eyes met, chains seemed to wrap around her brain, and she couldn't move or even blink. From Conner's loud gasp, she guessed the same thing had happened to him. A cruel smile appeared on the stalker's face, and a narrow beam of darkness shot out of his eyes, slicing through the light in the room.

Lexa—and Conner—screamed. It was the scariest thing

she'd ever seen: pure darkness shooting right at her. Worst of all, for the first time, the teachers looked scared too. They'd seemed calm during the whole fight, but now they sang and quoted louder and faster, appearing agitated and frantic.

The darkness hit the window and shattered it into a gazillion pieces. Lexa heard a raspy laugh and a harsh, hoarse voice. "I was nearly finished there. Thank you so much for your help. I couldn't have done it without you." Lexa tried to look away, but the stalker yelled, "Look at me!" Conner's head jerked up, and then something yanked Lexa's head up too. The darkness he shot at them grew, expanding until it formed a tunnel between them. The stalker stood at the other end in front of some kind of huge, swirling lightning storm. Outside the tunnel, the dim outlines of the three teachers shot faint blasts of light, which bounced off the walls of the tunnel.

"Now you will serve my Masters," the stalker hissed. "Come now, or I will break you until you beg me to take you."

"Oh yeah?" Conner shouted. "Tell your Master we won't serve him!" Lexa was pretty sure he got that from a movie.

The stalker shouted strange words. Lexa didn't understand them, but they made her feel dirty and awful and ashamed, as if her spirit was covered in slime.

A cold wind whipped through the office, yanking papers from Dr. Timberi's desk into the swirling blackness at the other end of the tunnel. The wind grew stronger, pulling at them, snatching pictures off the wall, and sucking the desk drawers out. As everything flew around them, Lexa grabbed the windowsill. Melanie grabbed a filing cabinet, and Conner grabbed Melanie. The stalker's ugly words got louder, the wind grew fiercer, and despair rippled through the air.

The darkness suffocated and smothered them, leaving no light to see, no air to breathe—only thick, heavy darkness and the churning storm at the end of the tunnel.

Lexa's fingers grew numb, and one hand slipped away from the windowsill.

"Lexa!" Conner tried to grab her, but when he let go of Melanie to catch Lexa, the wind caught him, and he flew out the window, gulped down by the swirling, hungry blackness.

Lexa and Melanie screamed, and Lexa struggled to keep her one-handed grip, but the wind was too strong. It felt like each hair on her head was being pulled out one by one. The wind pried her fingers away from the windowsill, pulling her into the tunnel as everything went black.

Alone, Melanie fought the suction. She struggled for a few minutes or hours, but the wind grabbed her with a hundred strong arms and dragged her into the darkness—total, complete, inky blackness. She couldn't see anything and knew she would be destroyed. Body, mind, and spirit—all would be completely gone.

And then, great burning blades of sizzling light sliced through the darkness, followed by a massive explosion, like two suns colliding. And then there was bright, furious, shimmering white light. Melanie heard a loud scream and then—

Nothing.

# CHAPTER 8

# Light and Dark

THE FIRST THING LEXA NOTICED WAS THE pattern in the ceiling.

"Oh, Lexa, you're back." Soft fingers stroked her hair, and Madame Cumberland's warm smile reminded Lexa of hot cocoa on a winter morning. "Just lie still for a few minutes."

"Okay." Lexa groaned. Her head felt like it was wrapped in a whole roll of bubble wrap, and she was dizzy and sick to her stomach.

Next to her, Mrs. Grant knelt by Conner and patted his cheek. "Conner. Conner! Can you hear me? Conner?"

"I'm here," he croaked.

"Oh." She sighed, and it looked to Lexa like two or three hippopotamuses' worth of worry jumped off her shoulders. "Oh, my."

Conner sat up and blinked. "Is it bad that I'm seeing stars?"

"You just sat up too soon." Mrs. Grant's voice was softer than Lexa had ever heard it.

Melanie sat on a chair a few feet away, wide-eyed and shaking. Dr. Timberi had a protective arm around her, and he spoke in a soothing, soft voice.

The teachers were wearing their normal clothes again—no more robes—but they still had a soft glow, much like the light around the moon on a cold night.

Madame Cumberland looked at Mrs. Grant. "Carol, it hasn't been all that long. If you wake everyone now, they may assume that they simply lost track of time."

Mrs. Grant nodded and flicked her red pen, and all of the silver cyclones reappeared, swirling back in reverse. When the last two merged, they vanished. Outside, Lexa heard Coach Thompson and the sixth graders start running again.

She glanced at the clock. It was only 3:20.

Dr. Timberi looked around his room. It was a major disaster—chairs blown apart, music scattered and torn, and big, ugly, black scorch marks all over.

"This will never do." Dr. Timberi raised his baton and hummed Beethoven's *Ode to Joy*. As he conducted, chairs that had been blown to pieces flashed, jumped up, and put themselves together again. Small whirlpools of light swirled around the scorch marks, erasing the spots, and everything returned to normal.

Or at least, mostly normal. About half of the scattered pages of music shot into the air, sorted themselves, and flew back into their cabinet slots. The pages the stalker had shot with his shadow-arrows didn't move.

As Dr. Timberi sang, Lexa felt like someone unwrapped layers of plastic from her woozy head, and by the end of the song, both the room and her stomach had stopped spinning.

While Dr. Timberi cleaned up the room, Madame Cumberland and Mrs. Grant worked on his broken office window. With a few flashes of light, the glass floated back into the frame like nothing had happened.

Dr. Timberi inspected the room, nodded, then smiled. He looked at his students. "Now, little goslings, we need to talk."

Melanie had finally stopped shaking when Dr. Timberi arranged some chairs in a circle and gestured for the others to sit down.

To get there, they had to walk through some of the music that had remained on the floor.

"Hey, isn't this music from the cabinet?" Lexa asked. "The stuff we sang in class today?"

There were no notes and no writing. The paper wasn't white anymore. It had turned an ashy gray color.

Lexa reached down and touched a piece. It crumbled into a pile of cindery dust.

"They have been Extinguished." Dr. Timberi's voice contained a funeral sermon. "Every bit of light gone. Remember that, and understand this is not a game. What we are going to tell you is deadly serious. Now please, come sit down. I imagine you have some questions."

Everyone sat, stared at each other, and stewed in silence for several seconds.

"*Awk*-ward," Conner said, and everyone laughed, which broke the tension.

"Um, so, what just happened?" Lexa's voice was rough.

"The answer, Miss Dell, is more amazing than you can

possibly imagine." A glint of light flashed in Dr. Timberi's eyes and sparked a smile on his face. "To understand any of this, you must understand some fundamentals, so please be patient as I try to explain. There are two basic powers in the universe: Light and Dark. Not daytime and nighttime, not the difference between a light being on or off. I refer to two very real powers. Light and Dark."

"Proper nouns, not adjectives, ya'll." Mrs. Grant punctuated her sentence with a nod.

"Exactly. Light fills the universe," Dr. Timberi continued. "Light radiates out and touches everything, infusing and governing all things, but it is so refined that you cannot always see it—like molecules of oxygen. So one who can guide the Light has great power—as you saw today."

"Is it magic?" Lexa asked.

"Certainly not!" Mrs. Grant sniffed.

Dr. Timberi's smile flashed at full strength. "Not exactly. There is a difference. But that is perhaps a bit deep for now. Think of it as magic if you like—magic with laws and rules."

"Middle school magic!" Lexa said. "I love it!"

Dr. Timberi chuckled. "If Light is good magic, understand that there is also Darkness—black magic. Darkness is a very real power that exists in opposition to the Light. They are in constant, eternal conflict, as are those who follow them."

"Who was that stalker guy? Why was he after us?" Lexa asked.

Dr. Timberi's hands flew up. "One question at a time, Miss Dell. The night of the storm, we believe that

Timo—the man you call the stalker—"

"Wait," Lexa interrupted, "you know his name?"

Dr. Timberi's voice snapped, a sharp whip-crack in the air. "That's none of your concern!" He took a deep breath, pushing the tension out of his face and voice. "We'll borrow your term and call him the Stalker. The Stalker came to your street. We assume the dogs were alarmed by the Darkness he carried and began to raise the alarm. Most likely that annoyed him, so he killed them."

"That is *soooo* sad," Lexa said.

"Yes, it is," Madame Cumberland said in a voice stuffed with sympathy. "The Dark doesn't care about who gets hurt."

"Um . . ." Melanie paused, trying not to be rude. "What *are* you?"

Madame Cumberland chuckled. "We're called Magi."

"Please note, ya'll, that 'Magi' is plural for 'Magus.' Magus is singular, Magi plural." Mrs. Grant spoke with the resigned air of someone who had been fighting a losing battle for a very long time.

"That's right," Madame Cumberland said. She dropped her voice and added, "But most people just use 'Magi' now—singular or plural."

"Okay, but singular or plural, what are Magi?" Melanie repeated.

"You might think of us as warriors for the Light. We fight for the Light, and in turn, the Light gives us great power," Dr. Timberi said.

"So, all the other weird stuff lately—Geoffrey's shorts and Zach flying—was that you?" Lexa asked.

"Goodness no, Lexa!" Madame Cumberland laughed. "That was you—all of you! You're Magi too. You've Kindled."

# VOICES

MELANIE STARED AT MADAME CUMBER-land, stunned into silence for ten seconds. During that silence, her familiar, well-organized world spun away, an insane amusement park ride gone wild—a ride she wanted to get off.

*What is she talking about? No way. She's joking. Or lying. Or she's crazy. But she can't be right. This can't be happening. Not to me.*

While she struggled to make sense of it all, Conner and Lexa exploded with questions.

"One at a time." Dr. Timberi held his hands up. "Mr. Dell?"

"So we're magic-Jedi-Knight whatevers too?" Fireworks went off in Conner's blue eyes.

Madame Cumberland chuckled again. "We're not exactly wizards, but the answer is yes. The three of you Kindled this week."

"We what?" Conner looked worried.

"Kindled. Your latent powers sparked into life. Congratulations." Madame Cumberland beamed at them.

"Some people are born with the ability to use the Light," Dr. Timberi said. "We call such people—us, or you—Adepts. Although Adepts are born with this power, they generally do not discover it until adolescence— around twelve or thirteen. For your entire life, you unconsciously gathered Light and stored it inside your soul. This soul fire, or virtue, grew and accumulated until it burst out. This first burst of your powers is called the Kindling."

"Wait, we all Kindled at the same time?" Melanie finally felt able to talk. "Does that usually happen?"

"Good observation, Miss Stephens," Dr. Timberi said. "No, it does not usually happen. You three are very unique. Possibly unprecedented, in fact. Any Kindling is special— but three at once is really quite remarkable. In fact—"

Cream, turquoise, and purple comets shot into the room, fading into Mrs. Sharpe, Mrs. Davis, and Coach Jackson.

"Something's wrong." Mrs. Sharpe glared all around.

"What do you mean?" Madame Cumberland asked.

"There's places in the Otherwhere where the Shroud is thin, like someone's hiding and just waiting to rip it open or something," Coach Jackson said.

"They've never used the Otherwhere like this before, and they shouldn't be able to tear through the Shroud like that." Mrs. Davis shook her head. "We think they might be coming to attack again."

"We need to get the children home." Mrs. Sharpe took charge with her brisk voice. "Morgan, you drive. Thomas, Mary, and I will go patrol the Otherwhere. Carol and

Mona, you go with the car. Daniel and Joe will follow as well. If anything looks suspicious or wrong, take them to the Sanctuary."

"But what about our parents?" Melanie asked. "They think we're in detention until five."

Dr. Timberi walked over to the wall and yanked the red handle of the fire alarm. "There is our excuse." He raised his voice over the screaming alarm. "Lexa, call your mother and let me talk to her. While I talk, we will go to your lockers and get your homework. Quickly now."

Lexa pushed a button on her phone, which worked now, and gave it to Dr. Timberi as they started walking. "Hello, Cathy? Morgan Timberi. So sorry to disturb you. The fire alarm is going off at the school. I'm sure it's a false alarm, but state law requires us to evacuate. Under the circumstances we will have to bring the children home immediately. I drive past your neighborhood on my way home, so it would be easy for me to drop them off." He paused and nodded. "No trouble at all, I assure you. Very good then. Good-bye." He handed the phone back to Lexa.

Everyone got their homework, then rushed out to Dr. Timberi's gold grandpa car, surrounded by teachers while Dr. Timberi made a similar call to Melanie's mother.

As they climbed in, two more comets shot by and became Mr. Miller and Mr. Duffy, turning in constant circles as they scanned the area.

While the students pulled their seat belts on, Mrs. Sharpe, Mrs. Davis, and Coach Jackson disappeared into some silver curtains hanging in the air, which then disappeared too. Dr. Timberi backed out and started to drive.

The other teachers ran. They got faster with each step, and in about five steps, they blurred into colored comets. As Dr. Timberi drove down the street, the blurs shot alongside them.

"Will we be able to do that too?" Conner asked.

"That would make you formidable on the lacrosse field, wouldn't it? Yes, you will be able to do that when you are fully trained. There are some wonderful things ahead of you. You will learn more tomorrow. Now listen, we haven't much time, and there is much to discuss. I'll arrange with your parents for you to stay after school tomorrow. Come directly to my room, and we will answer your questions and begin your training."

"Training for what?" Melanie blurted out.

"To be Magi, of course," Dr. Timberi said.

"But what if the Stalker comes back tonight to get us?" Melanie's questions surfed on the flood of her anxiety. "What if he tears a gash in the air and comes into our rooms and murders us?"

"We will not allow that to happen, Miss Stephens. We have guarded your homes for the past few nights and will continue to do so. Beyond that, after that explosion today, I can guarantee that the Stalker is severely weakened and will not trouble you anytime soon. He might even be dead." Through the rearview mirror, Melanie saw a shadow of heavy sadness dim his eyes. "But above all—listen, please—you will be safe as long as you do not tell your parents about any of this. That would put them and you in great danger."

"I knew it!" Lexa yelled and pumped her fists in the air. She stopped. "Why?"

"There's a very good reason, but I'm afraid we do not have time to discuss it right now. Please trust me." They rolled up to a stop sign. Dr. Timberi turned around and shot the students a deer-in-the-headlights stare. "The fact that Miss Stephens obeyed our instructions today and did not watch the battle when you two Dells snuck a peek is what saved your lives. This is serious. If you tell your parents you will put them—and yourselves—in grave danger. Their innocence in this matter creates a shield that will protect them, their homes, and consequently, the three of you."

He turned back around and continued to drive. "What's that up there? Where are they? Carol! Mona! Don't you see—?"

They heard a loud tearing sound outside the car. Dr. Timberi's hands choked the steering wheel, and he yanked it hard to his left. The colored comets got closer, circling the car at a dizzying speed. No matter how fast the car went, the blur of light maintained its orbit. After two minutes, Dr. Timberi's shoulders sank and his fingers relaxed their death-grip on the wheel.

"What just happened?" Lexa whispered.

"I think maybe they just scared away an attack," Melanie whispered back.

"I totally want to learn how to do that." Conner didn't whisper. "That is so cool!"

Dr. Timberi pulled into Melanie's driveway.

"Have a good evening, Miss Stephens. Go inside quickly and stay there. I need to get the Dells home and then go join the others."

When Dr. Timberi dropped Lexa and Conner off a few minutes later, they went straight to the kitchen.

"So, what do you think about all that?" Lexa opened the freezer to look for some ice cream.

"Alexandra Louise Dell! Conner Brent Dell!" The chill in their mom's voice made the air in the freezer feel warm.

They turned around. Mrs. Dell's voice was cold, but her eyes were burning.

"Detention?" Mrs. Dell's voice got louder and higher on each syllable. "Seven demerits? In one day?"

Lexa looked at the floor and muttered something about being sorry.

Mrs. Dell laughed, cold and bitter. "You have no idea how sorry you are going to be!" Suddenly the Stalker seemed less scary to Lexa than her mother. "Up to your rooms. Now! No Facebook, no iPod, no texting. Give me your phones." Lexa surrendered her phone, and Conner did the same. "I need time to figure out your punishment."

*Sheesh, Mom, you don't have to freak out!*

Lexa couldn't believe Conner dared talk to their mother like that, especially when she was this mad. His mouth was going to get her in trouble too. She looked over at him.

*We're fighting the forces of evil, and all we get from you is a bunch of yelling. Thanks for the love, Mom.*

He wasn't talking. His lips weren't moving. But she could still hear him.

As they walked upstairs to their rooms, Lexa tried a quick experiment and thought a message as loudly as she could. *Conner, can you hear me?*

# CHAPTER 10

# CONFERENCE CALL

**W**HAT DO YOU MEAN, CAN I—WAIT A *minute! Lexa, you're not talking.* Conner's voice rang in her head.

Lexa forced herself not to squeal.

*Neither are you,* she thought. *But I can still hear you.*

*No way! We can talk to each other in our heads? Whoa! Really cool.* Conner paused. *Or really awkward. Is this because we're twins, or can all the Magi do this?*

I don't know. I wonder if Melanie can do this too? How cool would that be? Anyways, at least this will make being grounded more interesting.

*Conner? Lexa? Is that you? Can I really hear you? Can you hear me?* Melanie's voice joined their conversation.

Hey, Mel! It's Lexa. Now we don't have to pass notes in English!

*I'm really glad you guys noticed it too. I was thinking all the stress had made my mind snap.*

*This is so awesomely cool! So, Mel, what did your mom*

*do when you got home? Our mom is soooo mad about detention, and we're probably grounded for life.*

*My mom is pretty upset too. She changed the passwords on my Facebook and email, and she took my phone. So far, I'm not really liking this whole Magi thing. What do you think about it? I mean, a battle going on between Light and Dark right around us in the twenty-first century? And people we know have these special powers? It's kind of weird. We still don't know why they made us go to detention. Did they want us to be attacked? And what if we don't want to be Magi?* Melanie's thoughts spun faster and faster, as though she was upset or mad.

*I want to be a Magi—I mean, a Magus!* Conner's thoughts shouted. *Did you see the way they were shooting? How cool would that be!*

*But there's more to it than shooting!* Melanie sounded like she was fighting tears. *Don't you get it? The Stalker was trying to kill us!*

She lost her battle with tears, and Lexa could sense her crying, which felt like being in a car on a bumpy road where the driver keeps losing control. Melanie's connection faded. After a minute, Melanie came back. *You guys, this is like a serious war. And they want us to fight without knowing anything about it.*

Lexa made her thoughts soft and gentle. *Mel, I know it's weird and kind of scary, but I know it's right. If I've ever known anything, then I know that. We've got to trust the teachers and follow what they tell us.*

*I think Lexa's right.* Conner's thoughts were gentle too.

*Maybe. But I need to know more before I just sign up. I mean, just a few hours ago, we were pretty sure they were trying to kill us.*

"Conner! Lexa! Come down here this minute!" Unfortunately, that was not a voice in Lexa's head—it was her very real, very angry mother.

"Dum-dum-*de*-dum-dum-*de*-dum-*de*-dum-*de*-dum," Conner hummed the funeral march as they walked down the stairs and into the kitchen. *Nice knowing you, Melanie.*

"You two are in so much trouble," Mrs. Dell hissed. "The rest of your lives are not long enough to ground you—"

The phone interrupted her, and she glared at the caller ID. Her frown got bigger. "Why would someone from the school be calling this late?" She picked it up. "Hello? Oh, hello, Mrs. Sharpe." As she listened, the red burned brighter in her face. "Oh, I see. Yes, I understand. Good-bye."

She hung up. "That was Mrs. Sharpe. Since your detention didn't happen today, she said you'll have to go tomorrow after school instead. You two better not even breathe wrong in the next few days. I can't believe you got detention! Your father and I are seriously thinking about canceling the trip to Disney World next week! You're grounded until further notice. Now get upstairs and do your homework."

*This is so unfair!* the twins heard Melanie shout in their thoughts. *I can't believe they are making us go to detention after all this! Why didn't they tell our parents it was all a mistake or something? Most people lie to get out of trouble. I'm lying to get in more trouble.*

*I guess they'll train us there, and this way they won't have to explain why we're staying after school,* Conner thought as the twins walked out of the kitchen.

*Detention!* Melanie fumed. *That goes on your permanent record! My mom is so mad at me. They can make me go, but they can't make me learn anything!*

*Come on, Mel. It might be fun. So what do you think we'll learn tomorrow?* Lexa asked.

*I'm serious, Lexa. I don't know if I want to go through with this. There's too much I don't understand. I'll have to see how things go tomorrow.*

The next morning, Conner came down to breakfast a little late.

"Hey, Mom—"

"Shhh!"

Lexa and his parents stared at the little TV in the kitchen.

". . . police say there is no connection between the cases. The three missing teens all attended different schools and resided in different parts of the city. Authorities have issued an Amber alert. If you see any of the missing children, please contact the police immediately. Again, three local teenagers are missing this morning. Jaime Martinez, Taylor Nelson, and Jeff Charles were all on their way home from various locations yesterday, but none of them ever arrived."

Three pictures flashed on the screen. They all looked like they were Conner's age, and he felt sick to his stomach. He also thought that the girl—Taylor—was beautiful.

*Lexa, if it hadn't been for our teachers, the Stalker would have gotten us, and that would be us on the news.*

*Yeah, I can see why Melanie's a little scared.*

*Me too.*

A series of honks in the driveway signaled the arrival of the Stephenses' minivan.

"Bye, Mom," they both yelled as they ran out.

# CHAPTER 11

# ILLUMINATIONS

ONCE IN THE CAR, LEXA SQUEALED IN Melanie's head. *Ohmigosh! Did you hear about those kids, Mel?*

*Just a little. My mom and dad turned the TV off this morning when Madi came in, so I didn't hear very much.*

*The police don't know a lot.* Lexa's thoughts flowed through in a dramatic tone. *Three kids never got home yesterday after school. They're about our age too.*

*That's so sad!* Melanie's smile faded, and she felt heavy inside.

*Do you think it has to do with the Stalker somehow?* Lexa asked.

*I don't think so,* Melanie replied. *Dr. Timberi said that the fight yesterday almost destroyed him.*

*Well, I don't know how all this works,* Lexa thought. *I just have a feeling that the Stalker has something to do with this. I'm glad we're going to get trained so we can defend ourselves.*

The minivan pulled up at the school, and they got out of the car.

Melanie remained silent.

*I mean, those kids on the news—it could have been us,* Lexa thought. *We've got to get trained.*

*I don't know, Lexa. I don't like that I can't talk to my mom about it. I feel bad lying and keeping it quiet. I don't like that they're making us go to detention, either. That really makes me mad.*

*Come on, Melanie. It will be boring if you're not there,* Conner thought. *Plus having one more person will help protect us from Dr. Timberi's scary-ness. Magi buds? Maybe we need a secret handshake or something.* He held up his hand for a fist bump.

Melanie bumped his knuckles and felt her face get warm. *Well, maybe I'll go and just see what it's like. But I'm not signing up to be a Magi. Magus. Whatever. I need to find out a lot more first.*

*Yay!* Lexa squealed inside her head. *We'll have so much fun!* She held her fist out, but Conner and Melanie didn't notice.

At the end of the day, they walked to the choir room. Lexa and Conner chatted about what they might learn, but Melanie maintained a cold silence.

"Now, little chicks," Dr. Timberi said, "we have a great deal to do today. I know you must have many questions, and I will try to answer some of them. However, ultimately, you will find your answers as you are trained."

Conner raised his hand. "Uh, trained for what? I mean, what are Magi? What do you—I mean we—do?"

A smile flickered on Dr. Timberi's face. "Light and Dark are locked in a constant struggle, and so are their followers. The Magi are servants, or warriors, of the light. We need to train you to fight the Darkness like we do."

"Okay, that makes sense," Lexa said. "But how did Melanie save us yesterday?"

Dr. Timberi thought for a second. "Miss Dell, right now the answer would possibly confuse you more than the question. Trust me, I will explain eventually."

"Okay, why was the Stalker after us?" Lexa said.

Melanie noticed Dr. Timberi's eyes grow sad. "Umbra is an evil organization, and the Darkhands, as we call them, would have felt your Kindling too. As I said, three Kindlings being so close in proximity and time is unusual. It would certainly have attracted their attention. They want to stop you from becoming Magi. It all comes back to the Kindling."

"So the weird things, like pushing Zach or having super-sensitive hearing, that's all just part of this Kindling?" Melanie's curiosity grew stronger than her determination to maintain her silence with the teachers.

"Yes, Miss Stephens. As you Kindle, the Light randomly amplifies various physical abilities. It seems especially tied to adrenaline. However, we know little about the process of Kindling. You see, everything we know about Lightcraft has come through observations passed down over millennia. Kindling remains a mystery because it happens without warning. Once someone has Kindled, it is too late to study.

"We presume that Kindling releases so much energy that nearly anything can happen, much like a power surge can cause a normally well-ordered electrical system to behave unusually. If we knew when someone was about to Kindle, we could observe them and get more definitive answers. But that is not possible, nor desirable, since the idea of sticking a human in a lab is repellent. And now—"

"Wait!" The emotion in Melanie's voice made it sound like a shout. "Yesterday all the weird things that made us get demerits and go to detention. Was that you?"

"Yes, Miss Stephens. And there was a good reason for that." He looked at his watch. "We haven't much time today, and there is so much to do."

"But my mom thinks I really got detention. We're all in trouble."

Dr. Timberi's voice softened. "I'm sincerely sorry about that, Miss Stephens—all of you. However, it is a matter of priorities. In a battle against the agents of Darkness, the small details of your life really do not matter very much. That is true for all of us. It is the burden of the Magi."

*Oh yeah? Well the details of my life matter a lot to me! And I haven't signed up to join the Magi yet*, Melanie fumed. *This is ridiculous.*

*Just give them a chance, Mel. Let's see what the training is*, Lexa thought.

Melanie frowned but eventually nodded.

"Very good. It's critical that you learn to control your powers, rather than vice versa. The first thing you must learn is how to connect with the Light. You have done this unconsciously and sporadically lately, but you must learn to do it consciously and consistently. Close your eyes and relax," Dr. Timberi continued. "Breathe deeply. Imagine the Light all around you—like the oxygen you breathe. Visualize that image clearly, and try to feel the Light."

Conner closed his eyes and took deep breaths. He squinted and stretched his mind, trying to see the Light with his brain. After several minutes, he felt the sensation of snowflakes tickling his skin. He concentrated harder, and soon his mind saw tiny, red sparkles of Light, like molecules, floating in the air around him.

Conner realized that Light was everywhere, but it was concentrated around him, the girls, and especially Dr. Timberi, as though they were Light magnets.

He tried to grab it and pull it in but was unsuccessful. He could feel but not touch it, and, for sure, he couldn't make it shoot.

*Lame!*

"The Light needs a way to enter your soul—a gateway, if you will," Dr. Timberi continued. "The gateway is different for all Magi."

"Is that why you each did something different during your battle with the Stalker?" Lexa asked. "Singing or speaking French or whatever?"

"Yes, Miss Dell. The beauty of the French language opens a gateway to Madame Cumberland's soul. For me, it is music. You each need to find your own personal gateway. Think of something that makes you truly, deeply happy, then remember the last time you engaged in that activity. Recall the details and sensory images."

"Once you have identified your—Yes, Melanie! That's it!"

Dr. Timberi's voice crackled with enthusiasm. "Well done!"

Conner opened one eye and peeked at Melanie. A line of pink Light flowed from her right finger to her left. Next to her, he noticed a notebook filled with equations.

He laughed. "Your gateway is pre-algebra, Melanie? That's just wrong!"

"Concentrate, Mr. Dell!"

Conner closed his eyes and thought about lacrosse. He felt Light swimming around him, like sparkly tadpoles, but he still couldn't get it to come inside of him.

"Focus on something that fills your soul with joy," Dr. Timberi said. "Find your gateway, and the Light will come."

Conner closed his eyes so hard that his eyeballs almost popped through the back of his head. Still nothing. Next to him, Lexa muttered under her breath, talking in a weird sort of rhythm.

*Lexa, what are you saying? It's distracting.*

*Shhh!*

*Are trying to rap?*

*Conner!*

*Hey, are you doing your lines from* Beauty and the Beast?

*CONNER!*

Conner closed his thoughts off and tried to find his gateway.

*Okay, this is not turning out to be very fun. I thought we'd get to shoot things and run super-fast,* he thought. *What's my gateway—?*

Lexa's squeals interrupted him. "I did it, I did it!"

Conner heard her bouncing up and down in her seat.

"Very good, Lexa!" Dr. Timberi's voice crackled with excitement. "Now, allow the Light to fill you."

"This is so cool!" Melanie said.

*Her voice is so soft,* Conner thought, deep down inside of his head. *Like her hair. Which is red and silky and smells like strawberries—*

Warm goose bumps jumped up all over him. His skin tingled, and happiness partied from his head to his toes. Even his hair and toenails felt happy. He heard a loud crackle, and his fingers got warmer and warmer—almost hot. He opened his eyes and saw a bright red, baby lightning bolt sizzling between his pointer fingers as each cell in his body shouted, "Yeah, this rocks!"

"My goodness, Conner." Dr. Timberi's eyes jumped wide open. "That came very quickly, which suggests an intense connection. Now that you have all learned to access the Light, you must learn to guide it, and truth is the steering wheel. Whether spoken aloud or merely thought, truth guides the Light. Essentially, you must create an action mentally and spiritually before it occurs physically.

"Please think of an object. The Light will respond to the truth in your thoughts by creating a representation of that object. This is called an illumination."

Dr. Timberi held his hands out, and a golden glow appeared between them.

"Swan," he said. The Light stretched out until it formed a gold swan.

He smiled and gave it a gentle push. The swan floated out into the air like a real swan swimming in a lake.

"I created the image in my mind—the truth of the

swan, if you will. That truth guided the Light, which created the illumination. While you are learning, it helps to speak the word out loud. As you become more experienced, that will not be necessary.

"Now, visualize a small object—anything at all. Concentrate on that object. This image will be the truth that guides the Light. As soon as you see the object clearly, imagine the Light between your hands taking the form of that object."

Conner concentrated as hard as he could. Nothing happened.

*Is anyone else having a hard time with this?*

*Yes,* Melanie replied.

*Yeah,* Lexa said. *I have a cramp in my head.*

*I think I'm going to pass out,* Conner thought.

After a few more minutes, Conner took a break. He looked over at Lexa, glaring at the Light between her fingers. Her Light got dimmer, and she glared harder. The Light faded and disappeared.

*I think you scared it, Lex,* Conner said. *You look a little like Mrs. Grant.*

Dr. Timberi walked over to Lexa. "Miss Dell, you focused so hard that you lost your connection to the Light. You shut the gate. Relax and try to open up to the Light. Remember, you cannot compel the Light. Light responds to truth, not to force. Try again."

Conner heard Lexa mutter something under her breath, and the Light reappeared between her fingers. This time, she didn't look quite so mad.

"Flowers," she said. The Light blinked, but nothing else happened.

"What kind?" Dr. Timberi's voice was soft. "Truth is specific."

She closed her eyes. "Roses."

Conner jumped as the Light in front of Lexa boiled and popped. It jerked and pulled itself into four jagged lines. At the end of each line, Light churned and swirled into a shape. Pretty soon a bouquet of four prickly blobs floated in front of her.

*I did it!* Lexa squealed in her thoughts.

*Did you mean to make your roses look like porcupines stuck on jagged sticks?* Conner asked.

"It's a start, Miss Dell," Dr. Timberi said. "Keep trying. Miss Stephens?"

Conner's heart skipped a beat as Melanie scrunched her nose. "Butterfly," she said. The pink light stretched out, then mushed together again. Melanie scrunched her nose harder, and each side of the blob flopped and shook, like a deformed, drowning Pac-Man.

The corners of Dr. Timberi's mouth twitched a little, and he coughed into his hand. "Keep trying, Miss Stephens. You're very close. Concentrate on the image. More detail. And now, Mr. Dell?"

Conner knew it was coming, so he was ready. "Football," he said. *I hope this works!*

The light wavered and flickered. Conner closed his eyes and tried to concentrate.

Still nothing.

"You're doing great, Conner!" Melanie said.

Conner's hands grew warm, and he felt power there, like he was pushing the same side of two strong magnets together.

He opened his eyes and saw a football made of red Light floating there.

*Football?* Lexa thought. *It looks more like a beach ball with a majorly serious allergic reaction.*

Conner shrugged. *Whatever. At least it's in the ball family.*

"Not bad," Dr. Timberi said. "Not bad at all."

"Morgan!" Madame Cumberland ran in. Conner had never seen her look so upset. She saw the students and stopped. "I'm sorry to interrupt—great Caesar's ghost! Illuminations already?" A faint smile appeared for a few seconds. Then her frown chased her smile away, reminding Conner of clouds covering the sun.

"Mona, what is it?" Dr. Timberi's face grew worried too.

The clouds on her face turned into a storm.

"I'm afraid something terrible has happened."

# CHAPTER 12

# MORE BAD NEWS

**W**HAT IS IT, MONA?" DR. TIMBERI ASKED. Conner had never heard him use such a gentle voice.

"Notzange hasn't returned my calls or emails for two weeks now. At first, I assumed she was on a mission or too busy. But when I still didn't hear anything, I got worried, so I contacted the Sodality. They told me they had no idea where she was."

"I'm sorry, Mona." Dr. Timberi's voice flowed soft and warm. "Would you like me to see if the Adumbrators know anything?"

"Would you mind terribly? I'm sorry to ask, I'm just so worried . . ."

"Not at all. We were nearly finished anyway. Please excuse me for a few moments while I send a message."

He walked into his office and shut the door.

"So what's wrong?" Lexa asked.

"My friend Notzange is missing," said Madame

Cumberland. "Notzange was my Guide when I Kindled, like Dr. Timberi is for you, so I've known her for a very long time. She's as old as the hills but sharp as a tack. Notzange is famous because she has a unique gift." She paused. "Oh my stars, you don't know about gifts yet, do you? So much has happened so quickly! A gift is something really special. As your powers develop, the Light gives you a special talent or ability. Notzange's gift is to sense Adepts before they Kindle. It's really remarkable. She can just touch someone and tell if they'll Kindle or not. She's the only one who can do that, so the Sodality sends her on missions frequently."

"So we'll get gifts too?" Lexa asked.

"Yes, Lexa, you will. You all will."

"What will they be? Do you know what my gift will be?"

Madame Cumberland smiled. "No one can tell you, Lexa. No one knows. It will be obvious eventually. Until then, you'll have to be patient."

Lexa grumbled and tugged her ponytail.

"So what does Dr. Timberi have to do with all of this?" Conner changed the subject.

"Many years ago, Morgan was an Adumbrator— which is like the Magi FBI or CIA. There's not much that happens that the Adumbrators don't know about, but they don't share information easily. Morgan still has friends in the office, so he can sometimes get information the rest of us can't access. I hope that Notzange is just somewhere on a top-secret mission for the Sodality. If she is, the Adumbrators will know."

"What's the Sodality thing you guys keep mentioning?" Lexa asked.

"The formal name of the Magi organization is 'The Sodality of the Midnight Stars.' For short, we call it the Sodality. This is our symbol." She pulled out a silver chain from her blouse. Hanging on the end of the chain was a long silver star with eight points surrounded by a curving, crescent moon. It was the same thing that had been on their robes during the fight the day before—and the same image that had burned in the compass courtyard the day of the attack.

"Why midnight stars?" Conner felt confused. "That sounds Dark."

"Knowing what you do about the Magi and the Darkness, can you guess?"

*I hate it when teachers answer a question with a question.*

"Well, it's dark at midnight, but there are still stars shining," Melanie said. Conner noticed that Melanie's dark eyes lit up like, well, stars at midnight. "So maybe the idea is that Magi are supposed to be like stars in the night. No matter how dark it gets, you're always there making a little bit of Light."

*She is so smart*, Conner thought.

"Beautifully put, Melanie." Madame Cumberland beamed. "You'll learn more about the Sodality later."

Dr. Timberi walked out of his office. "I managed to contact Veronique. She wasn't able to say much because Hortense came in." His mouth tightened. "But before we were interrupted, she told me they have not heard from Notzange and are apparently quite worried about her too. I'm sorry, Mona."

"Thanks for trying, Morgan. I'm sure she's fine." Madame Cumberland tried to make her face smile, but her eyes frowned with worry.

Dr. Timberi turned to Conner and the girls. "I think we should call it a day. We will withdraw from the Light now. Please do this slowly or it can cause some shock. Imagine your gateway closing in small increments."

*Okay, this is not so fun,* Conner thought. *Shutting my gateway feels like showering while the last of the warm water runs out.*

When his gateway closed all the way, exhaustion tackled Conner. He gasped. It felt like someone had turned all his energy off. He'd run cross-country, wrestled, and played football in Tennessee during August, but he'd never felt anything like this before. Total and complete exhaustion made him sway and stagger back and forth.

It wasn't just him—Lexa was as pale as Pilaf's legs, and Melanie shook like she was sitting in a killer massage chair.

*Every cell in my body just changed from, "Yeah, this rocks!" to dying a painful death,* he groaned in his thoughts.

"Now, little hedgehogs, as we continue, you will grow accustomed to working with the Light—including closing your gateways. Lightcraft takes a great deal of energy. Just as your body gets stronger with exercise, your soul, and the virtue therein, will get stronger as you work in the Light.

"In the meantime, please practice these skills. They are fundamental building blocks for anything else. Each night when you're in bed, open yourself up to the Light and form an illumination. Eventually, you will be able to do these things instantly."

"Okay." A fierce yawn distorted Conner's voice. "We'll work on it."

"Very good. We shall meet again next week. Have a good evening."

Conner's legs wobbled like retired bungee cords. Every muscle in his body screamed as though he had been running suicides for the last three days.

Lexa groaned as they walked down the hall. *I can hardly move.*

*Me, either,* Melanie added. *That was the hardest workout I've ever had. And all I did was make a few sparkles and a deformed butterfly. I'm not sure I can handle being a Magus, even if I decide to be one.*

Melanie dragged herself out of bed the next morning. She dragged herself down to breakfast. Then, she dragged herself to the car. When she got to Conner and Lexa's house, she noticed they dragged themselves out too.

*I'm so tired,* she moaned. *I definitely don't want to join the Magi if this is what it feels like.*

"You're all quiet this morning," Mrs. Stephens said. "Melanie came home last night and went right to bed. I could hardly get two words out of her. You must still be catching up on sleep from the play last week." No one said anything, so Mrs. Stephens turned the radio on.

". . . police are concerned by what appears to be another string of kidnappings. Once again, the missing children are the same age but from different parts of the city . . ."

She snapped the radio off and engaged Madi in a conversation.

*More kidnappings!* Lexa's thoughts squealed just like her voice. *Scary.*

Melanie didn't say anything. Lexa looked over at her and saw that she was asleep. She shook her and woke her up as they pulled up to the school.

"Have a good day, everyone." Mrs. Stephens stopped the car.

"Bye, Mommy!" Madi gave her a kiss and jumped out of the car. "Bye, Conner." She skipped and joined a pack of first-grade girls.

"Bye, Madi," he replied.

Melanie headed to her locker and reorganized her books. Lost in organizational bliss, she didn't pay attention to anything around her until Lexa tugged on her sweater.

*Mel, should we do something?*

*What?*

Melanie looked up, and Lexa nodded her head in the direction of Conner's locker.

Geoffrey stood next to Conner's locker. He talked at top volume to his posse but glared at Conner. "Coach said if you miss the clinics you're letting the whole team down. And if someone thinks he's too good to come to the clinics then he shouldn't even bother trying out."

The back of Conner's neck glowed bright red.

*Con, you okay?* Lexa asked.

"Some people talk big," Geoffrey continued, "but that's all they can do."

Melanie watched Conner's fists clench.

Right then, Pilaf turned the corner, taking baby steps and balancing a huge model of the circulatory system with a pumping heart and flowing blood. Geoffrey smirked. He nodded to his minions, and they moved away from Conner's locker. Geoffrey slid the end of his lacrosse stick across the floor to one of his friends on the other side of the hall. They held it a few inches above the ground, directly in Pilaf's path. Pilaf was five feet away from tripping and giving his science project a fatal heart attack.

Conner noticed that Geoffrey had stopped talking and looked up. He saw them getting ready to trip Pilaf, and he growled.

Melanie gasped as Conner got faint and blurry. For a fraction of a fraction of a second, he seemed to stretch out, reminding Melanie of a bite of cheese being pulled away from a piece of pizza. He appeared by the middle of Geoffrey's lacrosse stick, slammed his foot down, and shot back to his locker before Melanie heard the sharp crack. The broken ends of the stick fell to the ground. Everything happened in less time than it took for Melanie to blink her eyes.

"My stick! Who broke my stick?" Geoffrey screamed, holding up the broken pieces. "That's a brand new Warrior Titan Pro! Who did that?" He glared all around.

Pilaf stood several feet away, and Conner put his last book into his locker. Geoffrey and his buddies were the only ones near the stick. "Freaking idiot!" Geoffrey smacked his former accomplice with the net. "You broke my stick!"

Conner shut his locker and walked over to Melanie and Lexa. *Um, did you two just see something?* His blue eyes sparkled with diamonds of exhilaration.

*Ohmigosh, Conner!* Lexa nearly shrieked. *What did you do?*

*I'm not sure . . .* His thoughts trickled out slowly. *I was mad because Geoffrey was trash-talking—whatever. But then I saw that he was going to trip Pilaf, and I wanted to snap his stupid lacrosse stick in half . . . and the next thing I knew I was stomping on it, and then I was back by my locker. It happened really fast. Like in the time it takes to blink your eye. Did you see it?*

*Yeah,* Melanie replied. *You got blurry and then stretched out like a rubber band or something. I thought for sure everyone would see you, but I guess not.*

*Cool!* Conner said. *Maybe this is part of getting more powers? Do you think that was sort of the same thing as turning into a comet?*

"Conner!" Pilaf dodged the much larger bodies all around him. "Thanks for taking care of Geoffrey for me."

"What?" Surprise and guilt painted Conner's face.

"That was pretty cool how you snapped his stick in half. How'd you go that fast?"

"Uh, Pilaf, what are you talking about?" Lexa said.

"You know. The way Conner jumped on Geoffrey's lacrosse stick because he was going to trip me. Good thing you did that or my project would be ruined. I didn't see him."

Melanie froze, an icicle of shock. Conner and Lexa did too.

"Oh, I get it." Pilaf winked at them, eyes magnified by his huge glasses. Melanie thought of a praying mantis winking. "It never happened. I didn't see anything at all.

Nope. Nothing." He nudged Conner with his elbow. "Don't worry, I won't tell." He walked off, giggling through his nose.

*How did he see that?* Conner stared at the two girls. *He hasn't Kindled! I mean you have to Kindle to see this stuff, right?*

The first bell rang.

"Hurry, we only have a few minutes to get to class," Melanie said.

## · CHAPTER 13 ·

# IGNORANCE AND INNOCENCE

NO, NO, NO!" DR. TIMBERI SIGHED AND flicked his baton. It looked like he wanted to chop the singing off. "Basses, you do understand that in choral music there is a right and a wrong? You do realize that one does not just sing and hope to bump into the correct note? Mr. Gregory has asked us to sing at the dedication of the new athletic fields after spring break. We really must—"

The bell interrupted him. "Merciful heavens, not a moment too soon. Have a lovely weekend. Mr. Dell, Miss Stephens, Miss Dell? May I speak to the three of you for a moment?"

When everyone had left the room, he led them into his office. There were still no pictures on the wall. "I take it you heard about this latest wave of kidnappings?"

"Is it the Darkhands?" Lexa asked. "It has to be."

"We do not know what is happening, but there are clearly plans afoot we do not understand. Consequently, it is urgent to speed up your training. At a minimum, we must teach you some self-defense fundamentals in case of any future attack."

"Cool!" Conner said. "When do we start?"

"That is our problem. We must find a large block of time without making your parents suspicious. As it happens, I need to reorganize the costumes and scenery and move them to the new storage location under the field house. I thought I might call your parents and offer to hire you to help with that chore tomorrow. That will give us some good, uninterrupted time for training. I hate to ask you to give up your Saturday, and frankly, I do not like to give up my own, but we have work to do. What do you think?"

Melanie squeezed her words into her meekest voice. "Last night, when my mom asked about my day, I had to lie, and it made me feel bad. Plus, she's still mad about detention. And I don't even know if I want to be a Magus."

"Me too," Conner muttered. "I mean, me too that I felt bad about lying. I definitely want to join the Magi, though."

"I see." Dr. Timberi nodded and seemed to drop a layer of his constant emotional armor. "Lying to your parents *should* bother you. It bothers me too. However, there are important reasons for doing so. I alluded to this yesterday but was not able to do it full justice."

He paused, then started to talk again. "If a new student moved in over the weekend and came to school on Monday, would Mr. Duffy expect him to have the homework assignment ready for that day or be prepared to take a quiz?"

"No," Lexa said. "He didn't know about the homework, so it wouldn't be fair."

"Precisely. But after a few days, what will happen?"

"Mr. Duffy will expect him to start learning," Conner said.

"Correct. Mr. Duffy will hold him accountable from the time he begins to understand the expectations. That is the principle. Without knowledge or awareness, you have no responsibility. Awareness and understanding bring responsibility. Essentially, this is the stance of the universe regarding the battle between Light and Dark. Your parents do not know that there is a battle. Consequently, they are not involved, and the universe limits the Dark's ability to attack them through supernatural means—coming into your home through the Otherwhere, for example.

"However, once they know about this battle, even just a little, then the universe will hold them accountable. They cannot be neutral. They must choose sides, and if they choose the Light, the Dark may attack them. Do you understand?"

"I think so." Melanie nodded.

"This is why the Stalker could not take Melanie the other day. Conner and Lexa, when you watched the battle, you gained knowledge, which brought responsibility. You lost the protection of innocence. However, Melanie did not watch and so remained innocent. When the Stalker tried to take her, he unwittingly contravened basic, universal laws. The universe rebelled at this and turned his power against himself in a sort of cosmic short circuit.

"There is something else. The Dark can only control those who open themselves to its power. When you obeyed our instructions, all of our power automatically warded, or shielded, you. Your choice to disobey us severed that protection and put you in the Stalker's power. That was why we could not stop him at that point. The universe and all the elements recognized that your choices had given him power over you."

"Great, Lexa, we broke two major laws at once." Conner gave Lexa a rueful high five.

Dr. Timberi smiled. "When you progress further in your training, you'll be able to protect your families." His eyes got big, his chin started to shake, and his voice clenched in his throat. "Keep your families safe!" He turned around and took a deep breath. When he faced them, his voice and face were calm and even, if a little forced. "Consider the situation. You cannot yet protect your families. However, their innocence provides protection from the Darkhands. And since you live in their homes, you are protected as well. Telling them will remove that protection before you can replace it. What options do we have?"

*I don't really like it, but it makes sense,* Conner thought. *Did you notice how intense he got about protecting our families? I've never seen him like that.*

*I know,* Melanie replied. *That was a little scary. I hope he's okay. So, about our families, I don't like it, but I guess it has to be this way. At least until I decide what I'm going to do.*

"Okay," Melanie said out loud.

"Very good." Dr. Timberi smiled and raised his emotional armor again. "Now, run along to lunch or you will miss it entirely. I will arrange some time for us to work tomorrow."

After school, Melanie went home, ate, and dropped into bed. *Lightcraft—and all the drama it causes—is exhausting. Do I really want to join the Magi?*

"Melanie, are you awake?" Mrs. Stephens opened the door. "Dr. Timberi sent me an email about helping him move some things tomorrow. Did he talk to you about that?"

"Yes, ma'am." *But it's a lie. We're not really going to do that. It's just an excuse to get together and learn how to fight back if we get assaulted. But I can't tell you because if I do then creepy guys can tear a hole in the air in our bedrooms and kill us all.* Melanie took a deep breath. The stress of this secret twisted her soul.

"That's thoughtful of him," Mrs. Stephens said. "You can use that money at Disney World next week. I'll call Cathy and arrange the rides. Good night." She paused in the doorway. "Melanie, is everything all right?"

Luckily Melanie was on the side facing the wall, so her face—and the tears—were hidden.

"Yeah." She squeezed her voice into a bright sunbeam. "I'm just tired." *Another lie.*

Mrs. Stephens waited for a few seconds. "All right. Good night, Melanie."

"Good night, Mom."

Mrs. Stephens closed the door behind her. A bonfire of guilt roared through Melanie for about twenty seconds. Then she fell asleep.

# CHAPTER 14

# TRANSLOCATION

AT EXACTLY EIGHT O'CLOCK, MELANIE'S dad pulled up at the school. Dr. Timberi stood in the parking lot waiting.

"He doesn't look like he's dressed to get dirty or do much work." Mr. Stephens's voice was fully loaded with snark. "What a weird guy. So stuffy. Has he ever shown any emotion at all?"

*What's up with your dad?* Lexa asked.

*I don't know,* Melanie shrugged. *He's never liked Dr. Timberi. I don't know why. One more reason I'm not sure about doing this Magi stuff. If he ever finds out what's going on behind his back, he's going to seriously freak out.*

"You'll earn your money today," Mr. Stephens continued. "He's sure not going to do much. Look at him. Sheesh, he's even got his conductor's stick."

*Uh, your dad's kind of got a point.* Conner nodded his head in Dr. Timberi's direction. *Who wears khaki slacks and a button-up shirt to move stuff?*

*He rolled up his sleeves at least,* Lexa pointed out.

"Good morning, Frank." Dr. Timberi walked next to the car door and bent down.

"Hi, Timberi. When should I pick them up?" Mr. Stephens clipped his words as short as his military buzz cut.

"Will three hours be agreeable?"

"Sure. Work hard." Mr. Stephens looked at Melanie and snickered.

They got out of the car, and Mr. Stephens drove off.

"Shall we begin?" Dr. Timberi led them to the basement, where all of the school's props, scenery, and costumes were being stored. Platforms, stairs, walls, doors, and plastic bins overflowing with costumes were scattered all over the place.

"Hey, it's Conner's Beast head!" Lexa held up a big furry head from *Beauty and the Beast.*

"A marvelous show." Dr. Timberi smiled. "Nevertheless, we are not here today to bask in past glories. We have important work to do. Now, as you saw the other day, Magi can use the Light to move objects. We call this translocation, and it is a fundamental skill in Lightcraft."

He flicked his baton at the enormous wardrobe from *The Lion, the Witch, and the Wardrobe.* Light flashed, and the door flew open. Capes and cloaks floated out, sailed across the room, and landed in a plastic tub.

"The ability to retrieve an object is also very useful." He opened his hand, and a teakettle flew over to him. "You can, for example, reach into someone's house and snatch a pre-algebra book from their room." He smiled at Lexa, then Conner. "Or make a belt disappear."

"Oh, so that's how you got us in detention." Conner laughed. "I wondered about that."

Irritation built up inside of Melanie. "Why did you want us to go to detention?"

"Consider the situation, Miss Stephens. Your Kindling was disrupting the school, and the Stalker was trying to abduct you. We planned to get you three in detention, where I hoped to drop enough hints to provoke you into asking some questions, hopefully sparking a discussion. During that time, the other teachers intended to attack and get rid of the Stalker once and for all."

"Why didn't you just tell us instead of messing with our minds?" Melanie's annoyance flared into anger. "We thought you were trying to kill us!"

"And what would you have said if we had told you?" Dr. Timberi's unusually gentle voice extinguished some of her anger.

She hesitated and blushed. "That you were crazy."

"Exactly." Dr. Timberi nodded. "And that disbelief would have quenched your new powers. One must be extremely careful about giving information to new Adepts. Done clumsily, it creates doubt, which can destroy, or quench, their new powers. Do you understand?"

Melanie nodded. "I think so." *I need to think more about all of this later. Everything has been moving so fast—I need time to think!*

"Very good. Using Light, you can also manipulate objects from a distance." Dr. Timberi pointed at a large book on a shelf about ten feet away. The pages turned as if invisible hands were flipping them. "This allows you to bring chaos to even the very neatest of lockers. Technically, this is telemanipulation, not translocation, but that distinction is unimportant now."

"This is so cool!" Conner yelled. He pointed at a wig from *Annie* and waved his arm back and forth. Nothing happened.

"Before we proceed, you must understand the laws that control this power. So I must explain a bit of theoretical Lightcraft.

"In translocation, the size of the object and the distance you move it are irrelevant. The only important factors are the what and the where.[1] You must know *what* you want to move and *where* you wish it sent, or from *where* you want it retrieved. It is critical to have these two factors fixed clearly in your mind.

"The other day, I was able to retrieve Lexa's prealgebra book only because I had encountered it recently and had a clear image of it in my mind. I also suspected it was in your house. You cannot simply reach out into an unknown place and grab an unknown item. Now, open your gateways."

He paused for a few minutes while they opened themselves to the Light. No one seemed to struggle with it today. "Well done, little tadpoles! You will find that Lightcraft is like riding a bicycle. It can be difficult to start, but once a skill is learned, you can generally do it again and again with little difficulty.

"Please select a small prop or costume piece. Point your arm in the direction of the item you chose. Imagine

---

1. For the relevant portion of *Jurgen's Postulates on the What and Where of Translocation*, see Appendix A on the author's website: http://www.thekindlingbook.com.

the Light extending from your arm directly to the prop, forming a bridge between you and the object.

"Picture the Light as an extension of your arm. Imagine controlling the Light just as you control your own arm and fingers. Then, visualize the action you wish to accomplish. Go ahead and try."

Melanie concentrated as hard as she could, scrunching her nose until it ached. *Okay, this is really awkward. I don't really get what he's describing.*

"Well done, Conner!" Dr. Timberi's voice exploded. "Well done!"

Melanie opened her eyes in time to see a big, fake battle-ax floating through the air. Conner's eyes were closed, but pride had pasted a giant grin on his face. She looked over at Lexa jerking her arm like she was being electrocuted.

Dr. Timberi walked closer. "Miss Dell, less with your arm and more with your mind."

"Ouch!" The wooden handle of the battle-ax smacked Conner in the nose.

"You might want to open your eyes once the object is moving, Mr. Dell." Dr. Timberi hid a smile and then turned to Melanie. "Miss Stephens, I see a nimbus of Light around you, so I know you are connected, but I see no movement. What seems to be the problem?"

"Well, I understand what you're saying about the big Light-arm thing, but it doesn't make sense to me. I mean, it makes sense, but it feels strange."

"I see. Tell me how you open your gateway, Melanie."

"I do equations in my head."

"Very well. Instead of visualizing images, try to

approach this as an equation, a matter of physics. Channel enough Light to move a particular mass through space."

Melanie closed her eyes again and remembered concepts she'd learned in science. She focused on the distance, how much energy it would take to move an object that far, the correct angle, and so forth. While she focused on these factors, a whiteboard appeared in her head. It was covered with a traffic jam of strange mathematical symbols, but somehow, she knew what they represented. As she mentally manipulated the symbols around the board, something clicked, and she knew the answer.

A second later, a lantern from *Peter Pan* sailed through the air and landed in her hand.

"Nicely done, Melanie!"

Melanie looked up and saw Dr. Timberi's glowing smile. He stood next to Lexa, encouraging her while a small suitcase that said "Professor Harold Hill" bobbled through the air in jerky waves.

Lexa gasped, then started to shake like the suitcase. The suitcase crashed to the floor with a loud thud. Lexa's eyes rolled back into her head, and she collapsed too.

"Lexa! Lexa!" Dr. Timberi yelled, dropping down next to her.

# CHAPTER 15

# THE DELCIDIUS THEOREMS

LEXA'S EYES SNAPPED OPEN. SHE LOOKED around, and Melanie thought she looked confused.

"Lexa!" Dr. Timberi put his hand on her forehead. "Are you all right?"

"I'm fine." Lexa's words came out slow and muddy. "For a minute—I . . . I don't know. It was—" She shook her head, rebooting her thoughts. "I started to have a dream or something. I saw a face for a second, and then everything went fuzzy, and . . . I woke up." She looked up at Dr. Timberi. "I'm fine. Just tired. Keep going."

*Are you really okay?* Melanie asked.

*Yeah, I feel fine. I guess I just got dizzy or something. Kind of tired.*

Dr. Timberi looked at Lexa for a few seconds, then nodded. "Very well. But if you start feeling faint, please let me know. Would you like a drink?"

"Maybe some water?"

"Of course." He flicked his fingers. "It will take just a

moment. While we wait for our beverages, let me explain something else. Centuries ago, one of the Magi, a man named Delcidius, proposed guidelines for ensuring that the energy is not wasted. These guidelines are called the Delcidius Theorems.[2] I will paraphrase them. Delcidius noted that using the Light takes energy from your entire soul: heart, mind, spirit, and body. We call this soul-energy virtue. Using the Light, therefore, takes far more energy than using physical strength because it drains energy from more sources. This is why you have been so exhausted lately."

Dr. Timberi held out his hand, and a big feathered hat floated across the room. "It took far more energy to translocate this hat than if I had walked over and retrieved it. I was expending virtue, as opposed to merely burning calories."

Three water bottles and a diet Dr. Pepper floated into the air in front of Melanie. "Normally translocating drinks would be a trivial use of the Light. However, I felt Miss Dell needed water, and this came more quickly than I would have been able to furnish it on my own." He opened the Dr. Pepper and took a sip. "Drink your water while I finish explaining. Since using the Light requires so much energy, you must first decide if the task is worth the energy involved. Some tasks are easier to accomplish the normal way."

He flicked his baton and an overstuffed leather chair jumped up and disappeared in a silver shimmer in the air.

"However, the expenditure of energy is the same

---

2. For the text of the Delcidius Theorems, see Appendix B on the author's website: http://www.thekindlingbook.com.

regardless of distance. I used the Light to move it to our new storage facility five miles down the road, but it would take the same energy to move it five hundred miles or five feet. Obviously, this is much more efficient than renting, loading, driving, and then unloading a truck."

"How does it work?" Melanie asked.

"An excellent question. Do you remember asking how the Stalker could tear a gash in the air and appear somewhere? The answer is the same: the Otherwhere."

"The other what?" Lexa asked.

"The Otherwhere. Let me explain. As a boy, I loved to visit my grandmother. Her house was several stories high with a laundry chute running through the middle of the house. When you had laundry, you simply dropped it in the chute, and it slid down into the basement.

"There is a different dimension all around us, connected to and running straight through our own. We call this dimension the Otherwhere, and you might think of it as a laundry chute in space and time. One can use the Light to open a portal into the Otherwhere, and since it connects everything and everywhere, it is a universal shortcut. It is more complicated than that, but that is the basic idea."

Dr. Timberi pulled out some pictures of the new storage space.

"Since translocation requires an exact idea of the location to which you send an object, these will assist us. You know where the field house is geographically, but the pictures will help you visualize more specifically. We will place the larger set pieces in this corner, costumes over here, and small props on these shelves," he said, pointing to the photos.

"Wait a minute." Lexa felt confused. "I get how we move stuff across the room, but I don't understand how to get them to the storage place."

"Simply do what you did earlier. Imagine the Light picking the object up and moving it to the new location. You are merely sliding it through the laundry chute. It's not as difficult as it sounds. Now, let's give it a try."

He sang a Cole Porter song and flicked his baton. The large wardrobe shot down the aisle. A patch of air shimmered silver, like the air on a hot day, and the wardrobe jumped into the patch and vanished.

As Melanie watched the wardrobe disappear, the symbols whirred and clicked on the whiteboard in her brain. She looked at a bunch of fake flowers from Munchkinland and calculated the angle of flight, how much power they needed to lift off—boom! They sailed into the shining air and disappeared with a silver flash.

"Watch this!" Conner shouted as two swords jumped out of a trunk and hacked away at each other in the air. They swung and slashed, then dropped to the ground with a clattering clash.

"Whoa." Conner staggered like he was dizzy. "That got really hard."

"Yes, that is another part of what Delcidius said: any task done with Light is at least as difficult as doing the same task in the normal way. Try again—but keep it simple."

Before long, a crazy parade of props and costumes floated through the air: ruby slippers clicked, the Beast's head danced with Annie's wig, fish puppets moonwalked, and a tiger pelt wrestled with dwarf beards. Twenty minutes later, the room was empty.

Dr. Timberi smiled and looked around. "Well done."

The students all collapsed onto the floor. With their gateways closed, exhaustion pounded them.

"Catch your breath." Dr. Timberi looked at his watch. "We have two hours left. You will now blend two skills—translocation and illuminations. Specifically, you will use an illumination to send a message to Mr. Miller, who is waiting in the new storage facility.

"First, organize an illumination, then speak a message to it. Next, you will translocate that illumination to the destination. When sending a message, you may send it either to a specific location or to a specific person. It is possible, for example, to send an illumination to another Magus even if you do not know where he or she is. This is explained in *Lant's General Dynamics of Illumincy*[3]—however, I will not go into those details at this time. For now, simply give your images a message and translocate them to Mr. Miller."

"But I'm so tired," Lexa moaned.

"Miss Dell, would any decent coach ever accept that as an excuse? Open your gateway and connect to the Light—it will not be so bad. Now try."

Melanie groaned but connected. *He was right about that*, she thought. *Once I opened my gateway, I went from feeling dead to just being exhausted.*

She stretched her hands out and said, "Butterfly!" The

---

3. For *Lant's General Dynamics of Illumincy*, see Appendix C on the author's website: http://www.thekindlingbook.com

air crackled between her fingers, and a giant, pink butterfly flapped its wings in the air between her hands.

"Look, you guys! It looks more like one of Maddie's
Pokemon cards than a real butterfly. But at least you can
tell what it's supposed to be!"

Conner squinted at his hands. Red Light glowed
between his fingers, but there was no shape.

"You can do it, Conner." Melanie tried to sound as
encouraging as Madame Cumberland.

She heard a loud sparking noise, and a bright red football appeared between Conner's hands.

"Roses!" Lexa commanded. Bright yellow roses
popped up between her hands. The flowers got bigger and
brighter, but then Lexa gasped. Her roses disappeared, and
she fell down to the floor, shaking and trembling again.

Dr. Timberi dropped down next to her again.

"Conner, Melanie, quickly! Your illuminations!
Think a message into them and send them to Madame
Cumberland and Mrs. Grant. Now!"

"Please go superfast and tell Mrs. Grant to come right
now!" Melanie spoke as quickly and loudly as she could.
The butterfly glowed brighter, then flapped away into a
shimmery patch in the air, followed by Conner's football.

"Is she okay?" Conner knelt down next to Lexa.
Dr. Timberi had cushioned her head on a blanket he'd
found and was singing to her in a soft voice while stroking
her hair. He looked at Conner and shook his head, indi-
cating, "Not now, don't disturb me."

*This is really weird,* Conner thought.

*Yeah, I hope she's okay,* Melanie answered. *Why does she
keep collapsing like that?*

*Not that. I mean, that's weird too, but something just sort of hit me about Dr. Timberi. The way he's taking care of Lexa reminds me of my dad or grandpa or something. It's like he really cares about Lexa. I've never really thought of teachers having feelings before. Especially Dr. Timberi.*

Madame Cumberland streamed into the room in a blur of silver light. She wiped her hands on an apron all spattered with spaghetti sauce. Mrs. Grant arrived about four seconds later in a blue comet. She pulled off a floppy straw hat and gardening gloves.

"What happened?" Madame Cumberland knelt down by Dr. Timberi and Lexa.

"She started an illumination, then gasped and collapsed," Dr. Timberi replied. "I cannot calm her or bring her out of it."

Madame Cumberland put her hand on Lexa's forehead like she was testing for a fever. "It's all right. She's Seeing."

"She's what?" Conner asked.

"Seeing," Madame Cumberland replied. "Remember how we talked about getting a special gift or talent? I think that Lexa's gift is Sight. She can see things that others can't perceive, like in dreams or visions—she might also get premonitions or feelings."

"Theelings," Melanie said. "That's what she calls them—they're sort of thoughts and feelings mixed together."

Madame Cumberland smiled. "That's a wonderful way to describe it. These theelings are part of Lexa's gift. Those gifted with Sight can also have vivid visions or dreams, and Lexa is having one right now."

"So she's okay?" Conner asked.

*Conner is such a sweet brother*, Melanie thought.

"She's just fine." Madame Cumberland touched Lexa's forehead again but frowned a little. "I don't think her vision is very pleasant, though."

"How can you tell?" Melanie looked at Madame Cumberland.

"Have you ever noticed that Madame Cumberland always knows just what to say to cheer you up or make you feel special?" Mrs. Grant asked in return.

"Yes, ma'am."

"That's her gift. She can sense what people feel. She can feel what Lexa is feeling right now."

"I think she's coming out of it," Madame Cumberland said. "Keep your voices low. She may be disoriented for a few minutes. Lexa, you're safe," she said in a warm peach pie voice.

Lexa stirred. Her eyes opened and darted all over. It looked like she couldn't really see anything for a few seconds.

Conner grabbed her hand, and she looked up, then let out a long sigh. "Something really bad is happening."

# THE VISION

"TELL US, LEXA," MADAME CUMBERLAND whispered. "Tell us about it. What happened?"

Lexa took a deep breath and started.

"When I opened up my gateway, I got tackled by one of those illumination things. It was sort of a dream or a vision, and someone had sent it out, so it was flying around the Otherwhere like a trapped bird, looking for someone. Anyways, it was like downloading a movie into my head. I saw a tall woman with dark skin and short, white hair. She had an über-colorful robe with some matching fabric wrapped around her head.

"She was stuck in a cage in a black room—everything was black—and there were no lights. She had a big chain around one of her wrists, and it ran through the bars of her cage and hooked into a metal ring in the wall.

"A door opened in the wall, and four big guys in black walked in. Three of them were dragging prisoners behind them. Another woman in swishy black robes sort of swooped in behind them. Her skin was almost white, but her hair was the color of midnight, and it was coiled around her head. It reminded me of snakes getting ready to strike. She looked ice-cold—like your fingers would freeze if you touched her. This really weird, really little man followed her. He had big glasses and kept smiling and bowing.

"The fourth guard didn't have a prisoner. He walked to the cage and yanked the chain attached to the prisoner's wrist. She groaned and pulled herself up, then stumbled over and stuck both of her hands through the bars. It was like she knew exactly what they wanted her to do. The little man walked up and took one of her hands. He bowed at her, but she ignored him.

"The first guard shoved his prisoner up, and then everything changed. I got a fuzzy, blurry glimpse of people in beds and lots of other people in white coats and wires and lights—like a hospital or lab. Right then, I heard Madame Cumberland's voice, and everything faded and, ohmigosh, I am so freakily tired."

Lexa lay back down while the teachers stared at each other. Madame Cumberland stretched her hand out in front of her. The air shimmered, and a picture in a silver frame appeared, which she handed to Lexa. The picture showed Madame Cumberland sitting by an elderly woman with rich, dark skin and short, white hair.

"Lexa, the woman in your vision . . ." Madame Cumberland's voice was anxious.

Lexa felt so bad that she couldn't say anything. She just nodded.

"Oh, Notzange." Madame Cumberland moaned, and

Dr. Timberi put his arm around her shoulder. The quiet in the room got stronger.

Then something hit Lexa, and she sat up. "I know who the prisoners were!"

"Who, Lexa?" Mrs. Grant asked.

"Those kids—the ones who got kidnapped."

The quiet shouted now.

"I'll get the word out," Mrs. Grant said, breaking the silence. "The Sodality needs to know."

"Carol, we also need some extra help here," Dr. Timberi added. "We need to strengthen the guard on these three. I have a feeling we are not done with Darkhands."

Mrs. Grant nodded and left the room.

"What do we do now?" Conner looked at Dr. Timberi.

"I think we had better stop for today," Dr. Timberi said. "Lexa will be fine, but she needs to rest. I will tell your parents that we finished our work early. Melanie, please call your father." He pulled out his iPhone, and Melanie tapped in her dad's number. Mrs. Grant walked back into the room right as Melanie handed the phone back to Dr. Timberi.

"Hello, Frank? Morgan Timberi . . ." Lexa couldn't hear what Mr. Stephens said, but Dr. Timberi clamped his lips together. "No, as a matter of fact I am not going to keep them later. To the contrary, we are done early." He clamped his lips even tighter. "I see. Well, I am certainly sorry to inconvenience you."

*Great, you guys. What's my dad saying?* Melanie asked. *Dr. Timberi's using his soft, polite voice. That means he's really annoyed.*

"As it happens, Carol Grant is here today as well. I

believe she lives in your neighborhood. Perhaps she could bring them home on her way? That way you can play all eighteen holes." Dr. Timberi paused. "Very well then. Good-bye."

He pounded the "end" button. "Carol?"

Mrs. Grant nodded. "I'll just go home and get my car." She started to run, getting faster and faster with each step until she blurred into a comet and shot out of the room.

"It will take her a few seconds to get home and then a few minutes to get back with her car." Dr. Timberi sat down. "I'm unsettled about Lexa's vision. They're getting extremely bold, attacking the school the other day and now taking Notzange." He frowned the Grand Canyon of all frowns. "It is unlike them to be so direct. Something deep is afoot. While I do not comprehend their plan, they are clearly kidnapping teenagers, and trying to see if they are going to Kindle. I don't understand why they're doing this, but we must assume they'll try again to capture you.

"It's more vital than ever that you learn to defend yourselves. Tomorrow, please rest and renew your strength. Beginning Monday, you must stay after school for more training. Every day." He paused. "Do not worry—no more detentions! I suggest you tell your parents that you are attending after-school study hall to prepare for exams." He shrugged. "We're all uncomfortable with deceit, but I see no alternative."

"Okay." Lexa shrugged. Conner and Melanie looked at the teachers and nodded.

"Conner?" Dr. Timberi spoke in a featherbed voice. "I'm sorry—"

Conner shrugged. "It's okay. No big deal."

Dr. Timberi smiled at Conner and nodded. He looked proud. Then his face changed, and he shot a serious look at the three of them. "You really must be careful! Indeed, for the time being, you had best not go anywhere except school and home."

Lexa started to argue, but he cut her off. "Miss Dell, perhaps you would like to end up in a cage in a dark room?"

Lexa shut her mouth.

"If anyone invites you out, I suggest you tell them that you're preparing for your demanding midterms. Be extra cautious. If anyone seems suspicious or menacing, do two things. First, organize an illumination—something strong and powerful, like a lion. Imagine it attacking them. We shall practice this on Monday. Then form another illumination and send it to me immediately. Guide it with your thoughts as you did today, and it will find me."

"Hey, I have a question." Conner acted casual and cool, but Lexa could tell he was dying of curiosity.

"Yes?" Dr. Timberi answered.

"How is Mrs. Grant going to notify the Sodality? Is there some kind of special Light thing you do?"

"No, Conner. For this kind of communication, we have more efficient methods."

"Cool! What do you do?"

Dr. Timberi looked at Conner. "We send an email. Now, shall we go outside?"

Mrs. Grant pulled up in an old Volkswagen with peeling bumper stickers about recycling and clean water and President Obama.

*Are you okay, Lex?* Conner asked. *That was freaky when you collapsed.*

Lexa shrugged. *It didn't hurt. It was just kind of— intense. Hey, Con, today when Dr. Timberi told us to come after school next week, he got all quiet and said your name. Then, you said that something was "okay." What were you talking about?*

*Lacrosse.* Conner's thoughts dropped to a whisper. *I'll miss tryouts on Monday. Whatever. No big deal. Saving the world and learning how to protect ourselves is a little more important.* He pasted a big smile on his face.

He threw up a wall around his thoughts, but before he did, Lexa and Melanie heard what he was thinking, so they knew how he really felt.

Melanie reached over and patted his hand, and Lexa pretended not to see the tears in his eyes.

# REPRISE

"I ASSUME I'M TAKING YOU TO YOUR HOUSE, Miss Stephens?" Mrs. Grant asked from the front seat.

"Yes, ma'am," she answered.

*Hey, Mel,* Lexa thought, *do you want to come over for a while?*

*No thanks,* Melanie replied. *I'm so far behind in pre-algebra, it's not funny.*

*Me too, and pre-algebra is never funny,* Conner said.

*I'm way behind too. Like scarily, epically, lost, behind.* Lexa sighed. When they got home, she worked on her homework until eleven, shutting Conner and Melanie out of her thoughts.

When she finally went to sleep, she had a dream. She saw Notzange's dungeon again. Notzange was touching a prisoner's head, and Lexa realized it was Taylor—the girl who had been kidnapped. The guards yanked Taylor away from Notzange's cage and through the door, then dragged her down a dark hallway made of thick, black bricks.

They stopped at a black metal door. They pushed buttons on a keypad, and the door opened. A ray of light shot out, like it was trying to escape. They pushed her into a room full of people in white coats, who shoved her into something that looked like a round telephone booth made out of dull gold, covered with a tangle of wires and cables.

A few seconds later, Taylor screamed, and a huge flash exploded in the booth, which blinded Lexa and woke her up. Something bad was happening, and watching it upset her. She didn't know what it meant, but she thought Dr. Timberi should know.

Lexa cleared her mind and recited lines from the play until the Light filled her.

She wanted the message to go fast, so she thought of the fastest thing she could imagine. Yellow Light shimmered and stretched into the image of a flying cheetah.

"Go to Dr. Timberi, like speedily fast. Tell him my dream."

The illumination shot out of her room and disappeared.

A few seconds later, the air in front of her shimmered, and a golden swan appeared.

"I received your message about the dream, Lexa." Dr. Timberi's voice echoed in her room. "Thank you. I've sent the information on to the Sodality. And well done with the cheetah! Very impressive."

Lexa looked over her shoulder, expecting her parents to come running in when they heard a man's voice in her room.

His voice continued. "Incidentally, no one can hear or see this message unless they too have Kindled. Now, your illumination carried a great deal of anxiety and tension. May I suggest you relax? You need your rest." Dr. Timberi's voice sang a song in a strange language. Although she didn't understand the words, the song rolled over Lexa, covering her with warmth and washing away her fear, her . . .

The song relaxed her so much that she slept all Saturday night and most of Sunday—she stayed home from church and woke just a few times to eat or get a drink. Monday morning, she woke up early, which was unusual for her, feeling completely rested.

No one else was up, so she decided not to get ready. All the bedrooms were upstairs, near the bathroom, and she worried that running the shower and hair dryer would wake everyone up. She went downstairs and turned on the TV for a little noise and companionship.

A reporter stood outside a bakery. "This morning police have been overwhelmed with phone calls from local businesses. A rash of thefts occurred overnight in the Squirrel Hill area. Police say most of the stolen items were of minimal value, and they're baffled because none of the businesses show signs of forced entry. And, in a strange coincidence, they are all within several blocks of where Taylor Nelson lived. The widespread and apparently random nature of the thefts has left business owners and residents confused. Myrna Bilton owns the Sweet Nothings Bakery."

A tired-looking woman with brown hair and a big apron came on the screen and shook her head. "I just don't know what to think. First Taylor disappeared, and now our shop gets robbed. Do you know what they took? Two-dozen cream cheese Danishes and the tip jar by the cash register. That's all. It doesn't make sense. And you know what? Taylor used to come by and buy a cream cheese Danish for breakfast, and she was always a real good tipper. I just don't understand what's going on."

The camera went back to the reporter.

"Mayor Carlton and Chief Boscoe have scheduled a press conference later this morning. Stay with us throughout the day for more on this developing story. Back to you, Dave and Gloria."

Lexa turned the TV off while a throbbing theeling shouted that this news was important somehow—but she couldn't figure out why.

She wanted to talk to Melanie, but when Lexa reached out with her thoughts, she could tell Melanie was still asleep. Then it was time to get ready, and it was hard to connect with thoughts when a lot was going on. So even though it almost killed her, she kept everything inside until they were in the car on the way to school.

*Did you hear about the robberies?* she asked Melanie.

*Yeah, my parents watched it on the news.*

I have this super-strong theeling that it's majorly important.

What do you mean, Lex?

I don't know exactly. I just feel like it's important, maybe some kind of a clue, but I can't figure out what.

*Wait!* Melanie shouted in her brain. *Wait a second!* She stared away and scrunched her nose.

*What is it, Mel?*

After a few minutes, Melanie shook her head. *I don't know—for a minute something stuck in my mind. You know how sometimes your nose gets itchy and you almost sneeze, but then it stops? My brain just did that. I was about to have a thought, but it stopped.*

They pulled up at school, and Melanie's mom stopped the car, then turned around. "Cathy has a doctor appointment, so I'm picking you up after school. You girls go straight to study hall after school. Conner, when you're finished with lacrosse, you go to study hall too. Wait there for me until I text Melanie and let you know I'm here. Then come straight to the car. We just can't take chances with all these terrible things happening. Madi, I'll pick you up right after school. Stay with Mrs. Riley until you see me."

"Okay, Mommy," Madi said.

"All right then. Have a good day. I'll see you around 5:30."

Lexa stopped at her locker before settling in the English room, where she only survived the boredom of five-paragraph essays by having a thought conversation with Melanie for the whole period. Mrs. Grant shot annoyed looks at them every few seconds and seemed particularly unhappy.

When class finally ended, she tore through her locker like Hurricane Lexa, trying to find the folder for her next class. Loud laughter interrupted her, and she looked up. Geoffrey and his gang were clumped around Conner's locker again while Geoffrey pretended to talk to his friends. "So what do you call someone who doesn't try out for the team? Can you even be a quitter if you don't even try out?"

Conner stared into his locker. His jaw was clenched like a fist, and anger flashed across his face.

Lexa recognized that look. It was the expression that came right before explosions.

*Con, take a breath. Don't get in a fight.*

No answer.

Geoffrey continued, "Not even trying out—that's an epic fail. What's worse than a quitter?"

Conner's hand tightened on the locker door, and his knuckles turned white.

*Conner! Don't let him get to you. If you get in a fight, you'll be suspended!* Lexa started to panic.

"Maybe quitters know they can't really—"

Conner's hand squeezed even tighter, and a metallic clanking sound ripped through the hallway as he tore the locker door off the frame like a piece of toilet paper. Geoffrey froze as Conner turned to face him, and Lexa screamed in her thoughts.

*Conner! Don't hit him!*

# $\mathcal{S}$IGILS

CONNER GROWLED AND PUNCHED THE locker door from behind. The metal bent around his fist like soft wax.

"Geoffrey—" Conner folded the locker door in half. "You are the biggest, freaking jerk in this school. I'm seriously tired of you, and so is everyone else." Geoffrey's eyes stretched as big as Pilaf's glasses, and he shook all over, quaking and quivering until Lexa almost felt bad for him.

"Stop. Being. A. Jerk!" Conner slammed his fist straight through the metal like the football team breaking through a banner at a pep rally.

Mrs. Sharpe buzzed down the hall. "What's going on here?"

"Nothing, ma'am," Conner said. "Just a little accident with my locker. Sorry." He handed her the broken door, grabbed his books, and walked away. As he turned the corner, Lexa saw him shake his hand and mutter, "Ow."

Mrs. Sharpe raised her eyebrows and stared down at

the locker door, then watched Conner's retreating figure until she noticed everyone still staring. "Go to your next class, everybody. Quickly, the bell is going to ring."

As Lexa walked to her next class, she heard Conner's voice in her head. *Whoa! Did you see that?*

*How come you didn't answer me!* Lexa mentally smacked him. *I was so scared you were going to do something stupid and get expelled or go to jail or something.*

*I didn't hear you,* Conner said.

*I'm glad you're okay, Conner,* Melanie joined in. *That's weird you couldn't hear Lexa, though. Maybe the thought conversations don't work if you're distracted or upset.*

*That makes sense,* Conner replied. *Melanie's so smart—* He shut his thoughts off, so Lexa and Melanie didn't hear anymore.

After school, Lexa reported to Dr. Timberi's room, followed by Melanie and Conner.

"Are you all right, Conner?" Dr. Timberi's voice was unusual. Gentle. Lexa thought of warm towels from the dryer. "I heard about the locker door."

"Yeah, I'm fine." Conner nodded.

"Very well then." Dr. Timberi rubbed his eyes, and his voice changed from warm towels to a frayed, worn-out rag. "We have so much to do—so much."

"You seem stressed out. Are *you* okay?" Conner looked at Dr. Timberi.

Dr. Timberi's mouth did a shaky push-up into a weak smile. "You are kind to ask. We have been guarding your homes at night. That is tiring, and Lightcraft, as you have learned, takes a great deal of energy." He frowned. "The Darkhands have not slackened their attempts to get you. In fact, they have increased. Now come these kidnappings and robberies. Some plan is in motion, and I ought to be able to see it, but I cannot understand it." He rubbed his eyes again.

"Now, possums, we really must begin. It seems likely that you will need to defend yourselves in the near future. Since time is of the essence, we must jump ahead into advanced areas.

"There are two very important skills for you to master. First is something we call a sigil. A sigil is a symbol. Think of a knight's coat-of-arms in the middle ages, or the seal engraved on the ring of a king or queen. These emblems were symbols that represented the owner's identity. Likewise, the Magi use sigils—personal emblems or symbols. A sigil is your essence in concentrated form, and it's actually a part of your soul. Because of this, your sigil can act as a proxy for you and is more powerful than an ordinary illumination."

"Is your sigil the swan?" Melanie asked.

"Yes." Dr. Timberi smiled. "And as you have seen, a sigil can help you communicate. Whereas you need to tell an illumination what to say, your sigil is part of you, and it will do what you need it to do without being instructed. A sigil can also be a powerful weapon. When directed at an enemy, it confronts that enemy with the full force of all the Light and virtue in your soul.

"Since time is so limited, and this is such a versatile element of Lightcraft, we will focus on sigils. Open yourself up to the Light, please. Once you're connected, think of experiences that show you at your best. Think of what you hope to be, of what you hope to do. Ponder the truth of who you are when you are your best self. Reflect on that and let your thoughts run free while the Light fills you." He paused for a few minutes.

Light flowed through Lexa as she focused on who she thought she was and who she wanted to be. While she pondered, a river seemed to rush through her, running from her soul to her fingers, making her hands tingle and glow.

She opened her eyes and saw a neon yellow ocean of Light swirling between her fingers. A dolphin made of yellow Light jumped out of the ocean, smiled, and flipped in the air. Lexa felt like it was her doing flips and jumps.

She looked over at Melanie in time to see a delicate unicorn leap and prance out of the soft, pink Light between her hands. Melanie smiled as if it were Christmas morning.

"Yeah!" Conner shouted as bright, red Light flashed between his fingers. A red German shepherd jumped out, rolled over, and then bounded forward a few feet, panting happily.

The sigils were smaller than the real animals would be—Lexa's dolphin was just a few feet long—but they crackled and glowed with power.

Dr. Timberi's big smile softened the rigid stress lines in his face. "Well done! You are not prepared to fight, but this will give you a degree of protection and the ability to quickly send a message to any of us if you get into trouble."

"When will we learn to fight?" Conner asked.

Dr. Timberi laughed. "As soon as we can teach you.

For now, my priority is to teach you some basic defensive techniques.

"Let me emphasize something. Your sigil is a small piece of your soul, so it is easy to call up and does not require as much energy as an illumination. And because they come from your heart and mind, they know exactly what you want them to do.

"However, be cautious! Darkhands can harm you by harming your sigil. Sigil combat is extremely dangerous, and you must be careful. I cannot emphasize this enough: a sigil is a part of your soul, a piece of your essence. If it is harmed or captured or damaged, then you will be harmed or captured or damaged as well.

"There is, for example, something called a sigil trap, a Dark device that captures and paralyzes your sigil. It then forces your body to travel through the Otherwhere and reunites you with your sigil—thus capturing your soul and body. I've also heard of something called a Shadow Box, which uses your sigil to twist and pervert your spirit in a terrible way." Pain flared up in Dr. Timberi's eyes and voice, but he pushed it away. "Consequently, a sigil is not always the right thing to choose in combat. Use it only if you can make a direct hit with one attacker, or as a last resort if you are weak and have very little energy."

He took a deep breath, and Lexa realized he had been talking unusually fast. "Which brings us to attack illuminations. If you are fighting a large group of people, if you are not sure that you can hit your assailant, or if your assailant knows you well, then organize an illumination of a fierce animal and send it at your attacker. The shape you choose signals the Light that you need it to be aggressive and powerful."

"Wait," Conner said. "Did you use your sigil when you fought the Stalker?"

Sadness bloomed on Dr. Timberi's face. It took him a couple of seconds to answer. "No, I did not." He stopped talking, and the silence in the room felt heavy. "You may recall I used the Light to animate the music. There are times when that is the best strategy. For example, if you are tired or weak, a little energy can go a long way. The disadvantage in animation, though, is that it's not as strong as a sigil or illumination."

"Do attack illuminations have disadvantages?" Conner changed the subject.

"Good question, Mr. Dell." Dr. Timberi's voice still sounded tight. "An illumination is not connected to your soul, so if it is damaged or captured, it cannot harm you. At the same time, you have no control once it is released. You might think of your sigil as a sword and an attack illumination as a bullet or grenade.

"Now, imagine you are being attacked. Your first action will be to send an attack illumination at your attacker. Think of a ferocious beast or a powerful weapon of some kind. Pour as much energy into this initial attack as you can. Then send a sigil with a message for me. I will stand by my office door. Send your illumination at the back wall, then send your sigil to me. Mr. Dell, please go first."

Conner closed his eyes and held his hands out in front of him. His fingers glowed and a ball of red Light appeared between them. He shoved his hands forward, and the ball rolled and wobbled across the room, snowballing into a big blob of Light. Then Conner turned around and pointed at Dr. Timberi, creating a small, red poof—but nothing else.

"Whoa!" Conner collapsed into a chair. "In-freaking-tense."

"Were you trying to run your enemy down with a giant ball of pizza dough, Mr. Dell?"

"No, sir." Conner laughed. "I couldn't get it in the right shape. I was thinking about an elephant."

"Concentrate harder. The truth is specific and clear. Try again."

Conner took a deep breath and tried again. Lexa laughed as a baby elephant rolled through the air.

"Oh, how cute!" Melanie sighed.

"Mr. Dell! Pizza dough and now a stuffed animal? If you are attacked, perhaps you should simply fight your assailant with a locker door. Keep practicing. Miss Stephens—your turn."

Melanie scrunched her nose. Her hands glowed with pink light, and she shoved them forward. A possessed chicken made of pink Light flapped and squawked through the air, then smashed into the back wall and disappeared. Melanie turned around and sent a unicorn prancing toward Dr. Timberi, but after a few steps, the unicorn got blurry and dissolved.

Melanie swayed and grabbed a chair. "That's really hard."

"A chicken, Miss Stephens?"

She blushed. "When I was little, my grandma had a chicken that always chased me around the yard, and it gave me nightmares."

"I see. Very interesting. Miss Dell, your turn."

Lexa faced the back wall and muttered her lines from the play. She felt the Light burst and blossom inside of her, and she imagined a lion. But a violet window of Light flashed in the middle of the room, distracting her. A large bird illumination soared out, with shaky and wobbly wings. It flapped twice, pulled its wings back, and soared straight into her.

# · CHAPTER 19 ·

# FLIGHT OF THE CONDOR

CONNER YELLED AND RAN TO HER, BUT THE illuminated bird hit Lexa so fast that she fell unconscious to the floor before he reached her.

"Is she being attacked?" Conner asked.

"No, I do not think—" Dr. Timberi stopped. The glimmer of Light the bird flew through had been fading, like a TV after it's turned off. It had faded almost completely when a giant shadow-hand lunged through, missing the bird's tail feathers by an inch or two.

The hand grabbed at the air, groping for something it couldn't see. Then it reached for Lexa.

A ferocious look exploded onto Dr. Timberi's face. He slashed with his baton, and a big sword illumination appeared and sliced through the air into the shadowhand, shattering it into hundreds of little shadows. They fell, wriggled on the ground, then faded away. Another shadow hand came through the fading Light window and grabbed at Lexa too. Dr. Timberi swung his baton again, and the sword slashed toward that hand.

Right before the sword made contact, the window faded completely, and the hand vanished.

"Melanie, send sigils to Madame Cumberland and Mrs. Grant."

Two pink unicorns galloped into the air and disappeared. Lexa sat up as Madame Cumberland and Mrs. Grant blurred into the room at the same time.

"Great Caesar's Ghost, Morgan!" Madame Cumberland panted. "What happened? Lexa, are you okay?"

"Yeah, fine," Lexa said. "I got another message."

Dr. Timberi smiled. "When she opened up to the Light, a portal opened in the Shroud, and a condor soared in."

Madame Cumberland's face lit up like a birthday cake for a very old person. "A condor? Oh, Morgan, a condor?"

"Exactly." His smile swallowed his face, and Madame Cumberland laughed and cried at the same time.

"What's the deal about the condor?" Conner asked.

"A condor is Notzange's sigil." Mrs. Grant almost smiled.

"Notzange sent her sigil to attack Lexa?" Conner shook his head in confusion. "Is she working for the Darkhands now?"

"Heavens no!" Mrs. Grant said. "If Notzange sent her sigil out, that means she's still alive and well enough to do at least some Lightcraft."

"Why is it always Lexa?" Conner asked.

"Well, with that first vision, Lexa opened a connection between her and Notzange," Mrs. Grant said. "Notzange probably sensed that someone had seen it, so she sent her sigil to find that person again."

"There is some bad news." Dr. Timberi looked at the other teachers. "The Darkhands know the sigil came. I had to fight off their trace."

The other two teachers lost their smiles as he continued. "I believe the portal closed before they could fix an exact location, but they probably established a general vicinity. The Darkhands will surely infer that it came to one of you three."

"So, is that bad?" Conner hoped Dr. Timberi would say it really wasn't a big deal.

"I cannot imagine that Umbra will be happy that Notzange is sending messages that compromise their secrets. Since they failed to stop her from sending the message, I anticipate they will try to capture or kill the recipient of the message."

"Lexa, what was the message?" Madame Cumberland asked.

"Well, it was sort of broken up—like a call when your phone has a bad signal. She's really weak and tired, so her sigil wasn't very strong. But the kidnappings and robberies are all being done by the Darkhands. She was getting ready to say more, but right then the door opened, so she sent her sigil as fast as she could."

"She may not have sent the complete message, but she made the connection." Dr. Timberi's face fluctuated between a smile and frown. "And that will cost them."

"What do you mean?" Melanie asked.

"The fact that Lexa and Notzange have communicated directly means that Lexa can lead us to Notzange,"

Mrs. Grant said. "Just as Umbra traced Notzange's sigil here, the Sodality can trace it back."

"Seriously? How?" Lexa bounced like a spider monkey.

"Well, the pathway is established now," Madame Cumberland replied. "If you send your sigil to Notzange, it will find her. And we can follow your sigil through the Otherwhere—oh my goodness!" Madame Cumberland put her hands on her head. "Speaking of sigils, I completely forgot in all the excitement! Morgan, I got an email right before Melanie's sigil came for me. The Magisterium thinks we need extra help." She seemed almost giddy. "They're sending the Phalanx!"

Mrs. Grant looked shocked, and Conner thought Dr. Timberi might cry.

"Oh, Mona!" He let out a long sigh.

"The Phalanx?" Mrs. Grant repeated. "Here? The Phalanx?"

"Uh, not to sound stupid or anything," Conner said, "but what's the Phalanx? Isn't that some kind of bone in your hand?"

Madame Cumberland laughed like silverware clinking against china. "A phalanx is a military unit. The Twilight Phalanx is one of the most elite combat groups in all of history. They're the Navy SEALS of the Magi world. It means that the Magisterium takes your safety seriously."

"Magisterium?" Melanie raised her eyebrows.

"The governing council of the Sodality. It's like the White House. Or the Vatican," Mrs. Grant explained.

"This means that we will no longer have to patrol your homes all night and teach all day!" Dr. Timberi smiled. "Which means that the quality of both patrolling and teaching will improve dramatically." His smile stretched even bigger. "And since the Phalanx has the resources to protect both you and your families, I believe that we can tell your parents about all of this now."

"Why are they called the Twilight Phalanx?" Lexa asked. "Isn't it kind of dark at twilight? That sounds more like the Darkhands."

"Good question, Miss Dell," Dr. Timberi said, sounding surprised.

*Why do the teachers always sound surprised when me and Lexa say something smart?* Conner thought.

"Twilight is the moment of the last light before the night comes," Dr. Timberi continued. "Historically, the Phalanx has often been the only thing standing between civilization and complete Darkness."

"When will they get—" Conner was interrupted by a noise that sounded like the high pitch of a hundred speeding race cars. The noise was followed by a flash of lightning wrestling a sonic boom in the courtyard.

"Just about now." Madame Cumberland's face sparkled into one big smile.

Conner sprang to the window in time to see a massive, rainbow-colored hurricane zoom into the commons area. As it rotated, twelve small comets shot off, each fading into a person in midair. The twelve people flipped and landed in a crouched combat position. They all wore gray leather suits with the Magi emblem and had masks that covered their heads. Each of them gripped a long, silver staff.

After scanning the area in every direction, the person in front of the circle stood and pointed toward the school.

They ran, somersaulted, and flipped forward until they burst into the choir room, standing in two lines. The leader came in last, strutting down the center of the lines. His uniform was accessorized with cowboy boots and a wide belt with a big, silver buckle. He tugged his mask off, revealing messy, steel-gray hair. His bright, blue eyes crackled with energy as they scanned the room one more time and rested on the teachers.

A huge grin cracked his rawhide face, and a big voice, anchored by a heavy Texas accent, filled the room. "Shoot, Mona. What in Sam Hill's going on here? The Magisterium's been busier'n a hound dog at a flea convention trying to keep track of y'all."

# ·CHAPTER 20·

# THE TWILIGHT PHALANX

"LEE!" MADAME CUMBERLAND GRABBED HIS hand and laughed. "Oh, Lee, we're so glad to see you! My goodness, how long has it been?"

Lee gave her a one-armed hug and a peck on the forehead. "Longer'n a month of Sundays, for sure. Morgan, you old seven-times-son-of-a-gun, how the heck are you? Gained some weight, haven't you?" He punched Dr. Timberi in the shoulder. Conner was sure that would aggravate Dr. Timberi, but he laughed.

"Carol," Lee continued, "you're the same bewitching siren as ever."

Mrs. Grant lost the battle with a smile before managing to sniff and frown again. "My goodness, Lee, you look like you're a hundred. What have you been doing to yourself?"

Lee shook his head. "Well, I'll tell you, Carol. It's the Phalanx. One night in Morocco, next in Moscow. Alaska, then Algeria. That kind of thing ages a man. We're just blowing and going from can till can't. Where's Grimaldi?"

A short figure gave a sharp salute.

"Oh, rusty cowbells! Grimaldi, take off that mask!"

Grimaldi pulled the head-covering off, and long red hair poured out everywhere, like liquid fire. Behind her hair, dark green eyes smoldered. Conner's heart jackhammered his ribs.

*Conner!* Lexa snapped. *You're staring.*

He looked somewhere else, but those eyes stayed with him.

Lee pointed at Conner, Lexa, and Melanie. "So, are these the three jackrabbits causing all the fuss?"

"Yes," Dr. Timberi answered. "Colonel Lee Murell, meet Conner Dell, Lexa Dell, and Melanie Stephens."

"Pleased to meet ya'll. This is Lieutenant Miranda Grimaldi. Grimaldi's gonna head your protection detail. Don't let her size fool you—she could hunt a bear with a switch. She's that tough.

"Now, let's get us a plan here. Magisterium just sent us flying heck-bent for shoe leather. Gordon said it was urgent and we should deploy ASAP and just figure everything out when we got here. I assume Dell and Dell are one package deal, and Stephens is another?"

"Correct." Dr. Timberi nodded.

"Ancillary missions? Collaterals?"

"Mr. and Mrs. Dell, Mr. and Mrs. Stephens, and Melanie's younger sister, Madi."

Lee frowned. "We're just the advance guard—there's two more full squads coming, but they're up to their gills in another mission and won't be here 'til tomorrow at the earliest." He turned to Miranda. "Starting tomorrow, everyone gets a personal detail, round the clock. Until then, we're gonna be stretched a bit thin. Morgan, what's the defensive situation?"

"Currently their parents don't know anything, so they and the homes are shielded," Dr. Timberi said. "They Kindled last week and have started learning sigils and attack illuminations."

"Sigils already? Impressive. No keys, I assume?" Lee asked.

Dr. Timberi shook his head. "No, not yet."

"Can they stream?"

"No, I hoped to start them after sigils and attack illuminations," Dr. Timberi replied.

"Roger. Keep up the training. We'll do the rest. Grimaldi?" He nodded at her.

Grimaldi glared at the Phalanx soldiers. "Lin and Pollack, you take Mr. Stephens and Mr. Dell. Basic recon. Stay out of sight. This is a covert operation."

The first two people in the right line saluted and blasted away in colored comets.

"Whitford, Singh, Mendoza!" The next three soldiers in line stepped forward. "Your principals are Mrs. Dell, Mrs. Stephens, and Madi Stephens. Same orders. Dismissed." They saluted and shot out of the room as comets too.

"Oh, Lee, Lieutenant, one other thing," Dr. Timberi said. "Right before you came, Notzange sent a sigil to Lexa. However, the Darkhands did at least a partial trace. I worry they may be coming."

Grimaldi punched her right fist into her left hand. "If they do come, they're the ones who need to worry."

"Hold on there, Grimaldi." Lee chuckled. "I know you're itching for a fight harder than a bald wildcat with poison ivy, but let's not get cocky here. So Lexa got a sigil from Notzange?"

Dr. Timberi nodded.

Lee let out another low whistle. "Jehoshaphat! You'd better believe the Darkhands'll come after this little filly. We've practically got us a four-lane highway between Notzange and Lexa. Gotta tell the Magisterium ASAP. They'll be happier than gophers in soft dirt to hear this. Only thing that's got them more worked up lately than these three is Notzange being missing. Chu!" Another Phalanx member stepped forward. "I don't wanna risk a sigil. This is too classified. Get yourself back to HQ. Talk to Hortense directly. Tell her Notzange's sigil made direct contact with Lexa.

"After you deliver that message to Hortense, get up to Gordon. I want at least three more squads, and I want 'em two days ago. This is highest priority. Code Double Rainbow. Authorization: Charley Niner Able Delta Five Three Two. You got that?"

"Yes, sir." Chu saluted.

"Hurry! I want you back with two squads quick as a hiccup." He pointed at Lexa. "This little lady's a high-value target now, and we can expect one gollywhopper of a fight." He looked at the teachers. "Magisterium didn't know about Notzange's sigil when they deployed us, but it's a double-darned good thing they sent us when they did. You can just bet the Darkhands are gonna be around here like flies in a farmyard."

Grimaldi barked orders. "Johnson and Weinstein, you're with me. I want a patrol around the perimeter of the school right now. Chavez and De Meers, you're in the

Otherwhere. Let's go." They blurred into comets and flew out of the room.

Lee frowned. "Once we've got them home, I'm not worried. We'll ward their houses quicker than a one-eyed coon can blink. But driving makes them so vulnerable. That's where the Darkhands'll hit us." He shrugged. "Oh well, ain't nothing for it. We'll just have to fight through. I wonder where we'll get the best deal on location."

"What do you mean?" Conner asked.

Lee smiled at Conner. "Location is everything, son. If you have to fight a bear, you wanna do it on the ground or in a tree?"

"Um, honestly, neither option sounds great, but probably a tree," Conner said.

"Smart boy. A tree minimizes the bear's advantages and increases yours. Bear might win still, but you've got a better chance. You always wanna fight on the ground you choose. Ever seen pictures of old castles?"

"Yes, sir," Conner said.

"They could be defended by a handful of people. If a hallway's only wide enough for one person, it don't matter how many people are attacking. The enemy can only fight one at a time, so you've neutralized their advantage. If you're outnumbered, pick a spot that limits the enemy's ability to maneuver. Basic tactics."

Melanie's phone chimed, and she looked at the screen. "I'm sorry to interrupt, but my mom's in the parking lot. She wants us to come right now."

Lee frowned. "Well, so much for choosing the ground we want. We'll just have to make do. Ya'll go on to your momma. Your detachment'll be with you."

All the Magi vanished. No blurring or shooting—
they just disappeared.

"Where'd they go? Are they in the Otherwhere?" Lexa
squealed.

"We're still here," Dr. Timberi said.

"Does this have anything to do with why no one else
could see the Stalker?" Lexa asked.

"Yes, but we'll discuss it later," he replied.

They walked outside to the car and climbed into the
back row—Conner, Lexa, and Melanie. Madi sat in the
row in front of them.

They pulled away from the school and into the
street. Two members of the Phalanx shot along each side
of the car.

*You guys! Look!* Melanie yelled.

Conner turned around in time to see four shiny black
motorcycles roar out of a gash in the air. Each motorcycle
carried two riders dressed in black.

Mrs. Stephens looked in the rearview mirror and
jumped.

"Where did those motorcycles come from? They're
going awfully fast—"

Six more comets shot up to the car, followed by the
teachers' colored comets.

*Looks like the Darkhands underestimated a little.*
Conner felt smug.

"Look out!" Lexa screamed.

Mrs. Stephens screamed too.

*Or maybe not,* Conner added.

A big gash of darkness ripped open just a few feet
ahead of the car, and four more motorcycles roared out.

# Ambush

**M**RS. STEPHENS YELLED AND YANKED THE steering wheel, swerving to the left and just missing the gash.

The comets shot at the motorcycles, but the motorcycles turned and dodged.

One of the motorcycles sped about fifty yards past the car, flipped around, and shot back at them. A man in back of the driver stood up, swinging a rope with a big grappling hook.

A comet screamed by and turned into a Phalanx fighter in midair. He plowed into the man with the grappling hook, who fell off the motorcycle. The Phalanx fighter landed in a crouch, backflipped onto his feet, and then threw his staff like a javelin. It sliced through the air and slid between the spokes of the motorcycle's front wheel. Not quite a second later, the driver flew through the air in a way that ignored the law of gravity.

As motorcycles poured out of more gashes, the Phalanx and the teachers blurred back and forth, fighting one bad guy, then blurring and crashing into another one, then reappearing and fighting again.

*Epic!* Conner thought. *I wish I could see more—they're going so fast . . .*

Three more motorcycles zoomed toward the car.

Mrs. Stephens swerved hard to the right and knocked one of the motorcycles into the air. She slammed her brakes and let the remaining two bikes fly past, then floored the gas pedal and tried to ram the closest one. The driver darted onto the sidewalk and missed joining the bugs in the minivan's grille by about two inches.

"Melanie!" Mrs. Stephens shouted. "Call 9-1-1!"

"Okay, Mom." *Guys, do you think 9-1-1 can do anything?*

Two loud thumps pounded the roof, like man-sized pieces of hail. Two masked men dropped down over the passenger windows, hanging upside down from each side of the luggage rack on the roof.

They smashed the windows with clubs, and one of them reached for Melanie. Conner shoved his hands forward, and his sigil roared out. Growling and snarling, it pounded into Melanie's attacker—who fell off of the car and disappeared.

Conner beamed with pride. *Fail for you, big guy. Don't mess with my—*

His good feelings faded fast. He'd forgotten about the man at his window. Lexa screamed as a steel grip tightened around his neck. As the thick arms squeezed tighter, he started to see spots.

"Leave him alone!" Lexa shouted. Her dolphin appeared with a smile and a flip.

*Great,* Conner gasped. *I'm dying, and your dolphin does tricks. Maybe Shamu can come too . . .*

But Flipper morphed into Jaws and flew like a torpedo behind him. Next thing he knew, he could breathe again.

*Thanks, sis.*

*No worries.* Lexa gave him a high five.

"I don't know what you're doing back there," Mrs. Stephens yelled, "but whatever it is, I need some of it up here!"

Conner looked forward and saw a motorcycle barreling straight at them. When they were a few yards away, the rider on the back stood up and jumped toward the minivan.

*Mine!* Melanie thought. Her cute little unicorn became a bucking warhorse, galloping into the man as he landed on the car. His fingers left skid-marks down the hood as he slid down and disappeared.

*Yeah, Melanie!* Conner's high five lasted longer than necessary.

A hot rainbow exploded outside, and a massive comet appeared, spinning around the car. Mrs. Stephens must have sensed something, because she slammed on the brakes.

Gold light shot into the car, and Dr. Timberi appeared on the front passenger's seat.

"Morgan!" Mrs. Stephens screamed.

"Good afternoon, Elise. I apologize for alarming you, but we haven't much time. You and the children are in danger. We will fight a path clear for you. As soon as you see an opening, accelerate and drive home as quickly as possible. Once there, you should be safe."

He shot back outside, where things got crazier than the cafeteria on the last day of school, as the Magi kicked into action.

Three bad guys lunged at Miranda Grimaldi. She dropped into a somersault, then swung her staff out and whacked the first man in the kneecaps. Next, she pole-vaulted headfirst into the second man's stomach and took him down. The third man advanced, slashing at her with a knife in each hand.

She twirled her staff in front of her like a windmill. Her hands blurred and the windmill turned into a propeller. Miranda's staff whacked the man's left wrist, then his right wrist, and sent the knives flying. Next, the edge of her staff caught him in the side of his head, and he fell down for a long nap.

The fighting raged like this all around them. Somehow, the Phalanx opened up a pathway through at least fifty people.

Dr. Timberi shot back into the car. "Elise, push the gas as hard as you can and stop for nothing until you are home!"

She did, and the car roared forward.

"With your permission, I'll ride shotgun," he said. A big tearing sound split the air, and another gash opened up in the sky. Six people in black robes ran out, shooting big blobs of Darkness.

"Children, down on the floor!" Dr. Timberi ordered. "Elise, you really must put the pedal down all the way!" As Conner pulled his seat belt off, Dr. Timberi pointed his baton out the window. A gold eagle screamed into one of the men in black robes and took him down.

"How are they doing this?" he muttered to himself. "Impossible." His voice rose to a growl. "Where are those other squads? They should be here by now." He fired off a few swans, which looked pretty angry as they sailed away and disappeared.

Sirens screamed behind the car. Conner peeked up over the seat and saw a police car chasing them—which wasn't surprising, since Mrs. Stephens was going about four hundred miles an hour in a thirty-five zone.

Mrs. Stephens slowed down, but Dr. Timberi yelled, "Do not stop, Elise! They're not really police!"

"What?"

"Please trust me. They're imposters."

She sped up.

"How can you tell?" Melanie peeked over the seat.

"Have you noticed that when someone uses the Light, they glow?"

"Yes."

"We call that a nimbus," he said. "Whenever you work with the Light, your soul is illuminated and the nimbus shines through. Darkness leaves a similar imprint, a layer of shadow over one's soul. We call that a miasma. The two people in that car have clear miasmas." He frowned as the sirens got louder. "They will disturb the neighbors with all that noise." He flicked his wrist eight times. With each precise flick, one of the lights on top of the police car exploded, followed by each of the tires. The noise of the sirens stopped, replaced by some violin music. "Much better. Do you three know *The Four Seasons* by Vivaldi? A lovely piece."

The air in front of him shimmered, and a strand of dusty brown Light coiled into a rattlesnake, slithering in the air between Dr. Timberi and Mrs. Stephens.

*Man, your mom is tough!* Conner thought. *If a rattlesnake appeared by my mom, she'd scream like a madwoman. So would my dad.*

*So would mine, normally,* Melanie replied. *But I don't think she can see it since she hasn't Kindled. She probably can't see any of this except the motorcycles and maybe the Phalanx when they aren't blurring.*

"Everyone all right, Morgan?" The rattlesnake drawled with Lee's voice.

"Yes, and we're nearly to the Stephenses'."

"Good. Other squads just got here, and we sent the Darkhands packing. Chu says he got a few pretty angry swan sigils from you though." Lee laughed. "Get 'em inside, and we'll ward the house."

Melanie's mom pulled into the driveway, and Dr. Timberi said, "Quickly, in the house! Run and do not stop no matter what happens."

Dr. Timberi followed them in, walking backward, baton out, eyes darting in every direction. Once inside, he closed the door, and Melanie was blinded by atomic flashes of Light outside. She couldn't see anything for two minutes as hot static sizzled in the air and Light covered the house.

"What's going on out there?" Conner asked.

"The Phalanx is encasing the house in thick layers of Light—shields, basically," Dr. Timberi said.

Lee's rattlesnake appeared again. "All righty, house is warded. Ya'll are in there tighter than bark on a tree. Morgan, listen up. Hortense sent some folks, and they're looking at the adumbrations. They think the Darkhands're going after the family members that aren't there. We've gotta extract them from their current locations and get them to the house."

"I see," Dr. Timberi said. "What do you suggest?"

"Who is he talking to?" Mrs. Stephens whispered to Melanie.

"It's complicated," Melanie replied. "I'll explain later."

"Well, it's gotta be a car," Lee's sigil said. "They can't stream, and they can't go through the Otherwhere. You get 'em in a car, and we'll be on them like a duck on a junebug."

"Very well, Lee. Is Mona there?"

"'Course she's here." The rattlesnake grinned. "Jehoshaphat! I forgot how that woman can fight."

Silver strands of Light appeared in the air, twining and twirling into a bush. Roses swirled out all around, and Madame Cumberland's voice asked, "Morgan, is everyone all right?"

"A little shaken, Mona, but nothing worse. Lee says we need to get the Dells and Frank Stephens here. They know and trust you—could you be the driver?"

"Yes, of course."

"All right, then," Dr. Timberi said. "Give me a few minutes to work this out."

"Carol and I will come over now."

The illuminations faded, and Dr. Timberi looked up at Mrs. Stephens. "Elise." His voice flowed rich and warm.

"I know this must be difficult to understand. If you will give me a little more time, I'll explain everything. For the moment, though, we have reliable intelligence that the same people who attacked you may ambush Frank and the Dells. Your home is safe, so it's urgent that we get them here." He looked her in the eye. "Can you help me?"

"Well, I could call them." Her voice shook, and Melanie could tell she was trying to sound calm and controlled.

"Unfortunately, the energy protecting your house right now will interfere with all your phones."

*That must be why we couldn't use our cell phones in the cafeteria the other day,* Melanie thought.

"Well, I could write to Frank and to Cathy—" Mrs. Stephens jumped as Madame Cumberland and Mrs. Grant shot into the house. Her eyes got big, but she didn't say anything except, "Let me get something to write with."

She went into the kitchen and came back with a pen and some paper. Tension smothered all noise, so the house was silent while she sat with perfect posture and wrote a letter. Finally she said, "Mona, what's your phone number?"

"555-0192," Madame Cumberland said.

She wrote a few more words, signed it, and gave it to Dr. Timberi to read. Melanie looked over his shoulder and read:

> *Dear Frank,*
> *I can't explain fully, but you're in serious danger. This is not a joke. Please follow my instructions carefully.*

> *You need to get here as soon as possible, but you can't come on your own. It's complicated, but when you get this, please call Madame Cumberland immediately. Her number is 555-0192. Please don't delay! We'll explain more as soon as you are here with us.*
> *Hurry and call Madame C!!!*
> *Love,*
> *Elise*

"Now for the really hard one." She started writing again. Melanie looked over her shoulder too.

> *Dear Cathy,*
> *Everything is fine and the children are safe. However, there was a problem on the way home, and we were attacked. We are safe, but you and Brent are in real danger. Please, trust me on this.*
> *Mona Cumberland can help you. Call her immediately and make arrangements to get over here—and bring Brent too: 555-0192. I know it sounds crazy, but please trust me.*
> *Sincerely,*
> *Elise*

"I'd better get where I can be reached on my phone." Madame Cumberland smiled, blurred into a silver comet, and flew out of the house.

Dr. Timberi nodded. "Now we need to deliver the letters. A simple bit of translocation will do the job very nicely. Conner and Lexa, it would be better if only one of you did the letter for your parents. You might rip it if you both try."

"I'll do it," Lexa said.

"Whatever." Conner shrugged.

Melanie and Lexa both closed their eyes and opened their gateways. Melanie had a hard time because she was tired and stressed. But eventually her equations worked and the Light filled her. She thought of her dad, the air crackled, and the letter disappeared. Lexa's vanished immediately after Melanie's.

Mrs. Stephens's eyes grew wider, and her face became a pale china plate.

They waited for five minutes, though it seemed much longer. Finally, the silver rosebush appeared.

"It worked, Morgan," Madame Cumberland's voice said. "I'm on my way now to meet Frank and the Dells. We'll be there as soon as we can."

"Be careful, Mona!" Dr. Timberi's voice sounded urgent and anxious. He looked at Mrs. Stephens. "Your letters worked, Elise. They're on their way."

The house got quiet, except for Madi, who played with her dolls and sang Disney songs at progressively louder volumes.

"Hey, when are we leaving to Disney World?" she asked during a break between "Part of Your World" and "Heigh-Ho."

"In three days, sweetheart." Mrs. Stephens's voice sounded tight.

"And Conner and Lexa are coming too, right?"

"Yes, Madi. We're all going together."

"Are you excited, Conner?" Madi shouted. "Hey, do you want to go on the teacups with me? And the haunted house. My mom says it isn't really scary. Just funny-scary.

I don't like real scary things, but maybe I'll like funny-scary things. How can something be funny-scary anyway? Conner, do you think something can be funny-scary? Mom, can I have something to eat? I'm hungry."

"Come with me, Madi." Mrs. Stephens walked to the kitchen.

The room was silent, and time seemed to slow down.

*Awk-ward,* Conner thought.

About twenty minutes later, Madame Cumberland's sigil blossomed again.

"Here we come! Lee, open the shields."

Melanie and the others ran to the big front window. All she could see was a bubble of blinding Light surrounding the house.

"Here's your door, Mona," Lee's rattlesnake drawled.

One small patch in the Light faded until Melanie could see through it like glass.

Outside, a silver car raced for the open patch while Darkhands and Phalanx soldiers fought a furious battle all around it. Right before the car got to the opening in the shields, a shiny black motorcycle broke through the lines. These riders didn't bother with grappling hooks and ropes. They shot guns.

## CHAPTER 22

# The Parent-Teacher Conference from Heck

Conner watched as Madame Cumberland's car lunged toward the opening. The Darkhands shot one of the tires, and the car slid off course, skidding on three wheels.

Conner didn't think they'd make it to the opening, but at the last second, the opening slid over and caught the car as it fishtailed in. The patch flashed, and the Light bubble became solid once more. Outside, he heard a noise that sounded like a motorcycle slamming into a brick wall, followed by two large bugs hitting a giant bug zapper.

The car screeched into the driveway, smoke blowing everywhere. One of the tires was completely gone.

Madame Cumberland climbed out of the driver's seat, while several members of the Twilight Phalanx exploded through the wards in a white-hot blast.

"We're here," she said, smiling like she'd just finished riding Space Mountain or some other fun-scary ride at Disney World.

Mr. Dell climbed out of the car, pale and shaking.

"Conner! Lexa!" Mrs. Dell inhaled them in a fierce hug. "Are you okay?"

"Uh, Mom," Conner said in a muffled voice, "you're the ones who just got shot at. We're fine."

"Timberi!" Spit exploded out of Mr. Stephens's trembling mouth as he climbed out. "What is going on?" He bellowed like a wounded bull.

"Frank, I'll be happy to explain now that—"

"I've been shot at, and my house is surrounded by heaven-knows-what, and now you're holding my wife and my daughters hostage!" Mr. Stephens yelled. "What is going on?" He looked behind him at the Phalanx. "And who are all these jokers?"

Dr. Timberi's voice was slow and even. "Perhaps we can go inside and sit down—"

"I want answers NOW, Timberi, or I'll take this to the Board of Trustees, and you bet your sweater vests this will cost you your job!"

*This is so embarrassing,* Melanie moaned in her head.

Mrs. Stephens walked over and put her hand on Mr. Stephens's arm. "Frank, I think if we go inside the house, Morgan will tell us what's happening."

He opened his mouth, but Mrs. Stephens tightened her grip on his arm.

"Thank you, Elise," Dr. Timberi said. "I believe I can explain."

"Please, come in," she said.

Everyone went in and sat down while Dr. Timberi explained about Light and Dark, Kindling, and everything else. When Dr. Timberi stopped to take a breath,

Melanie's dad jumped up and yelled, "Are you crazy!"

"Frank." Mrs. Stephens spoke softly, but her message was clear.

"Morgan?" Mr. Dell raised his hand, and Conner felt grateful he wasn't shouting like Melanie's dad. "So you're saying our kids have magical powers of some kind?" He sounded polite but skeptical.

"Yes, Brent. They have powers, although this is not exactly magic."

"I see." Mr. Dell's expression and tone shouted that Dr. Timberi needed medication and a long, long rest.

"Honestly, Morgan, this is going to take all night." Mrs. Grant grimaced. She closed her eyes and vanished, followed by Madame Cumberland and Dr. Timberi.

The parents all jerked upright and babbled at the same time. Conner's dad jumped up and looked around, including yanking up the couch cushion he was sitting on.

*Good call, Dad. Three fully grown adults just slipped under the cushion you were sitting on and hid. Yeah, that's it.*

The teachers reappeared on the other side of the room, wearing their long Magi robes and hovering about three feet off the ground.

"Wait, how . . ." Melanie's dad spluttered.

"I don't understand any of this," Melanie's mom said when the teachers landed on the floor. "But, based on what I saw today, I have to admit that a lot of things are possible that I wouldn't have believed before. However"— her eyes slashed Dr. Timberi with a sharp look—"I have serious concerns about what's been going on behind our backs. What have you been doing with our kids? And why in secret?"

"Let me try to explain." Madame Cumberland stepped forward and smiled. She then explained about knowledge and innocence.

Mr. Stephens snorted so loudly that he almost blew his nose inside out. He started to say something, but Madame Cumberland shot a sharp smile at him and raised her voice just slightly. He settled down, and she continued without any more interruptions.

When she finished, Melanie's mom frowned and looked at the teachers. "You said these people couldn't harm us if we didn't know about them. I didn't know about them, but they attacked my car this afternoon."

"That is difficult to explain." Dr. Timberi frowned too. "It gets into some deep, theoretical areas. In fact, it is unprecedented as far as we know. However, Lexa received an important communication today, and they wanted to capture her very badly. They pushed the limits of what they could do to the extremes. Yet there were still limits. For example, they had to use paramilitary troops to attack you directly in this dimension. They did not simply appear in your car or home, grab the children, and disappear."

"Oh, well that's just great! We're supposed to be comforted because they used paramilitary troops to attack us in this dimension?" Mr. Stephens stood up and clamped his hands over his ears. "NO! NO, NO, NO! Melanie will not be any part of this! Get out of my house! This is crazy! You're all crazy. Get out of my house or I'm calling the police!"

"Now, Frank." Conner's dad stood up. "I don't like this a lot either, but let's discuss this calmly—"

"Calm? Brent, they could have killed these kids! Calm?

People shot at us today, Brent—real bullets! Did you ever get shot at before Timberi started interfering with your kids?" His eyes lit up. "Oh, I get it now. You must be involved in a drug ring or something."

Dr. Timberi's mouth got tight.

"You've got a lot of nerve, Timberi, messing with our families—especially when you don't even have kids! You have no idea what it's like to worry about your children being—"

The sudden silence that screeched into the room was sharper and more awkward than a big gasp. Madame Cumberland, Lee, and Mrs. Grant stared at Mr. Stephens like he had just shouted some really bad swear words.

Dr. Timberi's face burned bright red. He compressed his lips, and his left eyebrow twitched. For a moment, Conner thought he would blow up like an explosion in a fireworks stand.

Instead, he stood motionless.

"Mister," Lee growled, "you're as mean as you're ugly and twice as dumb." He walked up to Mr. Stephens and cocked his fists.

Dr. Timberi stepped between them. "That's enough, Lee." His voice turned cold and bitter as February, but his eyes flashed like summer lightning. "To the contrary, Frank. I know much more than you might think about that." Conner had never heard so much emotion in his voice. Dr. Timberi took a deep breath and turned to face the parents, shoving the emotion back to the hidden vault where he normally kept it. "I understand that this is unusual, upsetting, and difficult to process. Perhaps you can take some time to think and we can talk again—"

"Timberi, I don't need any time to decide that I don't want my child anywhere near you!" Mr. Stephens shouted. "I don't need any time to decide I want you out of my house. Now get out, or I'm calling the police."

Dr. Timberi stood up straighter. "I regret your decision. Nevertheless, you have made your feelings very clear. We will not persist in training Melanie against your wishes. But please allow us to provide security for your family. She—all of you—are in serious danger."

"No!" Mr. Stephens shouted. "Just stay away and everything will be fine. We'll be perfectly safe again when the drug dealers realize we're not helping you!"

"You're about as safe as a bug burrowed into a burning log," Lee muttered.

Dr. Timberi closed his eyes and pulled a breath deep inside of him. "Brent and Cathy?"

Conner's parents looked at each other for a minute. "Let's just forget all of this and move on," Mr. Dell said. Mrs. Dell nodded.

"Frank—" Madame Cumberland wrapped her softest voice in her biggest smile.

"NO!" Mr. Stephens yelled. "Get out of my house now. Not another word from any of you! You're all as crazy as Timberi! I'll have all your jobs! Get out now!"

Dr. Timberi's eyes were cold. "I think we had better go now."

The Magi all walked to the front door and turned the handle. The door opened, and Madame Cumberland walked out.

Mrs. Grant walked out.

Lee went out.

Dr. Timberi walked to the door. His foot crossed the threshold.

He stopped, then turned around.

"We will not interfere with your children against your wishes. Our laws forbid that." His voice got soft and silky. "But we will not allow you to interfere with our work."

*I can't believe this!* Conner yelled in his thoughts.

*We can't just let him go!* Lexa yelled back.

*Guys, what should we do?* Melanie cried. *Maybe I want to be a Magi after all—*

*You will do nothing at all.* Dr. Timberi's voice was very firm. But his lips didn't move. *You cannot serve Light by disobeying your parents' express wishes. That would allow Darkness to have power over you.*

Dr. Timberi looked at them with a sad smile, then walked out the door.

The door shut without making any noise, but Conner felt like it had been slammed.

*Yes, little possums, of course I can hear your thoughts,* Dr. Timberi continued from outside. *All the Magi can. My goodness, did you really think this was unique to you three? Ah, the boundless egocentrism of human adolescents.*

*Wait.* Conner thought, grasping for a ray of hope. *Is leaving a trick to make our parents think you're not going to keep training us?*

*No, Conner. You owe your parents your obedience. It is one of your most fundamental loyalties. If I compromised that, I would place us all in the Dark's power as surely as you and Lexa did when you watched the battle in the choir room.*

*You're really leaving? Just like that?* Lexa asked.

*Yes, Lexa. I'm deeply sorry. But the Light will not allow me to teach you after your parents have forbidden it.*

*But we want to be Magi!* Lexa yelled in her thoughts.

*Unfortunately, the universe does not care what you want. Your parents' wishes have placed a binding, unbreakable obligation on us. We have no choice.* He paused. *I need to go now. Please be careful. Your parents have forbidden us to continue your training. However, they did not forbid you to practice self-defense techniques on your own. Be careful, dear ones. Be careful.*

# THE BLACKS

CONNER HEARD THE FLIGHT ATTENDANT'S voice through his ear buds. "Ladies and gentlemen, we're encountering some turbulence. For your safety, the captain has turned on the 'fasten your seat belt' sign . . ."

Conner couldn't stifle a rueful laugh. The turbulence outside of the plane was nothing compared to the turbulence inside.

Next to him, Melanie's thoughts sounded defensive. *I just think it's interesting that the attacks stopped as soon as our parents made us stop training. How do you explain the fact that as soon as we stopped being Magi, everything went back to normal again? It's been three days since—*

*Who's stopped being a Magi—whatever you call them?* Lexa shouted back. *Not me! I practice every night, and I can do six or seven sigils in a row now. It's not fair, Melanie. You never even wanted to be a Magi and now your dad spoiled it for the rest of us!*

Conner shook his head. It looked like a long week in

Disney World with these two alternating between fighting and frosty silences.

"Ladies and gentlemen, the captain has turned on the 'fasten your seat belts' sign as we begin our final descent into Orlando. Please return your seats and tray-tables to their full, upright positions . . ."

Conner pushed his tray-table up and switched his iPod off. He shoved his backpack under the seat in front of him, where Mr. Stephens talked to a young couple.

"Oh yeah, there's lots to do," Mr. Stephens said, "even if you don't have kids. There's EPCOT, and MGM's a lot of fun."

"That's a relief," the man replied. "I was worried it was just going to be kid stuff and princesses for the next three days."

"Oh, stop it!" The woman laughed and kissed the man's cheek. "You're exaggerating." She looked over at Mr. Stephens again. "I'm so excited! I've always been the biggest Disney fan, but I've never been to Disney World! Kyle's never even seen a single Disney movie, but he planned this trip for my anniversary present. What a sweet husband." She smiled and kissed him again.

Conner tried not to gag. *Okay, kissing could be fun. Maybe. I mean, I'd totally like to kiss—uh, the right person. But these two are getting carried away.* Sitting behind them felt like eating straight sugar for two hours.

"No kidding!" Mr. Stephens said, bringing Conner out of the emotional sugar coma. "That's where we're staying too! What a coincidence."

"How fun!" The woman sounded like a cheerleader whose team just got a touchdown. "Maybe we can do dinner one night. We both love kids . . ." Her voice trailed off, and her eyes filled with tears. She smiled and dabbed her eyes with a tissue. "Sorry about that! Anyway, we both love kids, and we'd really enjoy it."

By now they had landed, and the people in the front of the plane had emptied out. Everyone stood up and tried to stretch.

Mr. Stephens gestured to the young couple. "Everyone, this is Kyle and Kelli Black. They're celebrating their anniversary and staying in the same condo units that we are. Kyle and Kelli, meet my wife, Elise Stephens. These are our good friends Brent and Cathy Dell. Elise and Cathy go way back—sorority sisters at Vanderbilt and all that."

"It's nice to meet you," Mrs. Stephens said as they walked off the plane and headed through the terminal.

Conner's mom smiled. "Did I hear it's your anniversary? Congratulations! How many years?"

"Four." Kelli beamed and showed everyone her massive wedding ring.

"These are our daughters, Melanie and Madi." Mr. Stephens pointed them out.

"Oh, what beautiful girls!" Kelli bent over and patted Madi on the head. "You are *soooo* cute! I may have to kidnap you and take you home with me!" Madi glowed at the compliment.

Conner's eyes kept getting stuck on Mrs. Black—Kelli. Long waves of silky black hair framed big, dark eyes, and she wrapped everything she said in a sunny smile and a heart-grabbing hiccup-giggle. She was short, and Conner could tell she worked out. Her yellow sundress emphasized her tan skin, and she carried a straw hat with a matching ribbon and bow on the back. It was difficult to force his eyes away.

"And these are Brent and Cathy's twins, Lexa and Conner," Mr. Stephens continued.

"It's nice to meet you." Lexa used her politest voice.

"Nice to meet you, sir." Conner extended his hand to Kyle, who crushed his fingers.

Kyle's muscles were as big as they could be for him to still look like a really ripped regular guy instead of a professional body builder. Conner guessed it must have taken hours to give his curly, black hair that wild, messed up look. His perfect, white smile seemed a little fake, as if he were a beginning model who'd been on a photo shoot for a few hours too long.

They all walked and chatted until they arrived at baggage claim.

"Well, we'll see you later," Kyle said. "We've just got our carry-ons, so we're not going to baggage claim. Nice to meet you." He flashed a dazzling smile, and they left.

"Nice couple." Mr. Stephens nodded with approval.

Conner felt like they waited for six months to get their luggage, but they finally had everything but one bag. It was Mrs. Dell's, and she refused to leave until she got it. It looked like another week or two in the airport, and Conner was tired. So he reached out for the Light. It took a minute because he still hadn't figured out his main gateway—and now he probably never would, thanks to Mr. Stephens's big blow-up a few nights ago.

*Jerk*, Conner thought.

He didn't know exactly where his mom's suitcase was, but he could imagine it clearly since he'd carried it to the car. He reached out and grabbed the suitcase with the Light, thinking about the luggage carousel. The air shimmered, and the suitcase rolled out.

"Oh good, I was starting to worry that it hadn't arrived," Mrs. Dell said.

"Okay, the car rental desk is just up here." Mr. Stephens pointed. "Brent, is it under your name or Cathy's?"

Conner tried to ignore the looks that Lexa and Melanie had shot him since the suitcase showed up.

*Conner, I don't think using Lightcraft is a good idea,* Melanie said.

*Do you want to wait all night for one stupid piece of luggage?* he retorted.

*No—it's just that—well, never mind.*

*What?*

She paused. *I don't want to start another fight.*

*Good call! I'm really sick of you two fighting! Lexa, promise Melanie you won't get mad if she tells me what she's thinking.*

Lexa tossed her head and glared, but in her mind, she said, *Fine. I promise.*

*Okay, Melanie. Lexa won't get mad. What were you thinking?*

*Well*—Melanie hesitated—*I wonder if using the Light attracts the Darkness. Or maybe it makes it push back—for every action there is an equal and opposite reaction. That kind of thing. So, if you don't use the Light, maybe the Darkness leaves you alone.*

*Yeah, but I've been practicing,* Lexa said. *And they haven't attacked.*

*Me too,* Conner added.

*I have another idea,* Lexa said.

*What?* Conner and Melanie both asked at the same time.

Well, I wonder if they're working on some complicated plan that's taking a while to get all set up.

*Now isn't this fun?* Conner thought. *Talking and working together—just like the good old days. You know, the good old days last week?*

"What do you mean canceled?" Mr. Stephens yelled, interrupting them. He sounded so mad, Conner thought Dr. Timberi might be around.

Mr. Stephens stood at the rental car desk browbeating some poor college kid. "I'm sorry, sir, but there's nothing here under that name."

"But I have a confirmation code!" Mr. Stephens waved a piece of paper in his face.

"Yes, I understand that, sir, but it's still not showing up. I'm sorry—"

"Excuse me, Frank?" Kyle Black and his perfect teeth stood there with a sympathetic smile. "Is there a problem? Kelli noticed you were still here."

"Oh, nothing too serious, they've just lost our rental cars," Mr. Stephens grumbled. "And apparently they can't make another reservation."

"Why don't you guys come with me and Kell? We've got a lot of room—they messed our rental up too, so we ended up with a twelve-passenger van."

"Well, I hate to put you out." Mr. Stephens looked back at the rental car person. "You're sure you can't rent me a car? I mean, that *is* what your company does, right?"

"I'm sorry, sir. The computers are frozen and nothing is working."

"Maybe we should try another rental company," Conner's dad said.

The airport went dark as the power went out.

"Oh, for crying out loud!" Mr. Stephens shouted.

"Never mind, Frank." Mr. Dell yawned. "No one's going to do anything without power. Let's just get to the condo tonight. We'll call and straighten it out tomorrow."

A few minutes later, everyone sat in the Blacks' van driving down the turnpike. Conner was 110 percent sure that Lexa and Melanie were blocking him from a mental conversation about how cute Mr. Black was.

"Tell you what," Mr. Stephens said to Kelli. "Since you're taking care of our transportation, let us get your meal tonight. We're going to order some pizza when we get to the condos. Why don't you come over?"

"Oh, we couldn't intrude." Kelli gave the most heart-breaking smile.

"This is your family time. We don't want to ruin that." Kyle sounded like an announcer in a cheesy commercial.

"Oh, stop that." Conner's mom swatted her objection away. "Sharing your car with us practically makes you part of the family!"

"Well . . ." he hesitated. "If you're sure. We'd love that, wouldn't we, Kell?"

"Oh yes! Thank you so much!" Kelli sounded like she was performing at a pep rally. "Melanie!" Madi called out in distress. "Help! I can't make my camera work. Hurry! What if we see Mickey?" She waved a pink digital camera.

Conner laughed to himself. *Let's see, if you count the time it took us to get to the airport from our house, our vacation is about four hours old. Since then, Madi has taken roughly four thousand pictures. It's probably overheated.*

"Let me see it, Madi." Melanie fiddled with the camera.

*Conner, stop it! You're staring!* Lexa snapped.

*What?*

*You're staring at Mrs. Black.*

*I am not.*

*You were too.*

*Was not. I was looking to see if Disney World was out there.*

*You know it's not there.*

*How would I know that? I've never been here before.*

*What are you guys arguing about?* Melanie finished helping Madi with the camera and tuned into the conversation.

*Nothing!* They both thought at the same time.

Lexa wanted to cheer when they finally pulled up at a giant condo complex. She was ready to get out of the van. And Conner had finally stopped staring at Mrs. Black, which was good.

*What were you and Conner arguing about?* Melanie asked Lexa.

*The way he stares at Mrs. Black. First Miranda Grimaldi and now Mrs. Black—honestly, brothers are sooo embarrassing. And it's not like Mrs. Black is nearly as cute as Kyle—she totally doesn't deserve him. Plus, she's waaaaay too perky and* chipper. *Like two liters of caffeine and sugar crammed into an eight-ounce can.*

Melanie's thoughts got very quiet, and all she said was, *Looks like we're here.*

The Dells' condo was on the far end of the third floor, the Stephens were right next door, and the Blacks were in the same building somewhere above them.

"Oh how fun, we're in the same building!" Mrs. Black giggled.

*She sounds so fake!* Lexa thought.

"What are the chances of that?" Mr. Stephens said. "We couldn't have planned it better. Let's get settled, and I'll order the pizza. Everyone meet back here in twenty minutes?"

Lexa shared a room with Melanie and Madi. She opened her suitcase and dumped everything in a drawer while Madi burned through another memory card taking pictures of the room. Melanie took forever to unpack and organize her stuff, so Lexa got bored. When the doorbell rang, she ran to answer it.

She opened the door and saw the Blacks, smiling and holding a couple of boxes of pizza.

"We found you," Kyle said.

Something startled her and sparked a bonfire of déjà vu. Lexa's mind flashed back, and she remembered standing in her doorway a few days earlier . . .

The Stalker stared right at them.

He wore a pizza deliveryman's clothes, and he held a pizza box, but it was him . . .

"I've found you," he whispered, then laughed—

Lexa couldn't breathe. She felt like she was in a movie

and someone had pushed "pause." Her brain kept reliving the experience with the Stalker and comparing it to what was happening now. Somehow, for some reason, the two experiences fit together, and a throbbing, burning theeling screamed: *Something is seriously, scarily wrong!*

# CHAPTER 24

# DISNEY WORLD

OUTSIDE OF LEXA'S TRANCE, MR. BLACK'S dazzling smile gleamed in the darkness. "We wrote your room number down wrong and went to the wrong floor at first—we were afraid we wouldn't find you at all."

"Who is it, Lexa?" Mr. Stephens walked out of his bedroom. "Oh, Kyle and Kelli, come on in. I'm glad you two found us. I think I gave you the wrong room number when we talked down in the parking lot."

Lexa moved away from the door, stumbling in a dreamlike state.

"We totally confused whoever is in the unit on the floor below you." Mrs. Black hiccup-giggled as they walked into the condo.

"I'm glad we found you on the next try," Mr. Black said. "I was worried we'd have to go floor-to-floor until we found you. When we got to our condo, we realized that we'd left something in the car, so we went back down and ran into the deliveryman. We thought we'd save him the trip and bring it ourselves."

They walked into the kitchen, and when Lexa could breathe again, she squeezed out a sigh of relief.

*Everything is fine. There's a perfectly logical explanation. They went to the wrong floor at first, so they were glad that they had found us. Nothing to worry about. I'm getting hyper-paranoid like Melanie. It was only a coincidence.*

*Right?*

Melanie paused between bites of pizza. She chose the tone of her thoughts carefully, not wanting to spark another argument. *I totally* understand *why that made you* nervous, *Lexa. I don't think you're being paranoid. I just wonder if it's a coincidence, that's all. What do you think, Conner?*

*Melanie's right. They don't really seem like the Darkhand type.*

*Let's watch them über-closely*, Melanie said. *But I don't think we should mention this to our parents. I mean, after the other night . . .*The memory twisted her face into a wince, and she stopped.

Melanie still felt bad about the way her dad had freaked out, and she didn't want to finish the conversation. So, she focused on Madi, who stood in the middle of the room singing Disney songs in her squeaky, little-kid voice. After each song, she bowed while everyone clapped.

"Oh, she is sooo precious!" Mrs. Black said, then started to cry. She got up and ran into the kitchen.

"Sorry about that." Mr. Black stood up to follow her.

"Is she all right?" Mrs. Dell asked.

"Yes." Kyle stopped. His voice got soft. "It's just that we've always wanted kids. It took a while, but about a year ago, we found out we were expecting. Things didn't work out, and Kell lost the baby. Since then, we get a little emotional sometimes. I'll just go make sure she's all right. Excuse me." He walked into the kitchen after her.

*Okay, guys,* Lexa thought. *After that, I really have a hard time thinking they're Darkhands. I must have imagined it. Forget I said anything.*

"What do you mean?" Melanie's dad shouted into his phone. "No cars? You have no cars at all? If I ran my business like this—" He hung up. "How is every rental car company out of cars?"

"Does that mean we can't go to Disney World tomorrow?" Madi's lips quivered.

"Of course not, sweetheart." Mrs. Black returned from the kitchen. Her eyes were puffy and red, but she smiled. "It just means you'll come with us. You'll all come with us. We've got plenty of room."

"Oh, we couldn't impose on you like that," Mrs. Stephens said. "We'll just wait until—"

"But, but I want to see B-b-b-belle!" Madi's quivering lips matured into full-on sobbing.

"It's no imposition." Mrs. Black's smile sparkled. "It would be our pleasure. We can't have Madi disappointed! As one princess to another."

"But what about your plans?" Lexa's dad asked.

"Our plans are to see Disney World," Mr. Black said. "And what could be more magical than to see Disney World through the eyes of a child?"

*He's so sweet!* Lexa thought.

Conner gagged.

Mrs. Black glowed. "Oh, this is going to be the best trip ever!" She knelt down and hugged Madi.

"What time would you like to leave?" Mr. Black asked our parents.

"Well, what time would you like to go?" Mrs. Stephens asked in return. "You're driving."

"How about if we leave at eight? That way we can park, get passes, and still be there when the gates open at nine."

Everyone agreed.

"Well, we'd better go then." Mrs. Black smiled at Madi. "I want to get enough sleep so we can have some serious fun tomorrow! Thanks for the fantastic entertainment."

"Good night, everyone." Mr. Black put his arm around Mrs. Black, and they left.

"What a sweet couple," Mrs. Stephens said.

"They sure are lifesavers." Mr. Stephens hung up with another rental car company. "Without them, we'd be going nowhere fast. This is the weirdest thing I've ever seen."

"Are we there yet? Is that it? How much farther? Is that it? Are we there? Is *that* it?"

Conner smiled at Madi's frantic excitement. It took twenty minutes to get to the Magic Kingdom parking lot from the condo, which was nineteen minutes too long for Madi. After parking somewhere in Georgia, they walked to the monorail station and waited in line for about six days. When it was finally their turn, they stepped inside.

On the way in, someone bumped Madi, and she dropped her camera outside the car. The monorail chimed to signal the doors were closing, but Madi leaned out to save her camera. Mr. Stephens grabbed her and the camera and yanked them into the car as the doors slid shut.

"Careful, Madi," Mr. Stephens said as the train started. "We almost lost you there."

A few minutes later, the monorail stopped. The doors opened, and the families went up to the booth, bought their passes, and walked onto Main Street, USA. Madi squealed in delight when she saw Cinderella's castle and broke away from the group.

"Madi, stay with us!" Mrs. Stephens yelled and ran after her.

"Hey, everybody," Mr. Dell said, "if anyone gets lost, let's meet again in front of the castle on that bench right there."

"I want to ride the teacups. Conner said he'd ride the teacups with me. And I want to do the haunted house. And I want to . . ." Madi came back, rattling off all the rides she wanted to try.

"All right, gang! Let's go get in line for some rides," Mr. Dell said.

While they walked to the Pirates of the Caribbean ride, Conner noticed an unusually grumpy-looking man. All the other visitors smiled, but this man looked like he'd eaten a storm cloud for breakfast and it was giving him indigestion. Conner didn't think too much about him, though, because he had to use the bathroom.

When he came out a few minutes later, Conner noticed the grumpy man staring at Lexa and Melanie and muttering into a phone. Then he realized something else that made panic jump into his throat.

He sauntered back to the group, trying to act casual and calm.

*Lexa, Melanie, check out that guy to the left about fifty yards in back of us.*

*He looks pretty unhappy,* Lexa said.

*Is that all?*

*Ohmigosh!* Lexa squealed. *What was that thing Dr. Timberi told us about? A my spasm or something?*

*I think it was a miasma.* Melanie managed not to giggle at Lexa. *That guy is definitely what he described—it's like he's covered with a thin, black blanket or something. What should we do?* Melanie's thoughts grew tense and brittle.

*Let's just keep watching,* Conner answered. *If we cry wolf on this one, our parents will seriously freak out. But we definitely need to be careful.*

They noticed at least two more visitors with miasmas while they wandered around Tomorrowland.

*Let's go somewhere else,* Conner thought. *Maybe go get lost in a long line or something.*

They ran across the park to Splash Mountain—a popular ride that always had long lines.

After an hour, Conner, Lexa, and Melanie finally got near the front of the line. A few minutes later, the next boat came, and the eight people in front of them got in and floated off. They moved forward as another boat came up to the loading dock.

"Next, please," the worker smiled.

Melanie and Lexa got in the two front seats, and Conner got in the row behind them. The people behind them started to climb in too, but the Disney World employee stopped them. "Sorry. You'll have to wait for the next boat." She smiled and said, "Enjoy your ride."

*That's weird*, Conner thought. *Why do we get our own boat? All the other boats were full.*

*I think we need to be super careful*, Melanie replied.

They sailed into the mountain and bobbed through the water. Toward the end of the ride, right before the big fall, the boat jerked to a stop, and it seemed as though someone were pushing the boat down in the water

*Are we moving kind of slow?* Melanie asked. *Something feels wrong.*

*Yeah*, Conner thought. *We're a lot lower in the water than we were.*

The boat started again, and they shot down the big drop, screaming as water went everywhere. They got out and stopped at the counter in the gift shop to buy the picture that a camera automatically took when riders went down the big drop. It was quite a souvenir—Conner, Melanie, and Lexa all yelling as they went down the big hill. There was one more thing: in back of Conner, there was a man in black with a knife in his hand. Luckily, he was in the process of falling out of the boat.

# CHAPTER 25

# It's a Small World

MELANIE FORCED HERSELF TO TAKE SLOW, deep breaths.

*You guys!* Lexa squealed as the picture trembled in her hands. *What the heck?*

*Remember how Magi can go invisible? Maybe Darkhands can do the same thing,* Melanie thought. *He must have lost his balance when we went down the hill, and that probably ruined his concentration, so he got visible again.* Now *should we tell our parents?*

*Yeah,* Conner thought back. *If he hadn't fallen off, we'd be dead—and this picture is proof.*

*Should we send a sigil to Dr. Timberi?* Lexa asked.

*I don't think he can do anything,* Melanie replied. *Remember how he said the Light wouldn't let him help us as long as our parents said "no." I bet this was why the Darkhands didn't attack us the last few days. They waited until we were away from the teachers. You were right about them working on some big plan, Lexa. Sorry I didn't listen.*

*It's okay. I was kind of a brat too.*

*It's a good plan. Good tactics,* Conner thought. *If they'd attacked us back home, the teachers would probably have sensed it. Now, we'll just have to protect ourselves. Can anyone do sigils and attack illuminations?*

*I can,* Lexa thought.

*Me too,* Melanie added. *I've been practicing.*

Lexa smiled at her. *I knew you hadn't really stopped being a Magi—guys, start moving.*

Melanie looked up and saw ten people with miasmas coming toward them from different directions.

They started walking as fast as they could.

*Do you think our families are safe?* Melanie worried about the way the Darkhands had ambushed them before.

*I think we're the main ones they want, but who knows?* Conner thought back. *We'll find them as fast as we can— then we better get out of here.*

They walked arm in arm, Lexa and Conner keeping watch while Melanie texted her mom to find out where they were. Mrs. Stephens replied a few seconds later.

*They're just getting off the Tomorrowland Speedway,* Melanie thought.

*Can we meet halfway?* Conner asked.

*There are more people following us.* Lexa's thoughts got shaky.

She was right. There were at least fifteen people following them now.

They jogged while Melanie looked at her map of the park to figure out where they could meet. She jabbed a spot on the map halfway between the Speedway and their location. Then she sent a text.

*Okay, I told them to meet us at the Small World ride,* she thought.

They dodged and wove through the crowd, trying to hide in a human maze. They ran to a fork in the road and darted up toward the Haunted Mansion. Right then, they got lucky. People were packed on each side of the road for a parade, so they shoved their way through the crowd and sprinted across the street, dodging the Disney villain float. They took as many twists and turns as they could and finally saw the Small World ride. Their parents, Madi, and the Blacks were waiting.

"Melanie, what's the matter?" Mrs. Stephens asked.

Melanie took a deep breath. "Remember the Darkhands that attacked us a few days ago? They're back."

"Melanie—" Mr. Stephens's voice rumbled, but when Melanie held up the souvenir picture from Splash Mountain, his jaw dropped, and he spluttered to a stop in the middle of the sentence.

"There are fifteen or twenty people after us," Conner said. "We've got to get out of here right now."

"How awful!" Worry distorted Mrs. Black's cutesy voice. "Maybe we can find some security people!" She looked at a security guard about one hundred yards away. He was covered with a shimmering miasma. "Officer!"

"No!" Lexa shouted. Then she dropped her voice. "He's fake—he's one of them."

"How do you know?" Mr. Dell asked.

"We'll explain later," Conner said. "Right now, we've got to get out of here."

The fake security guard looked up and saw them. He smiled and spoke into his phone.

"Now we really need to hurry," Melanie said. They started walking. Ahead of them, two people stepped out of the crowd. Miasmas. Between them and the security guard, they blocked the way out. Melanie looked over her shoulder. A few of the Darkhands they'd lost earlier had caught up and were only fifty yards behind them.

Three more Darkhands joined the fake security guard.

Fiery stings of panic burned Melanie. *What are we going to do?*

*We need a tree.* Conner thought.

*What?*

*Remember what Lee said? If you have to fight a bear, you want to be in a tree. Basic tactics. They've got more people, so we need to limit their ability to maneuver.* Conner looked at the Small World ride. *Here's our tree!*

"Come on, everyone," he said out loud. "Follow me. Hurry!"

"Conner," Mr. Stephens said. "I'm not sure—"

"Frank!" Mrs. Stephens's voice was sharp. "I don't understand this, but something's going on." She pointed at the gathering Darkhands. There were five of them in a group to the left and another five in a group to the right, walking toward them. "This doesn't make sense, but it's happening! And the kids know more than we do. Let's move!"

"Well said, Elise!" Mr. Dell said.

"We have a plan," Conner said. "Follow us!"

This time, everyone followed him, including the Blacks.

*We have a plan?* Melanie asked.

*Yeah,* Conner said, *right now our plan is to get inside so we're not out in the open.*

*And then?* Melanie asked again.

*Sheesh, do I have to figure everything out myself? For now, just get inside.*

They shoved through the line. "Excuse me, family emergency!" Lexa yelled. A few people muttered, but most of them just looked surprised. They pushed down to the front of the line, and the whole group jumped into a boat, floating forward through the opening of the tunnel that started the ride.

"It's a Small World" blared through the air as chipper British soldier dolls with tall black hats tapped their snare drums.

A sharp swish sliced the air, and a knife landed with a *thwack,* jiggling in the head of a French Can-Can dancer a few yards away. Two more knives followed a second later, sinking into the other dancers' heads.

Everyone screamed and threw themselves down. Melanie landed on Lexa as a blast of Darkness shot over them and exploded into an Irish leprechaun at the end of a rainbow.

"I wish Dr. Timberi were here," Melanie said, dodging leprechaun shrapnel.

"Me too," Mrs. Stephens replied.

"Would you give him permission to help us again?" A frail flutter of hope flickered in Melanie's heart.

"Melanie, what's the use? He's back in—"

"Mom! Just give permission. Hurry!"

"Well, okay, but—"

Melanie mentally grabbed on to her equations and felt Light crackle inside of her. She held her hands out, and a perfect pink unicorn jumped into the air. "Go to

Dr. Timberi!" It galloped a few steps and then vanished.

*Good thinking, Mel,* Lexa thought. "Dad, will you let Dr. Timberi help us?"

"Lexa, what difference—"

"DAD! Come on!"

"Well, sure, but—"

Lexa's yellow dolphin flipped into the air and vanished too.

The flicker of hope got stronger until Lexa interrupted Melanie's thoughts. *Melanie! Behind you!*

Melanie twisted and looked over her shoulder. Three men in black waded through the water about four yards behind them.

Melanie raised her hand again, and her pink unicorn charged into one of the men. He gasped and fell down. She sent another sigil at the man on his right, but he saw it coming and waved his hands. A big, black tarantula appeared and jumped onto her sigil. The spider shot strands of Dark webbing around the unicorn, and Melanie froze, totally paralyzed. She panicked because she realized that if the spider killed her sigil, she would die too.

The spider opened its mouth, but a red German shepherd tackled it while a yellow dolphin appeared and tore away the webbing. As soon as her unicorn was free, Melanie could move again. Three sigils crashed into the spider, and it disappeared. When it vanished, the man who'd sent it collapsed.

As they floated past some Swiss cuckoo clocks, blobs of Darkness smashed into each clock. The clocks exploded and sent splinters through the air. As everyone hugged the bottom of the boat a little tighter, they sailed through an arch into a new room.

*Help me block the entrance!* Conner thought.

They all reached out with the Light, and a few seconds later, happy, singing dolls and props were ripped from their native lands and flew into a multicultural heap in the arch behind them. The barricade burst into flames, while sparks from the newly exposed wires sizzled all around.

*Did someone do the flames on purpose?* Melanie asked.

*I think I did it on purpose*, Lexa thought. *But it might have been an accident.*

*Nice job, either way*, Conner replied. *Hopefully it slows them down a little.*

As the boat floated through a forest of giraffes, the long necks shook and jerked, then sliced down all around them, creating a spotted forest of executioners' axes. Conner, Lexa, and Melanie repelled the giraffes with blasts of Light, then paused for a breath. As they floated into the next section, a large elephant head on the arch above them started trembling and shaking. It slipped and fell, plummeting down with sharp tusks aimed straight at Madi.

As the head rushed closer and closer, blasts of red, yellow, and pink Light slammed into the elephant head and blew it away.

They entered the next area of the ride, where happy penguins in bolero hats whirled in circles across from a South American marketplace.

*Guys*, Lexa thought, *we need to get out. Right now. They're coming in the other way too.*

*How do you know? A theeling?* Melanie asked.

*Yeah, a big one.*

"Everyone jump out here." Conner was a little surprised when everyone obeyed and jumped out.

"Take cover!" Lexa yelled.

Everyone scattered and hid behind market stalls and baskets of props.

*Great,* Conner thought, *the only thing between us and death is a few bushels of fake fruit.*

Loud splashes echoed from the tunnel in front of them.

*There's a lot of people running toward our hiding place,* Conner thought.

A huge crash echoed from the tunnel behind them, followed by more splashes and shouts.

*I think they got through our barricade,* Lexa thought.

*What do we do now?* Melanie asked.

*We wait until they're here,* Conner replied. *Then we shoot sigils and attack illuminations like crazy.*

## CHAPTER 26

# RETURN OF THE MAGI

THE NEXT FEW SECONDS IMITATED YEARS AS shouts and splashes moved closer. Conner plugged his ears. *That song! Over and over and over . . .*

*Do you think Dr. Timberi got our sigils?* Melanie asked. *What if they didn't work?*

*Should we send more?* Lexa asked.

*Let's save our energy. I'm already tired, and we haven't even started fighting,* Melanie replied.

Three men splashed through the archway in front of them. Each man got a sigil in the chest and fell down unconscious.

"Nice shot, Con! Way to go, Lexa—whatever you just did!" Mr. Dell yelled, as if they'd just made back-to-back foul shots.

Five more people stomped through the arch behind them.

*We'd better be careful with the sigils,* Conner thought. *Remember how Melanie got paralyzed earlier.*

He waved his hands, and a red alligator illumination jumped up out of the water and attacked the closest person. It took her by surprise, and she went down. The other four people kept coming—unaware of the glowing yellow fin slicing through the water in back of them.

Lexa hummed the *Jaws* theme song under her breath and a huge shark leaped out of the water and chased one of the Darkhands away.

The remaining three people took a few more steps, then froze. A horrible screech drowned out the lyrics about sharing the world, and a giant, pink chicken appeared. She flew all over the place, flapping, pecking and scratching. The bad guys screamed and ducked as Conner vowed never to eat at KFC again.

More people splashed in. And more. And more—at least twenty or thirty people in each archway now, all coming toward them. Conner, Lexa, and Melanie sent illuminations flying all over the place, but they were much more difficult than sigils. They filled the air and water with them, but there were always more people. And that song! It kept going and going.

*This has to be the only battle in the history of the world fought while happy children sing about world peace*, Conner thought.

Their enemies pushed closer, and the young Magi retreated a few steps back, huddling closer together. Conner found himself fighting exhaustion as much as he was fighting the bad guys.

"Get away from them!"

Conner looked over his shoulder. His mom yanked a prop ladder from the marketplace and smacked a guy in the stomach. Melanie's mom joined her, whacking people on the head with wooden pineapples. His dad punched someone in the nose, while Mr. Stephens did some legit tae-kwon-do.

They all fought—but the bad guys kept coming closer.

Conner tried another attack illumination, but instead of a T-Rex, he got a newt. Exhaustion was winning. Fast.

*Maybe we better go back to sigils*, Melanie panted in her thoughts. *Illuminations are too hard.*

*Good idea*, Conner replied.

When someone tried to tackle Lexa, Conner sent a fuzzy German shepherd plodding into him.

When someone grabbed at Conner, Lexa sent a squiggly yellow blur through the air. Her sigil looked more like a tadpole now. Exhaustion had reduced Conner's German shepherd to a Chihuahua and Melanie's unicorn to a toy pony.

Conner wiped the sweat out of his eyes. Melanie staggered and fell. He grabbed her hand to help steady her. As soon as they touched, a German shepherd the size of a Clydesdale thundered out of his hands and slammed into the next five bad guys.

Melanie's hand slipped out of Conner's. He looked up and saw a big, dark glove at the end of a big dark arm grab Melanie's hair. She struggled, but the man was huge and gripped her with hands like demon pliers. She managed to twist around and kick his shins really hard. He bellowed with rage and grabbed her throat. While Conner struggled to get to her, Melanie's face grew red, then purple. Soon, she stopped moving.

That was when a gold comet shot through the air and smashed into the man.

"PUT HER DOWN!" Dr. Timberi's voice roared through the tunnel like a lion. His eyes flashed, and his gold robes seemed to be woven from flames. His baton flew in a blur of motion, sending blinding, furious blasts of gold Light exploding everywhere.

"Watch out," Lexa yelled. The man that had grabbed Melanie got back up and ran at Dr. Timberi.

Dr. Timberi's eyes narrowed, and his nostrils flared. He slashed his baton and sent a huge eagle illumination screeching into the man, who fell down for good. A sound like a falling bomb shrieked through the tunnel as two more comets shot in, becoming Madame Cumberland and Mrs. Grant, pointer stick and red pen blazing.

On the other side of the river was a rainforest made out of long strips of plastic. Mrs. Grant muttered about transitive verbs and flicked her red pen, and the streamers came alive. Stretching out like the tentacles of an octopus, they wrapped around any bad guys they found.

Madame Cumberland landed next to some penguin dolls on a spinning turntable. "Aux armes, citoyens! Formez vos bataillons . . ." She sang out "La Marseillaise," whirling around in circles, sending swirling blasts of silver lightning all over the tunnel.

Meanwhile, Dr. Timberi dodged and ducked, jumped and spun, shooting blasts of Light and attack illuminations all over the place.

*For an old guy, he's pretty amazing*, Conner thought.

About five minutes later, the bad guys either were knocked out or had run away.

"Is everyone all right?" Dr. Timberi asked. Everyone mumbled that they were fine, and Lexa indulged in a sigh of relief. "Listen please. We have just a few moments at the most. The Phalanx is coming to take you to safety. As soon as Lee is here, go with him. They should be here any minute. Until then, stay down. Is that clear?"

"You beat the Darkhands. What's wrong?" Lexa asked.

"My dear Lexa." He smiled and shook his head. "Those were not real Darkhands. They were simply thugs with some minimal training. When their masters discover that they failed, they will certainly send—"

A loud tearing sound shredded Lexa's relief. Black flames rushed out of a gash in the air as a man in a black cape with a twisted club limped out. A hot gust of wind blew from behind him and whipped his long hair. His smile seemed to torture the rest of his face.

The Stalker was back.

The Stalker waved his club, and the water boiled and popped. Huge pillars of angry, black water shot up twenty feet into the air, twisting and twining into six giant snakes. One of the snakes coiled back and sprang at Dr. Timberi, who hummed something and flicked his baton, as an enormous golden ax swung down and shattered the snake into millions of fragments.

Madame Cumberland smiled at another snake. A silver rose bush appeared and shot dozens, then hundreds, of long, thorny vines, lassoing and snaring the snake. As soon as the snake was wrapped with vines, roses burst into bloom, and the snake dissolved.

A third snake spit steaming black liquid at Mrs. Grant, who scowled. She pushed her red pen up in the air, and a blue Light umbrella popped open above her, blocking the snake's venom. The snake hissed and sprang for her, and Lexa screamed, sure it would swallow her whole.

Mrs. Grant threw her umbrella like a spear. The snake dodged back to avoid it, giving Mrs. Grant time to drop to the ground and roll away. The snake lunged forward again and missed Mrs. Grant by a few inches, slamming its fangs into the floor of the marketplace, which began to boil and steam and melt.

Mrs. Grant stood up and glared. Her fingers flew, like she was tying a bow on a gift. The snake froze for a blink, and then its head jerked backward toward its tail. Head and tail twisted together until the snake was tied in an elaborate knot. "Glad I listened in Girl Scouts," Mrs. Grant muttered.

*Do you think we can help?* Melanie asked.

*Can't hurt*, Conner replied. *Let's take the one on the left.*

The snake on the left was the smallest—only about ten feet tall instead of fifteen or twenty. It swayed and darted around Dr. Timberi in a black blur while he tried to fight another snake at the same time.

Three sigils charged into the air and stampeded the snake. They were still weak, so they only slowed it down, but the snake's slower speed allowed Dr. Timberi enough time to slash at it with his baton. A gold gash opened just under the snake's head and spread until the head fell off and the snake disappeared.

All three teachers turned to the remaining snake,

which got slammed with blasts of gold, silver, and blue Light. The snake vanished like a birthday candle being hit with fire extinguishers.

Lexa took a deep breath, but before she exhaled, she heard more tearing noises, and five more Darkhands appeared. Huge, hungry bursts of Darkness flew through the air, met by brilliant blasts of Light. Each time Light and Dark collided, a terrible explosion shook the walls.

"Run!" Dr. Timberi yelled, and everyone splashed through the water into the next room, where three Hawaiian hula dancers welcomed them with big smiles and the umpteenth verse of the "Small World" song.

When another Darkhand appeared in the air in front of them, Lexa and Melanie sent their sigils jumping out at her, but the Darkhand flicked her fingers, and the sigils disappeared in a blast of shiny black fire. The girls both staggered backward—Lexa felt like someone had knocked the wind out of her, and heat burned in, around, and through her.

Mrs. Grant appeared in a burst of bright blue Light and waved her red pen. A blue ballerina appeared, spinning in graceful circles around the Darkhand. The ballerina twirled faster and faster, circling the Darkhand with blue flames that flared up in a tight circle. The Darkhand howled before vanishing in an explosion of blue Light.

The light blinded Lexa for a few seconds, and before she could see, she heard another tearing sound. When her eyes focused again, a huge gash had been torn in the air. A high-pitched whine screamed, and five Jet Skis shot out, bouncing across the water, coming right at them. Everyone screamed and scattered, running for the shore.

The air crackled and sizzled, and the room filled with a blazing rainbow comet. Lexa cheered as the Twilight Phalanx shot into battle. It got so bright that she couldn't see. The battle raged as people huddled behind different props and set pieces. And then, it ended. The noise, explosions, flashes, and blasts—everything stopped.

Dr. Timberi limped through the smoke. His clothes were torn, dirty, and still smoldering in several places. He stumbled on a little puppet head, which was still singing "It's a Small World." He gave it a sharp kick, and it bounced into the water, chirping about smiles and friendship before it sparked, fizzled, and finally sank.

"Is everyone safe?" he asked.

A tan comet furiously exploded right next to Dr. Timberi, and Lee appeared. "Fire department's on the way, Morgan, so we'd best be getting on out of here." Lee stopped and glared at Mr. Stephens. "Oh yeah, mister, you were just as safe as could be. You didn't need our help, no sir. You had it all under control. Yep, you—"

Dr. Timberi held up his hand. "That's enough, Lee."

Lee bit his lip and looked away, still muttering.

Dr. Timberi faced Mr. Stephens and pulled himself up to his full height. "The English language is a marvel of expressive potential. Yet there are still times when words cannot do justice to one's feelings." He pulled his fist back, swung it in a wide arc, and punched Mr. Stephens in the face.

As they all staggered out of the building, a group of firemen ran in. "Is everyone all right? What happened?"

"Explosions—all over," Dr. Timberi said.

"Must be some short circuits." Mrs. Grant wilted the fireman with a glare.

Everyone had been evacuated, so the area outside was empty.

"Where's Madi?" Melanie's mom asked.

"And Conner?" Mrs. Dell added.

Lexa looked around. "And the Blacks?"

Panic gnawed at Melanie.

It had to be a horrible mistake. She looked around.

They weren't there.

While the paramedics checked the families, the Phalanx made themselves invisible and went through the ride twice.

They weren't there.

All the Magi blurred into comets and scoured the park. Everyone else ran to the rendezvous spot in front of the castle.

They weren't there.

Electric chills stung Melanie's skin, and a panic too aggressive for tears squeezed her heart. Right then, Mr. Stephens's phone rang.

"Hello? Yes, this is Frank Stephens. What? No, really? Oh thank you, thank you!" He put his hand over the speaker and yelled, "They have Madi! Security has Madi! She's okay!"

Melanie's heart jumped, and the panic faded.

"What about Conner? Do they have Conner?" Mrs. Dell shouted.

"Do you have a boy too—Conner Dell? Thirteen years—" Mr. Stephens's face fell and pulled everyone's hopes down with it. When Melanie saw his expression, her heart died in slow motion. "I see. Well, thank you. We're on our way now." He looked at the Dells as if he was in pain. "Brent, Cathy, I'm so sorry."

Mrs. Dell sobbed, and Mr. Dell put his arm around her. His eyes pooled, and his lips trembled. Lexa ran and hugged her mom and dad, crying too. Everyone stood there and cried. Then Conner's mom wiped her eyes and said, "What are we doing? We need to go get Madi."

Melanie's emotions bungee-jumped between relief that Madi was safe and despair that Conner was not. She and the others listened in silence as Madi told her story, safe in the break room of the Disney World security office. "Conner made a red dog appear, and it tackled Kyle . . ."

*Lexa, did she see Conner shoot a sigil?*

That's what it sounds like.

But how?

Lexa shrugged and didn't reply, so Melanie listened to Madi finish her story.

". . . and Conner pushed me so hard that I flew out of the doorway. The leash broke, and I flew out, and the doors shut, so I didn't go with them. Where did they take Conner? Will we see him again?"

No one answered her questions.

*Lexa! Melanie!*

Melanie sat straight up as Conner called out in her thoughts.

*Guys, I'm*—his connection faded.

*CONNER!* she yelled in her head. *CONNER!* But it was too late. He was gone.

"We just heard Conner," Lexa said. "But then he faded out."

Melanie's dad turned to Dr. Timberi, pale and shaking. "He saved my little girl. Get him back, Timberi." His voice softened. "Please. I don't care what it takes. Just get him back."

Dr. Timberi's jaw clenched. For just a minute his lips quivered. When he spoke, his voice was husky. "I will," he whispered. "Oh, I will."

# CHAPTER 27.

# ᴛʜᴇ Oᴛʜᴇʀwʜᴇʀᴇ

Aᴡʜɪᴛᴇ ᴄᴏᴍᴇᴛ ᴡʜɪꜱᴛʟᴇᴅ ɪɴ ᴀɴᴅ ʙᴇᴄᴀᴍᴇ the Phalanx member named Chu. He saluted Grimaldi. "Lieutenant, Magisterium HQ just sent a classified sigil. The Adumbrators say Umbra is massing for a major counterattack. There may be only minutes before the park is overrun."

"All the innocent people here," Mrs. Grant moaned. "We need to get the Stephenses and Dells out of here right away."

"Morgan, we've gotta get 'em to a sanctuary," Lee said. "It's the only place that's gonna be safe."

"But don't we need to be here in case the police find something?" Mrs. Dell asked.

"Oh, Cathy." Madame Cumberland's voice was a hug, a sunset, and a sad song on violins combined together. "The police aren't going to find anything."

"That's true, Mona," Mrs. Grant replied. "But it would look strange if the whole family just vanished. At least one of them probably needs to stay here."

"Where are you taking us, exactly?" Mr. Dell asked.

"To a Sanctuary. It's a special place, completely blocked off from this dimension," Madame Cumberland said.

"Take Cathy and Lexa. I'll stay here and be the contact for the police," Mr. Dell said.

"And we'll guard him," Lee nodded.

"Brent, no." Mrs. Dell grabbed his arm. "If anything happened—"

"Cathy, please. I need to do this. Especially after Conner . . ." Mr. Dell's voice cracked, and his eyes misted again. He forced a smile. "I can't let a thirteen-year-old show me up like that, now can I? You two go. I'll be fine."

"Don't you worry, ma'am." Lee patted Mrs. Dell's hand. "The Phalanx will guard him. He'll be safer than a catfish in a rainstorm."

Mrs. Dell's face tightened, but she didn't say anything.

Mr. Dell hugged Lexa, then Mrs. Dell.

When he finally pulled away, he nodded at Lee. "I'm ready to go." The Phalanx surrounded Mr. Dell.

"Now, to get the rest of you to the Sanctuary," Dr. Timberi said. "The Guardians will not like this, but we certainly cannot risk a car—far too easily ambushed."

From around his neck, Dr. Timberi pulled out a small golden chain, which had five or six small keys. He grabbed one of them and pushed it into the air. The key disappeared inside an invisible lock. He turned it, and a shimmering, silver gap appeared in the air, as if someone had opened curtains.

"Quickly now, through the portal," he said. "Once you are inside, do NOT move or touch anything."

Mr. and Mrs. Dell hugged one more time, then everyone walked through the opening. Dr. Timberi came last, pushed his key back into the air, and turned it again. The curtain closed, and he replaced the chain inside his shirt.

When the curtain closed, the quiet became so intense that it felt loud. Mrs. Stephens stroked Melanie's head as if she were comforting a small child, but she was the one shaking.

They stood in a corridor about ten feet square. On each side of the square, an arch soared twenty feet into the air. The arch they'd come through was made of polished wood. The arch across from them was made of bright, gleaming gold. The arch on their left glowed soft and silver, and the archway to their right was pearly. Each arch was covered with carvings that had Light flowing through them like tiny rivers.

Thin, shimmering curtains covered the opening under each arch. They looked silver, but one of them rustled, and a brilliant ballet of rainbow colors danced across the fabric.

There were no walls or ceilings. The only thing between and above the arches was a deep purple sky glowing with lightning-bright stars, moons, and planets. Whatever floor they stood on was covered with swirling mist that rose to Melanie's knees.

Music floated through the curtains in front of them, and Melanie realized it was the song they'd heard Dr. Timberi sing when he fought the Stalker—but more powerful and intense.

The music reached deep inside of her, caressing her

heart and soul. She wanted—she needed—to go to the music. She stepped forward.

Firm fingers on a gentle hand touched her arm. "I know, Melanie." Dr. Timberi gave her a sad, knowing smile. "I know. But you must not."

"Where are—" Lexa started to ask.

"Please." Dr. Timberi held up his hand. "Not now."

The gold archway in front of them trembled and shook. The curtains rustled and crackled, and the mist below hissed and boiled. A thundering waterfall of a voice roared into the corridor.

"Who is there?"

The arch glowed like melted gold, and the curtains burned with a white-hot light.

The voice came again, even louder. "Who is there?"

The arch grew so bright, Melanie could barely see. They all squinted and covered their eyes. Except Dr. Timberi. Through a tiny crack in her fingers, Melanie saw Dr. Timberi stand straighter and look straight at the light and the voice.

"I am Morgan Timberi. I follow the Light. I seek passage through your domains."

She heard a low rumble, like giant waves crashing on rocks, and then the voice came again.

"We know you, Morgan Timberi. You have the key. You may pass. But who are they? They have no keys. And some do not even have eyes that see." The bright light focused around the parents.

"Please, it is an emergency." Dr. Timberi's voice was low and even. "They were attacked by Umbra, and one of their children was taken. I believe they are in grave danger, and their presence will endanger others."

The rumbling came again—Melanie thought of two giants trying to whisper to each other.

"What do you seek?"

"I must take them to a Sanctuary," Dr. Timberi replied.

More rumbling. Now she thought the giants were arguing instead of whispering. And they didn't sound very happy. Melanie gulped her rising anxiety down. This didn't look very good.

"Morgan Timberi, we do not approve. Nevertheless, the battle with Darkness rages beyond normal bounds. So we allow your request. They must stay in this corridor and go into neither the Beyond nor the Between. They will be watched carefully and if they stray . . ." The rumbling didn't finish the sentence.

"Yes, I understand." Dr. Timberi gulped. "Thank you." He bowed.

The light faded out, and the area became silent again.

Dr. Timberi's shoulders dropped three or four inches. "Thank goodness. One never quite knows with cherubim." He released his breath slowly. "Follow me, and *please* touch nothing. Especially on that side." He pointed to the side the voices had come from. "They are serious about that."

The pearl arch on Melanie's right glowed, bright but gentle, like starlight. The curtains over the opening glowed and parted, and the group walked through. Dr. Timberi went first, Melanie and Lexa followed, and then came Mrs. Dell, Madi, and Mr. and Mrs. Stephens.

When they passed through, the curtains closed, and

the arch disappeared completely. They found themselves in a long, curving hallway about five or six feet wide. Melanie couldn't see where it started or stopped. There was still no ceiling, and the walls of the hallway were curtains made of the same kind of fabric as those in the first corridor. The curtains hung from arches set every five feet or so. Each arch was made from different materials— wood, gold, stone, and others she didn't recognize.

Nobody said anything. Melanie didn't even think about talking. Somehow, the place demanded silence.

About twenty yards later, Dr. Timberi pushed his key into a section of the curtains on his right. The curtains opened, and everyone went through.

They stepped out through an opening in a high wall of thick clouds and entered their world again. Behind them, the curtains blew in the breeze, then closed, faded, and disappeared. When the opening vanished, the wall of clouds was unbroken.

They stood at the end of a long driveway, which led to a large, white Victorian house embraced by a wrap-around porch. The house was surrounded by a neatly trimmed lawn, bushes, and flower beds overflowing with colorful flowers. In back, Melanie noticed the lawn rolled down a hill into dense woods.

That was all—house, yard, and woods—everything surrounded by the thick circle of clouds, which spun constantly in a slow, counterclockwise orbit. It was early evening, and a few birds provided the only noise. A deep river of calm washed over her.

"Welcome to Mockingbird Cottage." Dr. Timberi smiled.

# CONNER

WHEN THE JET SKIS BURST THROUGH THE gashes, everyone scattered to avoid being run over. A Jet Ski cut between Conner and everyone else, and he had to jump to the left. He flew through the air like he was tackling a quarterback but landed at a strange angle and sprained his ankle.

Lights flashed everywhere, so it was difficult to see. But between flashes, he thought he saw the Blacks leaving the tunnel. With Madi.

*That's weird.*

He yelled, but the explosions from the fight drowned him out, and Lexa and Melanie were too distracted to hear his thoughts.

The Blacks and Madi were gone now, out of the tunnel. He ducked to avoid being hit by a flying comet and a few stray blasts of Darkness.

*Lexa, Melanie!*

There was still no answer. The fight must be too

distracting. With no one else to help, he ignored the pain in his ankle and followed them, limping as fast as he could.

He saw them each grab one of Madi's hands and run to the loading dock. Madi pulled away and stopped, like she was arguing with them.

Madi started to run away, but Kyle grabbed her and threw her over his shoulder. She kicked and screamed as they ran up the ramp to the exit.

"Put her down!" Conner yelled.

Kelli saw Conner and yelled, "Faster!"

They were too far ahead for Conner to catch up, especially with his hurt ankle. He remembered the time when he'd traveled at light-speed and smashed Geoffrey's lacrosse stick.

He thought about that and focused on it. Nothing.

He thought about it more and focused harder. Nothing.

Sour panic boiled up in the back of his throat.

*What are they doing to Madi?*

He felt worry rage through him, and—

Conner felt himself stretch out for a second, and then he was with the Blacks in some kind of back-alley, Cast-Members-Only place.

Kelli and Kyle both jumped and screamed when he appeared.

"Run, Madi," he yelled.

Conner raised his hands, and his sigil charged out, barking and snarling. It plowed into Kyle and knocked him down.

"That's enough!" Kelli shouted, and Conner heard Madi cry out.

Conner looked back. Kelli had Madi by the hair with one hand. In her other hand she gripped a knife.

"Call your sigil off," Kelli growled.

Conner dropped his hands.

"Any more stupid tricks like that, and the kid's dead." Kyle got off the ground and wrenched Conner's arm behind his back. Hard. "Get a collar on him."

"Let me get the kid first," Kelli snapped. She reached into her bag and pulled out a child safety harness parents use to keep their kids close in public places. She latched the harness around Madi and handed the leash end to Kyle.

She reached into her bag again and giggled, then pulled a metal necklace out. She slid it over Conner's head and hid it under his shirt. Then she snapped it shut, locking it around his neck. It was just big enough to hang down inside of his shirt but too small to fit over his head.

When the metal brushed his skin, the Florida sun seemed to stop shining, and Conner felt locked in a portable prison of cold, heavy darkness.

"Kind of a fun little thing." Kelli giggled her formerly-attractive-now-evil giggle. "A refraction collar bends the Light into Darkness, sort of the opposite of solar panels. Oh yeah, and it causes excruciating jolts of pain." She shoved Conner at Kyle. "Be careful how you hold him, or someone will get suspicious. We've still got a long way until we're out of here."

"I thought someone was supposed to meet us and tear a gash," Kyle grumbled.

"Yeah, well, that was the plan, but obviously they're a

little busy back there," Kelli snapped. "That battle wasn't supposed to be such a big deal."

*Hah! Our fighting skills ruined their plans,* Conner thought. *Epic fail for the Darkhands!*

His excitement didn't last long. Kyle grabbed Conner's arm so hard that he felt Kyle's fingerprints being pressed into his bone. Kyle put his stupid white teeth up to Conner's ear and whispered. "If you even think about any more tricks, I'll be seriously mad. And I'll take it out on Madi." Conner felt a sharp poke in his back.

"I promise not to do anything else. Just let Madi go. I'll do whatever you want," Conner whispered back.

Kyle laughed. "Quite the little hero. Well, the problem is that Madi's our main target—you're just icing on the cake." Kyle laughed. "Did you think this was about you and those freak girls? Self-focused, egocentric teenagers." He laughed some more.

Ahead of them, Kelli walked, gripping the leash with one hand and clutching Madi's shoulder with the other. Her blood red fingernails gleamed in the sun.

*JERKS! How did I ever think she was hot? What kind of people would do this to a first grader? Should I yell for help? Maybe I can get some attention before Kyle guts me like a trout. Better not. I can't risk Madi's life on some crazy Hail Mary pass. If it doesn't work, I'm dead—and so is she.* Coldness washed over him. *Seriously, really, truly dead. Forever. Maybe Kelli's wrong about the collar. How much can she know about Light anyway? I can handle a little pain.*

Conner opened his gateway a fraction of a fraction of an inch, and pain rushed through him, burning in every cell in his body, as if he were the floor for tap-dancing elephants in red-hot metal shoes. Pain tackled, sacked, and pinned Conner, slamming his gateway shut.

He cried out, his knees buckled, and he fell down. The pain was worse than anything Conner could describe, and he knew that more than a few seconds of it would either kill him or make him pass out.

Kyle yanked him back up and laughed. "They never believe us about those collars."

*What am I going to do? I've got to give Madi a shot at getting away.* Conner thought about tactics and battles.

*How can I fight the Blacks without the Light and still maximize my advantages? Too bad I can't beat them with a locker door.* Conner assumed his strength was inside of him and that he didn't need to connect to the Light to use it—the way he could play a song downloaded on his iPod without being connected to the Internet. But he had no idea if that was true or not.

"Excuse me, would you mind taking our picture?" A smiling woman held out a camera to Kyle. A huge, extended family stood in front of Cinderella's castle wearing matching T-shirts that said, "FamJam."

Kyle put his arms around Conner, like Conner was sick and Kyle was supporting him.

"Open your mouth, and it's all over for Madi," Kyle whispered. He looked at the lady and spoke loudly. "Sorry, he's not feeling well. Stomach flu." The lady stepped away as fast as she could.

The strangeness of the situation hit Conner. *They're laughing and taking pictures with their cameras, and I'm about to take a one-way trip on the monorail.*

Pictures.

Cameras.

Monorail.

The whole plan flashed into Conner's head. He knew exactly what to do. It would take a few seconds, and he might need the Light. He said a silent prayer that he could push through the pain long enough to do what was needed.

They left the park and got in line for the monorail. Conner took a deep breath. *It's game time.* The monorail pulled up. Sweat poured down his face, and his heart pounded like a psychotic baker kneading bread dough. If he missed this by even a few seconds, it was all over. They'd have Madi, and there wouldn't be a second chance.

Conner paused. He wasn't sure he could handle that pain again, and a thought flickered in the back of his mind. *If I don't try to save her, who would even know?* He hadn't even finished the thought before he felt ashamed of himself.

The doors opened, and the people ahead of them shuffled forward. Kyle shoved Conner in. The car was crowded, and they stood near the door, which increased the odds of his success. As they walked inside, Kyle relaxed his grip on Conner just a little, and Conner noticed that there was some slack in Madi's leash.

The bell chimed, signaling the doors were about to close. Conner took a deep breath, said another quick prayer, and gathered all his strength. He yanked away from Kyle and shoved Madi as hard as he could.

At that point, everything seemed to switch to slow motion.

The doors were a quarter of the way closed, as Madi

went flying toward the opening. Kelli grabbed at the leash.

The doors were halfway closed and Madi was still a few feet away.

Kelli caught the end of the leash.

The doors were three-quarters closed.

The leash went tight.

Madi was still a few inches away from the door.

Conner connected to the Light, and pain washed over him. He couldn't breathe. He started to see spots swimming and flashing in the air. He tried to focus, tried to ignore the pain for just a few seconds.

He felt himself passing out, his consciousness running away like deer in a forest fire.

His legs went limp.

Madi's leash went completely tight.

He imagined the Light slicing through the leash.

The gap between the doors was only two feet wide.

He forced everything he had into the image of the Light slicing the leash.

And then he passed out.

Conner woke up in back of the Blacks' rental van, pain still raging through him. His whole body throbbed, and even worse, a cloud of grogginess stole his ability to think.

*Can you get a hangover from pain?*

Because he wasn't thinking clearly, he reached out to send a message to Melanie and Lexa, forgetting about the consequences.

*Lexa! Melanie! Guys, I'm—*

The pain overwhelmed him, and he passed out again.

# · CHAPTER 29 ·

# ℳockingbird ℭottage

"Y OU'RE SAFE NOW. DARK THINGS CANNOT come here." Dr. Timberi smiled and Melanie thought he looked younger. He lifted his baton, and a big, golden swan shimmered into being, then swam away through the air, disappearing into the clouds. "That will let them know we have arrived safely."

"Where are we exactly?" Mrs. Stephens looked around with big eyes.

"This was once a piece of land just outside of Nashville. However, the Magi have made it a Sanctuary. That means that the Otherwhere has surrounded it completely, forming an island in terms of time and space. Happily, the infrastructure that existed when the Sanctuary was created has remained functional. So, we have running water and electricity. A contact in the local utility office makes sure that no one asks too many questions."

The door to the house opened, and a lady with wispy gray hair walked out carrying a tray of lemonade. A worn

227

denim blouse and skirt hung from her spare frame, and her clothes were punctuated by turquoise Indian jewelry everywhere.

"'Lo, Morgan. Welcome, everybody." Her Southern accent rolled out, as soft and comfortable as her faded denim. "Anyone want some lemonade?"

"Thank you, Sadie. That is most thoughtful." Dr. Timberi took a glass. "Everybody, this is Sadie Frye, the caretaker of the Sanctuary."

A shy smile peeked across her face. "I better get supper goin'." She looked at Madi. "Would you like to help me, sweetheart?"

"Yes, ma'am!" Madi grabbed Sadie's hand and followed her into the house.

"She'll be quite safe," Dr. Timberi replied to the worried look that haunted Mrs. Stephens's eyes. "But you may certainly follow her in, if you would prefer." She nodded and went in after Madi.

Dr. Timberi looked at Mr. Stephens and Mrs. Dell. "Mona and Carol have gone for specialists who can help us track Conner. They should be here soon." He gestured to the furniture on the porch. "In the meantime, why don't you two relax while I show the girls around the Sanctuary."

Melanie and Lexa followed him down the steps that led from the porch, around the side of the house, and past more flower beds stuffed with colorful plants. They walked over a small creek, through some rose trellises, past a vegetable garden, and into the backyard. A long, gentle hill of smooth, green grass flowed down to the forest, and it looked like the trees went for a long way before meeting the boundary of swirling clouds.

In the branches, birds sang good night to their friends. All over the yard, flashes of light pierced the dusk as thousands of fireflies flickered on and off, a city of Christmas lights talking in Morse code.

"How are you doing?" Dr. Timberi's voice was soft.

Neither of them said anything.

"Where do you think Conner is?" Lexa asked. "What will they do to him?"

When Conner woke up again, he found himself sprawled facedown on a dirty, orange bedspread in a dirty, brown motel room with at least twenty years of cigarette smoke trapped inside of it.

"What do you mean, the plan has changed? Someone was supposed to come get him a long time ago and get us out of here!" Kyle shouted in his cell phone.

Conner noticed Madi wasn't in the room. *Did she make it?*

Kyle yelled into his phone again, adding a few words Conner was not allowed to say. "That's not my problem! We did our job! Now get the kid and get us out of here! Pass *that* on to your supervisor!" He hung up and looked at Kelli. Conner pretended to be asleep.

"The battle turned out to be a pretty big deal, and they lost a lot of people. They're trying to figure out how to get someone here to tear the Shroud for us, but they said they're spread kind of thin."

Kelli swore too. "I've been working for Eclipse for five years, and they've never been this disorganized—"

A loud tearing noise interrupted her. Conner opened

his eyes as a gash appeared in the air by the TV and a strange-looking man stepped out. Some people look stranger at first, but the longer you look, the less weird they seem. This man was the opposite. The longer Conner looked at him the stranger he appeared.

He was grandpa-old and maybe four feet tall. He had bushy, messy eyebrows, which he should have combed but didn't. Long, wiry hairs wiggled out of his nose, and he wore a brown three-piece suit with gray and orange squares on it that was ugly even back in the '70s.

He smiled and cleared his throat, then looked at the Blacks through rectangular, black glasses that sat on a long, beaky nose.

"Hmmmccck." He coughed and cleared his throat again. "Operatives Kappa and Delta?"

"Yeah," Kelli said. "And this is the Adept."

He looked down at a piece of paper in his hand and made a coughing noise. Conner thought he might cough up a hair ball. "Hmmmck, according to my notes, you should have a little girl." He coughed and cleared his throat again.

"Yeah, well, that was the plan, but we had a complication," Kyle said. "The kid crashed the party and freed the girl."

The short man checked his notes one more time. "Hmmmccckk, but you were ordered to bring the girl. She was an important element in the master plan." His smile froze Conner.

"Yes, we had her." Kelli spoke very slowly, like the man was deaf or stupid. "But like Kyle said, she escaped. The kid helped her get away."

"Hmmmcckk, so you failed." The man lifted his hands and pointed them at the Blacks, who collapsed onto the floor, screaming and writhing.

*Ouch. I almost feel bad for them even though they are the biggest, freaking jerks in the whole world.*

After a minute or so, the man lowered his hands, and they stopped shrieking. "Lady Nightwing will not be happy that you failed. Hmmmckk, hopefully for your sakes, she will accept the punishment I just gave you." He chuckled. "But she may not."

He waved his hands, and another gash opened up in the air with a loud tearing noise. "You may take this opening to the safe house. Wait there, either for new orders or—hmmck—for your punishment."

The Blacks stood up, gasping and dizzy, and hurried into the second gash, which closed behind them just as Conner remembered to close his eyes again.

"Hmmmckk, so you are the Adept who ruined the plan." The man grabbed Conner's ear and pulled him to his feet. "Lady Nightwing will be very angry with you. Very angry, indeed. Now, come with me. If you try anything, hmmm, anything at all, I will kill you. I'm Mr. Stanley, by the way." He smiled and bowed, like he was Conner's best friend's grandpa. They stepped into to the remaining gash, which was like stepping into a tsunami of black ink. Since it was so dark, it took Conner a minute to realize that they were in a tunnel. At the far end of the tunnel, he saw another pair of torn curtains.

As they walked through the darkness, Conner noticed brilliant white flashes outside of the tunnel. "Hurry."

Mr. Stanley pushed him along. "The cherubim are restless."

A blast of hot, white Light shot through the walls of the tunnel and flooded the tunnel. A deep voice boomed, "You may not pass through our domains!"

Mr. Stanley grabbed Conner's wrist and started running while yelling in a strange language.

Blazing bonfires of Light appeared at each end of the tunnel—Light so bright that the blackness melted away, and Conner could now see that the tunnel they stood in cut a diagonal line across a big hallway, like an ugly, black scar. The hallway was about five or six feet wide and seemed to go on forever. It was made of silvery-white curtains hanging on arches on each side.

Two bright, angry lights came closer. Mr. Stanley muttered and waved his hands faster.

Right before the lights hit him, two blobs of darkness shot out from the far end of the tunnel, making a loud screech. The lights flashed and collided with the dark blobs. The roaring and screeching continued as they clashed.

The lights grew dim for just a second. Then, more lights shot in and attacked the dark blurs together, defeating them like Conner's football team had destroyed Montmorency Pell Academy's team last season. They flew at Mr. Stanley, and he disappeared. Two of the lights came over to Conner. He felt like he was trapped in a hyperactive sauna, and the light was far too bright for him to see.

Before they got too worked up, he said, "I come in peace."

The lights got brighter, and he felt Light shooting

through his body and soul. Then a low, rumbly voice said, "You are young but have the look and feel of the Magi. You travel in shadows with those who summon demons?"

"Demons? Is that what the dark blobs were? Wow. So I was kidnapped by Mr. Stanley. He's the guy who called the demons. I'm not his friend. Or the demons' friend. To tell you the truth, I don't like them at all."

Another light shone over him, and he heard a different voice in his head. It was a female voice—strong and powerful but lighter and calmer.

"We see you speak Truth. Conner Dell, time grows short. The Demonfriend means to take you to a place of great Darkness. We can return you, Conner Dell, to your family and friends, if you choose."

"Okay, that sounds good. Thanks." He paused and waited. "So do I have to answer a riddle or what?"

"Do you wish to go on to the Dark place or go back to your family?"

"Ummmm, is this a trick question? Why would I want to go to the Dark place?"

"Because, Conner Dell, the Light has chosen you to help destroy the Dark place and free those who are imprisoned there. A great evil festers there, an evil that will cause much destruction if it is not stopped. But if you go, you must go willingly."

"I'm going to destroy the Dark place?"

"If you go, your presence may bring about a series of events that will destroy the Dark place."

"*May* bring? May? Like this is only a maybe?"

"Most of the great things on which mortals pin their hopes depend on choices being made at the right time.

There are no guarantees. Time grows short. You must make your choice. We must close this invasion of our home and purge the Darkness from our realm."

"What if things go wrong?"

"Then you may die. Certainly, you will suffer."

"Wow. A guy doesn't get an offer like that every day." Conner's thoughts sprinted to his mom, his dad, and Lexa. *Lexa can be annoying, but she's mostly cool, and it's fun being in the Magi with her. Mom and Dad are about as cool as old people could be.*

He thought of Melanie's laugh and the way she scrunched her nose. He thought of her red hair and brown eyes and her pink unicorn sigil.

*Imprisonment, pain, and possible death. Hmmm, tempting, but maybe I'll just click my heels three times and say, "There's no place like home."*

Then he thought of Melanie again.

In the garden at Mockingbird Cottage, Dr. Timberi looked at Melanie and said, "This is one of the most difficult experiences any Magus endures. Given the battle in which we are engaged, we have all lost friends. Sometimes very close loved ones. It is"—his voice dropped, and he paused—"difficult."

"Why do we keep fighting, then," Melanie asked, "if people get hurt or disappear? Is it worth it?"

"A fair question, Melanie." Dr. Timberi's voice faded into silence. When he spoke again, his words were a frail curtain that barely covered a room crammed with terrible hurt. "Many years ago, something happened to my . . ."

His voice tripped. "To someone I cared about." The muscles in his neck and face stiffened, as he wrestled for control of his voice. "This led me to question the value of my work. I considered leaving the Sodality, something one does not do lightly."

"What happened?" Melanie touched his arm with gentle fingers. He looked so unspeakably sad, so terribly hurt. It seemed like the right thing to do.

A small smile flicked at the corners of his mouth, and he patted her hand. "First of all, I realized that Darkness is essentially, eternally aggressive. The Dark and its servants will always try to conquer whether we fight back or not. You have studied World War II in history, I believe?"

"Yes," Melanie nodded.

"Had Great Britain not fought back when attacked, would the Nazis have gone away and left them alone?"

"Probably not," she said.

"Correct. The Nazis, like all servants of the Dark, did not want to live alongside with others in peace. They wanted to control and dominate. Everyone who serves or is influenced by the Darkness is much the same.

"I realized that evil would not stop simply because I stopped fighting it. Rather, it would have just that much more freedom to operate and be that much freer to make people suffer. By fighting the Darkness, I hope to make it more difficult for it to hurt others. If I succeed, then any cost or pain I bear because of my work may reduce what someone else will have to endure. That was the answer I found then, and it has given me strength in the subsequent years."

"What else happened?" Lexa asked. "You said there were a few things."

"A wise friend suggested a change of pace and helped me find another job within the Sodality. That proved to be excellent advice. And my new work helped patch some of the holes that had been torn in my life."

"Who was that friend?" Lexa asked.

He smiled. "A young Mona Cumberland. I first met Mona when I was with the . . ."

While Dr. Timberi talked, Melanie's mind wandered. Since the kidnappings first started, a few things had bothered her. But before she had time to really think about them, Umbra attacked, then her dad stopped her from joining the Magi, and then they went to Disney World. All those interruptions had pushed everything else away. But Conner's kidnapping sparked a fire in her brain that gave just enough light to reveal some deep shadows—things she didn't understand. Missing puzzle pieces lurked in those shadows, unsolved equations on her mental white board—sharp itches she couldn't scratch.

The first thing that bothered her went back to the morning the kids in their city were kidnapped. Lexa had a theeling that Darkhands were behind it. No one really knew then if she was right. But her vision established a connection and proved Lexa's intuition was correct. *Ever since we started this Magi thing, Lexa's theelings have always been right. Every time.*

*So why would the Darkhands want all those kids?*

That question flared and triggered other thoughts. Memories flashed in her mind—Boom! Boom! Boom!

Boom! She remembered Madame Cumberland talking about Notzange: "Notzange's gift is to sense Adepts before they Kindle. It's really remarkable. She can just touch someone and tell if they will be an Adept or not. She's the only one who can do that."

Boom! Dr. Timberi saying, "If we knew when someone was about to Kindle, we could observe them and get more definitive answers. But that is not possible, nor desirable, since the idea of sticking a human in a lab is repellent."

Boom! Lexa describing her dream about Taylor: "They pushed her into a room full of people in white coats that looked like scientists or doctors."

Boom! The bakery owner on the news: "First Taylor disappeared, and now our shop was robbed. And do you know what they took? Two dozen cream cheese Danishes and the tip jar by the cash register . . . Taylor used to come by every day or two and buy a cream cheese Danish for breakfast, and she was always a real good tipper."

Boom! Dr. Timberi teaching them about translocation: "You must know *what* you want to move and *where* you wish it sent, or from *where* you want it retrieved. It is critical to have these fixed very clearly in your mind."

The whiteboard came alive. The figures in the equations hummed and whirred faster and faster. Then, like the pieces in a kaleidoscope, they clicked into place and stopped. The answer hit her so hard that she fell down. She almost passed out.

"I know what they're doing!" she shouted. "I know what their plan is!"

Dr. Timberi looked a little alarmed. "Melanie?"

"I know what the Darkhands are doing! The kidnappings, the robberies, Notzange—oh my gosh, it's terrible! We *have* to stop them."

"Melanie," Dr. Timberi said, his voice smooth as an ocean sunset. "Tell me what you know."

Conner paused and chewed his lip. *Comfort and safety, family and friends, or darkness, suffering, and maybe death. Tough choice.*

But then he thought about Melanie. And about looking at himself in the mirror for the rest of his life.

"I'll go with Mr. Stanley."

Shrieks and screams interrupted Conner's hero moment. Kyle and Kelli Black flew past him, surrounded by comets of light. They kicked and flailed, but it was their eyes Conner noticed. Big and wild, filled with burning, raging panic.

"Help, Conner!" Kelli shrieked. "Don't let them take us! NOOOOO!"

They all vanished in a flash of light.

"Just out of curiosity, where are you taking them?" Conner asked.

"That is not your affair, Conner Dell. They were trespassing in our realm. They will be dealt with according to our law."

*I'm really glad not to be Kyle or Kelli Black.*

"Hey, can you get rid of this?" He pointed at the Light refractor collar around his neck.

The necklace began to glow yellow, then red, and finally white. He winced and prepared for it to burn, but it never felt hot.

"We have reversed the effect of this device. For a time, it will enhance your ability to use the Light. In the Darkness to which you go, you will need the extra assistance. Go now, Conner Dell. May you travel in the Light."

"Um, thanks. May the Force be with you." *Okay, that was lame. But I don't know any official Magi greetings.*

The lights disappeared, and Conner tucked the refraction collar back inside his shirt. Mr. Stanley was crumpled in a heap on the floor of what was left of his tunnel. He stirred and sat up.

"Hmmmcckk, the cherubim. What—?" He looked around.

"I think your demon blobs scared them off," Conner said.

Mr. Stanley smiled and laughed through his nose. He sounded like a buzz saw with a cold. He grabbed Conner's hand. "Hmmmckk, come on. Lady Nightwing is waiting."

He dragged Conner through the rest of the tunnel and the torn curtains at the end. They walked through a gateway carved out of black rock. Spirals of copper wire slithered all over the rock, and big spikes were attached in a hundred different places.

"This way." They walked through halls of black stone, finally coming to a dead end blocked by a huge metal door. Glowing buttons on a keypad lit up on the wall next to the door.

Mr. Stanley punched some buttons, and the door slid open with a sharp hiss. He pushed Conner into a huge room with white walls, white floors, and a white ceiling. It was some kind of laboratory, stuffed with tables, chemicals, beakers, and hospital beds.

When Mr. Stanley walked in, a tall woman in black robes looked up. "Stanley, it's about—" She stopped when she saw Conner. "Where's the girl?"

Mr. Stanley bowed. "They failed, my lady. The girl was rescued by this Adept."

The woman walked over and grabbed Conner's chin, yanking his head up toward her. Her skin was white and cold, and she made Conner think of a razor-sharp icicle. "Conner Dell, I believe. You have caused me a great deal of trouble lately."

She moved so fast that he didn't see her hand until it smashed into his cheek. His vision went blurry for a few seconds, and he tasted the salty tang of blood in his mouth. "Quite the little hero. Listen to me, boy. I'm busy today and don't have time for games. You've already Kindled, so you are of no use in my experiments. But from the reports I read, I gather you show great promise. Join us, and I can show you how to unlock far greater power than you have ever conceived."

"Never."

His other cheek got the back of her hand this time. She pulled her hand back to hit him a third time, but the door slid open, and four guys ran in, dragging a kid about Conner's age with them.

"She says he's going to Kindle any second now," one of the guards yelled.

"Get the induction chamber ready for energy capture!" Lady Nightwing commanded. People in white coats ran all over, and the guards pushed the kid to a round booth made out of copper.

*I'm not sure what's going on, but it can't be good. I really*

*don't think I should let them do . . . well, whatever they're
about to do.*

Conner reached out to Light, which was not easy since
Darkness was everywhere. The collar beneath his shirt
grew warm and Light flowed into him.

Using Light, he sent the hospital beds crashing into
the guards. He knocked a table full of chemicals over and
made a row of computers hiss and spark. Conner looked at
the round booth and concentrated all the Light he could
around it. It glowed and trembled. Smoke poured out of
it, and a series of explosions went off up and down it like
popcorn in a microwave.

Two guards tackled him from behind. He hit the
floor, the breath knocked out of him. Alarms and bells
and whistles started screaming. He noticed the other kid
was glowing.

"NO!" Lady Nightwing yelled. "No! No! He was our
last one! Quickly, check him and make sure!"

A woman in a white coat held some kind of scanner
up to the boy. It clicked, then chirped and lit up.

"I'm sorry, Lady Nightwing. It's too late."

Lady Nightwing turned back to Conner. Bright red
burned in her freezing white skin, and the whites of her
eyes swallowed up her dark pupils. "You will regret that,"
she hissed. "You've ruined my equipment and wasted the
last Kindling. Take him to the Shadow Box."

Melanie took a deep breath and tried to calm down.

"Take your time, Melanie." Dr. Timberi's soothing
voice was a cup of emotional chamomile tea.

She opened her mouth, and the words spilled out. "Remember how you said when someone Kindles, there's so much power that it basically overrides the laws that are usually in place—the laws that govern Light?"

Dr. Timberi frowned. "Yes, that's correct."

"And you can only use Light to move objects you know or from places you've been?"

She took a deep breath. "They're using Notzange to find kids who are about to Kindle. I think they just kidnap whoever they can and then take them to Notzange to see if they're going to Kindle. If they do, they somehow use the power it releases to do bad things that normally Light can't do. Remember how all the shops that got robbed were places Taylor had gone to? That's why. She could only translocate items she knew from places she knew. They're experimenting with little things like Danishes or tip jars to figure out how to use the power of Kindling to do big things no one can stop."

Dr. Timberi's skin turned to a snow-white pallor. He closed his eyes and took a deep breath. "Curse me as the blindest, most blundering idiot!" His anger blazed hotter than Melanie had ever heard from him. "How could I have been so criminally stupid, so unseeing and obtuse? In the chaos of the past weeks, I completely missed the obvious!" Real anguish burned in his face. "If they learn to manipulate the energy from Adepts who are Kindling, then they would be unstoppable. There's virtually nothing they wouldn't be able to do. That is why they've been able to use the Otherwhere so frequently. And no wonder they wanted you three so badly. Three very powerful Kindlings within twenty-four hours." His voice tightened to the breaking point. "Those poor children."

"What do you mean?" Lexa asked. "I mean, I know it's bad to be kidnapped by Darkhands, but . . ."

Dr. Timberi shook his head. "Trying to use the Light for Dark purposes is an act of spiritual violence that could cause major damage to the soul—or mind. It is unprecedented. The good thing, if there is one, is that finding Conner will most likely lead us to Notzange and the other kidnapped children. That streamlines matters. And, thanks to Lexa, we have a link to Notzange."

Right then, silver Light shimmered in the air and swirled into a rose bush. Madame Cumberland's voice said, "Morgan, they're here."

The guards dragged Conner into a room full of Darkness and a silence more threatening than any noise he could imagine. The only noise present was the echo-y sound of water dropping into water. As his eyes grew acclimated to the darkness, Conner could tell he was in a round room, about twenty yards in circumference and maybe a hundred yards high.

The guards shoved him along a catwalk that ran around the edge of the room. He still couldn't see much, but above him, he could make out chains, hooks, and pulleys hanging down from the ceilings.

*That looks like it might be for something really painful.*

Another drop of water fell from the ceiling, followed by a splash. He squinted and looked down. All he could see was something that looked like boiling darkness, with some steam.

He shivered as fear and the dark dampness began to soak into him.

*What are they going to do to me?*

"Water is very interesting," Lady Nightwing said. "It's almost impervious to Light, and if Light waves do manage to pierce through, the water bends and twists them. At the same time, water amplifies darkness. This sets up an interesting relationship with Darkness. Water doesn't obey Darkness, exactly, but water can be manipulated in"—she smiled—"interesting ways."

She pulled a lever near the wall, and Conner's ears were assaulted with the screech of creaky, rusty chains moving. A large, rectangular box lowered in jerky bobs from the ceiling and hung in the middle of the room. As soon as it was level with the catwalk, Lady Nightwing pushed the lever, and it stopped.

"The Shadow Box," she whispered. Her wide eyes glowed in the darkness. She turned a crank, and an extension bridge groaned out from the catwalk. It extended to the middle of the circle, up against the box.

Lady Nightwing pulled Conner forward to the box. It was about the size of a phone booth—or a coffin—and had a shiny black surface covered with black iron bands. Pieces of black iron formed a complicated pattern all over the four sides. It disturbed Conner to look at it. He didn't understand the pattern, but he felt evil and darkness emanating from the box.

Lady Nightwing stroked it as if it were a favorite pet. She muttered something, and pieces of the iron patterns whirled and spun. The front opened up with a loud click.

The back of the Shadow Box was lined in black silk.

The other three sides were mirrors.

"Go in, Conner," she whispered. He resisted. "Come in, and I might go easy on the other kids in the lab."

He stopped struggling and let her push him in against the back wall. Iron bands shot out of the fabric and pinned his ankles and wrists to the box. Then she opened an iron band and snapped it shut around his forehead. The band was attached to a chain that ran into the back wall of the box.

Cold waves of panic flooded through Conner, and he would have collapsed if it hadn't been for the iron bands holding him against the wall.

"You may be wondering what I'm going to do to you." She smiled. "Nothing. I will do nothing to you. That's the beauty of the Shadow Box. I'm sure the Magi have taught you about sigils. This is the same idea." She laughed now. "Except completely opposite."

She pushed the door shut, and Conner heard the whirring and twirling noises, followed by a loud click, and then he couldn't hear anything anymore. He felt a tug on the box, and it started to descend. Panic rushed into his body, and his mind wrestled with the scream trying to break out of his mouth.

# CHAPTER 30

# THE ADUMBRATORS

"THANK YOU, MONA," DR. TIMBERI SAID. "We'll be right there. Come, girls."

Dr. Timberi sprinted back to the cottage, and Melanie and Lexa followed. They burst through the back door and into the kitchen, where Madi and Miss Sadie were stirring chocolate chips into a big bowl of cookie dough with a wooden spoon.

"Melanie!" Madi's eyes were bright fireflies. "We're making chocolate chip cookies! Miss Sadie said that I'm a really good cook."

"Good job!" Melanie gave Madi a hug and walked into the front room. Coach Jackson, Mrs. Grant, Madame Cumberland, Mrs. Sharpe, Mrs. Davis, and Mr. Duffy were all there, as well as Lee and Grimaldi.

Madame Cumberland glowed as though she were at her high school prom again. She was smiling and chatting with three people Melanie had never seen before. Mrs. Grant looked like the teacher who got stuck chaperoning. Melanie's parents and Lexa's mom nodded politely as Madame Cumberland introduced them to a young man and woman in their twenties and to a middle-aged woman.

Dr. Timberi cleared his throat. "Here they are."

Lexa felt the power of everyone's stares, and the room went silent.

"Awk-ward," she said.

Melanie pushed a lump out of her throat. *That's what Conner would have said.*

The younger man and woman laughed and walked over.

"Hey!" The guy extended his hand. His arms were skinny, but when he shook Lexa's hand, he had a firm grip. "I'm Donovan." Spiky, messy black hair crowned his head, and he wore jeans and a black T-shirt that said, "Vampire Weekend."

"And I am Veronique." The girl's light accent gave her words an exotic flavor. "I am so happy to finally meet you." A Bluetooth phone piece blinked behind her long, black hair. Her dark eyes blinked as well, highlighted by her pale skin.

"It's nice to meet you too," Melanie replied.

"You guys are Magi?" Lexa sounded really surprised.

"Yes." Veronique smiled.

"But you're so young—you're not—" Lexa stopped and winced. It had popped out before she'd thought about it, but now it was too late. "Uh, not, well, not—"

"What you mean is that they are not old and decrepit like the rest of us." Dr. Timberi laughed. He steered Lexa and Melanie over to the middle-aged woman by Madame

Cumberland. "You met Donovan Kent and Veronique Danton. Now, may I present Hortense Benet?" His voice became a stiff tuxedo.

Hortense squeezed Dr. Timberi a polite smile. Something made Melanie think that Dr. Timberi and Hortense didn't like each other very much.

Hortense's short, gray hair emphasized her deep tan. A long, white blouse hung over a crinkled pink skirt, and she walked in a cloud of strong, flowery perfume.

"You don't know much about the Sodality yet"— Madame Cumberland beamed—"so their titles won't mean anything to you, but these are really important people, and they're here to help us. Hortense is one of the most gifted Seers the Sodality has. She's the head of the Adumbrators, which I told you are like the Magi CIA. Donovan and Veronique are some of her best people."

"I was just speaking with Melanie and Lexa," Dr. Timberi said, "and I believe that Melanie has discovered something important."

He explained what Melanie had told him outside, and everyone either got wide eyes or became tight-lipped or both. When Dr. Timberi finished, Lee shook his head.

"Little lady, I just bet you're right. This thing is crookeder than a barrel of snakes."

"This only makes it more important to trace the sigil that Notzange sent to Alexandra." Hortense's French accent gave her words the zest of lemon in water.

"Lexa," Lexa blurted out. Then she remembered her manners. "Please."

"I beg your pardon, in which *Lexa* saw Notzange." Hortense walked over to Lexa and smiled. "My dear, your visions. May I have permission to inspect them?"

Lexa stared at her. "Uh, sure, but I don't have them written down or anything."

Hortense looked confused.

"We've had very little time, Hortense." Madame Cumberland touched Hortense's arm. "There's a lot they don't understand. Lexa, with your permission, Hortense is going to tap into your memory and look at your visions."

"Like I'm a TV or something?"

"Well, yes, I suppose that's one way to describe it."

"Will it hurt?"

Lexa was one of the toughest people Melanie knew. She could handle pain without blinking. But she hated the idea of being hurt more than anyone Melanie had ever met. No one dreaded pain more or felt it less than Lexa.

"Certainly not." Hortense said, bristling.

Lexa shrugged. "Okay, then. Sure. Go ahead."

Hortense reached out and touched Lexa's forehead. "Now, Lexa, please concentrate. Open yourself up to Light and then try to remember all that you saw."

Hortense closed her eyes. She and Lexa started to glow. Hortense nodded and swayed for five minutes. Then she flung her eyes open. "Remarkable! Her visions—they are unusually vivid and strong for one so young. You have a great gift, my dear."

"Thank you." Lexa tripped through a curtsy.

"It was most certainly Notzange," Hortense said. "And everything that Melanie supposes about what the Darkhands are doing fits with what Lexa saw."

"What about Notzange?" Madame Cumberland sounded anxious.

"She is alive, but I do not like it at all. They are very clever, these Darkhands. She's in a dark room with no light at all. When this vision came a few days ago, she was already looking weak and tired. I cannot imagine that the last few days have been good for her."

"How about the Darkhands—anyone we know?" Donovan asked. He and Veronique pulled out small, white laptops. "Anything that might give us some kind of clue about location?"

Hortense shook her head. "The one in charge of everything has pale skin and dark hair. I do not recognize her. But in the vision, when Notzange thought about her, she seemed to think something about the night. The night and a bird possibly? And the man, he was short."

Veronique and Donovan pounded their keyboards, then Veronique looked up. "While we're waiting to see if we have anything in the archives, tell us more about that man. According to the reports we read about Lexa's initial vision, this man watched Notzange when they brought the kids to her. What do you suspect he was doing?"

"I do not know." Hortense shook her head again. "But if I had to guess, he has some empathic abilities. We assume Notzange is determining whether or not the children have powers, and are going to Kindle. He must sense what she is feeling and can confirm to the Darkhands whether she is telling the truth."

Veronique and Donovan both kept typing.

"Hmmmm." Donovan looked up. "Hortense? Lexa?" He flipped his computer around. A fuzzy picture of a woman with dark hair froze on the screen.

"That's her!" Lexa shouted.

Hortense looked carefully for five seconds. "Yes, that is the woman."

Donovan frowned. "Not good."

"Who is it?" Madame Cumberland asked.

Donovan shook his head. "Calls herself Lady Nightwing. Real name is Emily Jacoway. She has a background in physics and was once a Magus. She was disciplined several times by the Magisterium for experiments that were dangerous and unethical, finally expelled from the Sodality ten years ago. She's brilliant, unstable, and completely without a conscience—kind of a mad scientist. No known locations."

"All righty," Lee said, "no use wasting time. Let's do the sigil trace and get this show on the road."

"Will it hurt?" Lexa asked.

# · CHAPTER 31 ·

# THE SHADOW BOX

ONNER FELT THE BOX HIT THE WATER. IT bobbed on the surface for just a second or two, then sunk to the bottom with a thud.

As soon as the box submerged, the iron bands around him glowed with Darkness. It wasn't physically painful, but Conner shivered and shuddered. It gave him a feeling that he didn't like. Intense and strong, it was slightly sweet, but hot, like a spoonful of sugar mixed in several cups of cinnamon. It reminded him of being tickled for far too long.

Hisses and whispers echoed in the box—soft at first, then louder and louder, as loud as hisses can be: "Conner, Conner."

The mirrors glowed, then grew transparent so he could see out into the water. Dark shapes swam through the murky water, circling the Shadow Box.

"Conner! Conner! Come and join us," the shapes hissed. "Free the shadows in your heart."

"No!" he yelled.

The shadows laughed, then took form, twisting into human bodies. Conner gasped as some of the shadows turned into everyone he loved most—his parents, Lexa, Melanie. The other shadows started attacking them, tormenting them. One of the shadows took the form of the Stalker. Or maybe it was him for real; Conner didn't know.

His worst fears and nightmares buffeted him. His pulse pounded, and sweat broke out all over. He was pretty sure he was having a panic attack, which seemed to make the shadows stronger.

Melanie screamed. Was it really her? Or just a shadowy imitation? He couldn't tell. It was so real, so confusing.

The Stalker pulled out a long, slender knife, glittering with black Darkness. He laughed and grabbed Melanie by the hair. She struggled and kicked, but there was nothing she could do.

The Stalker laughed louder and moved the knife.

Conner screamed. "NO!" He panicked and shot out a sigil.

The shadows cackled and shrieked as his bright red German shepherd hit the mirror. It bounced back and forth, ricocheting across the other mirrors like a rubber ball.

Each time it hit one of the mirrors, it faded, growing dimmer and darker.

After about five bounces, it stopped bouncing and floated through the last mirror, and Conner could see through its eyes. It was in the pool, surrounded by dark, roiling water and shadows.

It tried to chase the shadows, but it couldn't move very

well. It felt like it had taken cold medicine, and everything was slow and sluggish.

Long strands of black shadow snaked out from all through the pool and wrapped around the sigil. It struggled, but the shadows got tighter and tighter, and soon the sigil couldn't move at all. Inside the box, Conner felt like chains had wrapped around his spirit.

Two shadowy forms floated over to the paralyzed sigil and started stroking it. Each time they stroked it, a cold chill ran through Conner. He felt darker and darker and noticed his sigil grew darker as well, turning from dark red to a deep wine color. It continued to darken until it was a shadow too.

Ugly, cruel, dark thoughts rushed into Conner's mind and heart. Things he'd never thought of flooded into his soul like an overflowing sewer. They appalled him—and, deep down, appealed to him. He felt as if someone had poured a sweetly flavored poison inside of him.

He tried to resist what he was thinking and feeling— the images and ideas that formed in his brain. He tried to stop, tried to fight back, but he felt like a baby wrestling a giant.

He saw his family and saw the shadows tormenting them.

And then he did terrible things. Things he had never thought of, things he couldn't have even imagined. And now he had not only imagined and thought them, but he had also done them—awful, evil, ugly things.

Guilt flared inside of him and became searing coals on his raw, bleeding conscience.

Racking sobs shook his body.

He felt a jerk on the box and then the box being pulled

out of the water. He strained and marshaled every bit of self-control he had, forcing himself to stop crying. The bands that held him snapped open. He heard the whirring and clicks as the box opened.

Mr. Stanley opened the door and laughed.

"Not such a hero now, hmmmmckk."

Conner shrugged and concentrated on not looking upset.

Mr. Stanley chuckled and looked at him. "Oh, I see. You're going to be brave. Very good. We could use more like you."

"What do you mean?"

"You're a Darkhand now. One of us. Congratulations."

Mr. Stanley's words shattered Conner's false apathy. Fiery guilt and shame rampaged through Conner's heart and mind as the words sunk in.

*I can't be a Darkhand!* But he remembered the things he had done in the Shadow Box.

Despair jumped out and pummeled him while guilt held him down.

*I'm a Darkhand now.* He started to cry again. Hot, bitter tears burned his cheeks as Mr. Stanley led him back to the lab, where four guards strapped him down on one of the beds.

"Never." He forced himself to say it. But he didn't believe it.

"As you wish. In that case, Lady Nightwing has some special experiments planned for you." He giggled. "But at the moment, she's busy. Don't worry, she'll be free soon."

Conner didn't care anymore. In fact, dying sounded like a good option. He just cried and cried.

Mrs. Grant looked at Lexa and smiled, then spoke in a gentle mother-hen voice. "No, Lexa. It won't hurt."

"What exactly are you going to do to her?" Lexa's mom asked.

"Cathy, Lexa is going to send a bit of her soul out to find Notzange and lead us to Conner," Dr. Timberi said.

"Think of it as if Notzange and Lexa were phones," Veronique explained. "Since Notzange's soul sent Lexa's soul a message, Lexa has her number on speed dial. We're going to have Lexa call her, and we'll trace the call so we can find out where Notzange is. Does that make sense?"

"I guess—as much as any of this does. But a piece of her soul? How dangerous is this?"

"Lexa will be vulnerable to attack, and it is possible her soul could be captured. However, we'll guard her carefully."

"Mom," Lexa said, using her most persuasive tone. "It's the only way to get Conner back."

Mrs. Dell didn't say anything. She just nodded.

Donovan came over to Lexa. "We'll ask you to send your sigil to find Notzange. Because you received her messages, your sigil will be able to find her. Have you ever done a sigil before?"

"Yeah."

"This will be a little different because you'll be linked to your sigil. Your body will be here, relaxed and calm as though you're asleep and having a dream, but your sigil will travel and your mind will follow along. It's a little like how the doctors can put a tube down your throat and look into your stomach—you're sending your sigil out to be your eyes and ears.

"Hortense will monitor you," Donovan said. "Veronique and I will send our sigils along to help with the tracking, and Lee and Miranda Grimaldi will go along for security. We'll be right with you at all times. Lee?"

Lee nodded. "Now, Lexa, honey, once you start poking around that rat hole, you'll be vulnerable as a bald porcupine. If anything happens, just call out, and me and Grimaldi'll be there and as ready to fight as two bucks in the spring."

"Any questions?" Donovan asked.

Lexa shook her head and tried to look brave.

"Lexa, they'll be with your sigil, and we'll be right with you here." Madame Cumberland patted her shoulder.

Hortense stood behind Lexa, then put her fingers on Lexa's temples. "Now, Lexa, open to Light. When you're ready, call up your sigil."

Lexa took a deep breath and held up her hands, but tension and stress shoved Light away and slammed her gateway shut.

She tried again, and this time a tiny, yellow flicker appeared in the air. It faded.

"I'm sorry," she squealed. "It's a way lot of pressure. Everyone's depending on me, and it's stressing me out."

"Try again, Lexa," Madame Cumberland said soothingly. "You can do it."

She did—but she couldn't.

Dr. Timberi's rich voice filled the room with a song from *Beauty and the Beast*, and Lexa joined him. Three measures later, her dolphin jumped out and flipped in the air.

"Well done, Lexa!" Madame Cumberland squeezed her arm.

"Now, Lexa," Hortense said, "imagine a cord running from your mind to your sigil. Nothing can break it." Lexa imagined what Hortense described, and as soon as she did, she could see through her sigil's eyes, like she was looking through a telescope.

"Well done, my dear," Hortense purred. "All right, everyone."

Donovan waved his iPhone and neon green electrical cords snaked out, while Veronique's Bluetooth glowed and shot a series of dashes into the air, followed by a big, light-blue Pac-Man. She smiled at Lexa. "I like classic video games."

Lee's belt buckle seemed to catch fire, sending his rattlesnake slithering through the air with the other sigils. Finally, Miranda Grimaldi did a quick karate move, and a big cat leaped into the air.

"Send your sigil to Notzange, but hold on to the other end of the cord with your mind," Hortense whispered.

Lexa nodded, grabbed her ponytail, and thought directions to her dolphin. The sigils vanished with a rainbow flash.

The dolphin became an extension of Lexa, so she saw through its eyes and was barely conscious of her body anymore. She could tell when the sigils left normal time and space. It—or she—swam through the air in a see-through tunnel of some kind.

It was disorienting, and her body started to feel faint. Back at the cottage, she swayed and staggered, but Dr. Timberi and Madame Cumberland grabbed her hands,

which helped, even though it felt like they—and she—
were a million miles away. She soared between stars in
space and dived between drops of water in the ocean. *This
is dizzily cool!*

Lexa realized that she was always between things—big
things and small things: one minute she swam between
microscopic cells and the next minute she soared between
giant mountains—the scenery around her changed, but
she was always between whatever was there.

Several times she passed bright flashes, heard deep
voices rumble, and saw fiery eyes burning behind flames.
*I wonder if those are cherubim.*

Finally, she pushed through the wall of the tunnel and
came out in a tiny room darker and stinkier than the boys'
locker room in a blackout. The room from her vision.

"Quickly, Lexa!" She wasn't sure if she heard Hortense's
voice with her ears or in her mind. "You haven't much
time. Go outside. Try to see where you are—notice any
landmarks you can find that might give us a clue about
the location."

Moving through the darkness felt like walking
through thick, thigh-deep mud, and the longer she stayed
in the room, the deeper and thicker the mud seemed.
Gooey Darkness slowed her dolphin down, but she managed to push through the walls into a hall with some dim
fluorescent lights. She shoved through another wall, then
another, and finally she found herself outside.

It was bright, and she sensed heavy heat but couldn't
see anything but lots of sand and the big pile of rocks
she'd just come through.

A sudden, sharp tug and icy cold feeling on her tail

distracted her. She tried to move, but something had grabbed her. She twisted and turned but couldn't break free. She flailed in the air and saw that an enormous shadow cobra had grabbed her with its tail. She thrashed around, but it tightened its grip. She tried to scream, but panic squeezed her throat so no sound came out.

She heard a loud rattle, and Lee's rattlesnake appeared, then sprang forward. Sparks flew through the air, and the grip on her tail relaxed.

"Go back, Lexa! Hurry!" Lee's voice shouted.

Her dolphin smacked the air with its tail, and she swam through the air as fast she could. Risking a look over her shoulder, she saw the cobra and the rattlesnake lock their fangs in each other, tails whipping and slashing through the air.

"Lexa, quickly, follow us!" Dr. Timberi's swan appeared in front of her, followed by a rose bush and a ballerina. They surrounded her and nudged her forward. Somehow, Lexa knew she had to go back the way they'd come: through the building hidden in the rocks, and that thought made her want to cry.

"Almost there, Lexa." Mrs. Grant's ballerina leaped through the air next to her. More cobras sprang out of the shadows between the rocks and sand.

One of the cobras jumped at Lexa, but a long, thorny vine shot out of the rose bush and coiled around the snake's body, while another vine wrapped around its mouth.

The ballet dancer spun a graceful pirouette, which turned into a double back flip, then went into a ninja-gymnastics routine as she flipped and jumped all over, delivering sharp kicks at two snakes. The swan performed a complicated dance of its own, flying forward, then pulling back—leading the rest of the shadow snakes away from her.

*Lexa, go now! Go back the way you came,* Dr. Timberi's voice clanged in her thoughts. *You are not trained in sigil combat. It is imperative you get back to the Sanctuary.*

Lexa flipped her tail and dove through the rocks back into the building. The thick darkness made it harder and harder to move—like swimming through rubber cement.

A shadow alligator jumped up and snapped his jaws, missing her by just a few inches. Lexa dodged and rolled away, barely escaping a second attack. She felt herself slowing down, her reactions taking too long. The alligator snapped at her again, and she managed to dodge his teeth, but a second later something smashed into the side of her head. She saw the alligator's tail swing away as everything went blurry, and she fell to the floor. A pack of shadow rats skittered beneath her, baring their ugly little shadow teeth. She got weaker and weaker and felt like she was fading—not just her sigil, but her whole soul. Everything went dark, a curtain falling over her vision. She tried to force herself to swim up higher in the air, but she couldn't. The shadow rats snapped their teeth just below her.

Conner was strapped to a hospital bed. He had stopped crying at some point. Now he drifted along on a sharp current of guilt and shame from the Shadow Box.

Something shook the current and pierced the fog that surrounded his mind and heart. Lexa? It was! Lexa! She was close. But something was wrong. She was fading. Her Light was almost out.

*Whatever.*

He started to sink back into the abyss of Darkness that swirled in his mind and heart.

Lexa. His sister.

Somewhere, deep inside of him, a spark flashed. It was small but strong enough to push away a small bit of the guilty blackness and make him care again. At least about Lexa.

*I need to do something.*

He shook himself out of his stupor and reached out to the Light. It seemed far, far away and felt distant and strange. He couldn't make it work, couldn't connect. But then his necklace got warm again, and Light filled him. It pushed away some of what the Shadow Box had done. He thought of Lexa, and more Light came, pushing a little more of the Darkness back. Trembling with the effort, he managed to call up enough Light to send a sigil to find his sister.

Lexa had almost faded away completely when an enormous red German shepherd exploded through the air, gnashing his teeth and snarling. He clamped his jaws on a shadow-rat and shook it twice, snapping it in half. The rest of the rats scurried away.

*Lexa! Hurry, get out of here!* Lexa heard Conner yell as his dog tackled the alligator and buried his teeth in its neck. The alligator thrashed back and forth, roaring and growling.

*Conner, come back with me.* Lexa's consciousness flickered back.

*I can't Lexa. Just get out of here! Hurry! Tell Mom and Dad I—* His sigil vanished, and his thoughts stopped.

Lexa tried to flip her tail, but she was still going in slow motion and getting slower. She was fading, leaking Light as a real dolphin would leak blood.

Everything went black, and she was
falling,
falling,
falling . . .

Darkness started to swallow her—mind, body, and soul. Then, faraway, a pale, pink spark pierced the darkness. It came closer and grew into a slender, pink unicorn, which bent down and gave her a gentle nudge.

The unicorn sang the words of Lexa's song, and Lexa's brain followed along. The Darkness vanished, and Light rushed through her. She flipped her fins, swished her tail, and shot through the Darkness like a shooting star.

And then the strongest theeling she'd ever had grabbed her and shook her back and forth.

*Go back and get Conner. NOW!*

She turned around.

*Lexa!* Melanie sounded frantic. *Where are you going?*

I've got to help Conner.

Lexa shot back through the air as fast as she could.

## · CHAPTER 32 ·

# LADY NIGHTWING

**A**FTER CONNER SENT HIS SIGIL TO HELP Lexa, it didn't take long for Lady Nightwing and some guards to run into the lab, followed by people in white coats.

"Just can't stop, can you?" Lady Nightwing sneered. "You're making it worse for yourself. Still, I'll say this for you. It's not easy to call up a sigil this soon after the Shadow Box. Practically impossible. You are unusually strong. This will be interesting." She pushed a cart of gleaming silver surgical tools up to the bed. They looked sharp. "No one has studied the real-time effect of pain on an Adept's ability to use the Light." She picked up a scalpel and held it up to the light. "Not yet."

She tugged on the straps that held him to the table "Hold him down. I don't trust the straps—and he'll definitely be thrashing around soon."

The guards pushed Conner down. One guard slapped

his hands on Conner's chest. "He's got something around his neck."

Lady Nightwing pulled the collar out but screamed and dropped it, sucking her fingers. "It's a refraction collar, but something's wrong. It's full of Light." Her eyes narrowed. "So that's how you've been using Light while you've been here. I'll need to study this more carefully. Remove it," she ordered. One of the guards yanked it off and threw it on the floor.

"Just to make sure you don't cause me any more trouble, let me introduce you to a sigil trap." She waved her arms, and a thin pillar of Darkness appeared. It ran from the ceiling to the floor, passing through Conner's chest and pinning him to the bed. Conner felt Darkness pulsing through his body, radiating out from the trap.

"Very useful things, sigil traps. Quite efficient at inhibiting the use of sigils or illuminations. Now, we can begin."

As the scalpel sliced down toward his chest, something inside of Conner woke up. *I don't think so! I'm really getting tired of you, freaking witch.* He thrashed and kicked as hard as he could.

Melanie's sigil paused in the Otherwhere. *Lexa's right,* she thought. She hated herself for hesitating. *We can't leave Conner alone. I'm not sure what we can do. But I have to try.* She galloped ahead, following Lexa out of the Otherwhere into a rank sewer of a room. The Darkness grabbed at her sigil and pulled down on it. Lexa's sigil seemed to know the way, so Melanie tried to ignore the Darkness and follow her.

They floated through a tangle of dark hallways until they came to a heavy-duty door made out of shiny black metal. A keypad on the wall glowed with buttons and switches.

They pushed through the door into a white room. It looked like a lab, full of beeping machines, bottles of chemicals, and wheeled beds with straps. The beds were empty, except one at the far end of the room.

*Conner!*

He was strapped to the bed, thrashing around. Four guards tried to hold him down while three people in white coats rushed around. A narrow column of shiny, sparkling darkness ran from the ceiling down through his chest and straight through to the floor.

"Stupid boy!" Lady Nightwing shrieked as Conner's arm hit her. Her voice reminded Melanie of a wild animal. She dropped a wicked-looking silver scalpel, and it clanged on the floor.

Conner thrashed harder and broke one of the straps on his bed. He pulled an arm free and punched two of the people in white coats, sending them rolling.

The woman shrieked with frustration as the guards tackled his arm and pushed him down again. She pointed at a woman in a white coat. "Inject him!"

"What dosage, Lady Nightwing?" The woman fumbled with a bottle and a syringe.

"Idiot! Who cares about the dosage!"

"But the experiment—"

"Forget the experiment! Use the whole bottle! Kill him. Just hurry!"

✳ ✳ ✳

Two sigils shot forward and crashed into the woman in the white coat. She and the bottle hit the ground at the same time, and the bottle smashed on the rough stone floor.

Next, the sigils charged the four guards holding Conner down. The unicorn and dolphin smacked into the first two guards, who fell down. That startled the other two guards, but they didn't have time to react before they fell too.

With no guards to hold him down, Conner tore through the straps and sat up, bringing his head and whole upper body inside the Dark column. He looked pale and dizzy.

*Lexa, Melanie, don't! It's a trap—*

Melanie sent her sigil into the Darkness to see if she could help him somehow. Lexa followed.

The Darkness around Melanie flashed like black lightning, and her sigil was paralyzed—frozen in midair.

It wasn't just her sigil. Back at Mockingbird Cottage, her body froze too—completely paralyzed. Neither her body nor her sigil could move or even blink. She felt like a rubber band that had been stretched out as far as it could go and then frozen. One end of the rubber band was her sigil and the other end was her body back in the Sanctuary.

Lady Nightwing said some strange words. Melanie felt like someone let go of the body-end of the rubber band. Her body was yanked away from the Sanctuary and flew through the Otherwhere. There was a crashing flash, and her body landed in the lab, reuniting with her sigil.

A second later, Lexa appeared too, and they were both imprisoned inside Dark columns, like Conner.

Lady Nightwing laughed.

"A sigil trap!" She screamed through her laughter. "You really just walked into a sigil trap? Seriously?"

She pulled out a long knife from her robes and walked toward Lexa. Melanie and Lexa raised their hands to send an illumination at her, but nothing happened.

*It doesn't work*, Conner thought. *I think we're on our own.* Melanie noticed that he kept his head down and didn't look at them.

Lady Nightwing lunged at Lexa. Conner jumped off his bed and tackled her. She sprawled across the floor as her knife skipped over the stones.

The door hissed open, and eight big men ran in. Six of them tackled Conner and choked him in a headlock. The other two grabbed Melanie and Lexa.

Lady Nightwing stood up and brushed her robes off. Her eyes smoldered, but her skin looked colder than ice-crusted snow. She started to say something, but then a series of explosions shook the walls and made the lights flicker.

"Take them to the cage. I'll get to them later. Quickly! We're being attacked." She vanished in a stream of foul-smelling smoke.

The guards dragged them out of the lab, through some halls, and into the room with the cage. In the center was Notzange, who was collapsed in a heap on the floor.

The guards unlocked the cage and threw Melanie, Lexa, and Conner inside too. Notzange didn't move or look up, but her eyes flickered open.

"Notzange!" Lexa crawled over next to her. "We're friends! We know Dr. Timberi, Madame Cumberland and Mrs. Grant. I got your sigil the other day, and the

Sodality and the Phalanx are tracking me, and I think they're out there right now."

Another explosion shook the building.

Notzange tried to smile, but she was too weak.

"Please . . . water," she croaked. Conner grabbed a bucket on the other side of the cage and pulled it over. Melanie knelt down and tried to hold Notzange's head up.

When Melanie touched her, a blazing flash of Light banished the darkness. Notzange glowed a rich, deep yellow. She smiled, sat up, and looked at Melanie. "You have a great gift, my dear."

"Me? What?" Melanie blinked. Surprise chased away any rational thoughts. "Excuse me?

"But surely you know, child? You are a remarkable Augmentor."

Conner's and Lexa's confused faces echoed Melanie's thoughts.

Notzange said, "You do not know this? Your own inner strength and virtue augments the Light that others can feel. Has no one told you? Surely someone has noticed that when you are around, their ability to use the Light grows stronger?"

"We're kind of new at this," Melanie replied.

"We'll talk more later. It's time for us to leave this place. Keep touching me, please." Notzange narrowed her eyes, and the links of chain around her wrist exploded. She glared at the bars on the front of the cage. Steam hissed from them, and they dissolved.

"Stay with me, children." Her voice was strong now, a rich mahogany polished by an elegant accent. She looked at Melanie. "And you, please keep hold of me."

An explosion shook the floors, and everything around Melanie melted into smoke, fire, and flying debris. Notzange threw a shield up, so nothing hit them. When the smoke cleared, there was a hole in the wall, and Phalanx members, led by Lee, poured in, doing flips and ninja rolls until they lined both sides of the hall.

A swan appeared in the air. "Lee! Lee!" Melanie had never heard Dr. Timberi sound so worried. Not even the night before *The Hobbit* when no one knew their lines.

"They're fine, Morgan," Lee drawled. "Safer than a—"

A gold comet exploded into the hallway, and Dr. Timberi appeared. He ran up and clamped his arms around his students. Dr. Timberi's shoulders shook, and all he said was, "Oh," while repeating their names over and over.

"Morgan, I hate to break up the reunion, but this party ain't over," Lee drawled. "We got the ball, but it's only halftime, and the other team's gonna push back hard."

"Thank you, Lee." Dr. Timberi broke the embrace. "Quickly, follow me. We need to get away from here. The only way is through the Otherwhere, but we dare not try to enter from this place. The taint of Darkness is too strong. If we open a portal here, the cherubim might mistake us for Darkhands. And, given the high traffic through their realm lately, they're a bit edgier than usual." He smiled. "So, possums, let's run for it."

They ducked through the holes the Phalanx had blown in the walls. As soon as they got out, the brightness overwhelmed Melanie. She hadn't realized just how completely dark it had been in the lair. She savored the sweetness of the sun—even though it was hot.

They ran in a scared-rabbit, zigzaggy path as fast as they could. Explosions crashed and shook around them, and Dr. Timberi paused three or four times to shoot attack illuminations.

When the explosions had been left in the distance, Dr. Timberi stopped. He smiled, and his shoulders dropped. "Safe at last. And, once the Phalanx is finished there, I'm confident that there will be no more attacks for—"

A human-sized cloud of Darkness appeared and slammed into him. He fell down to the ground with a grunt, and Melanie heard a dry, husky laugh. Darkness shimmered in the air, and the Stalker appeared. He laughed again. "Always making a speech, aren't you?" He saw the students and raised his fingers with a snarl.

A golden swan appeared and flapped around his face, distracting him.

"That was your warning," Dr. Timberi wheezed. He was very pale. He pointed his baton at the Stalker with a trembling hand. "Leave us," he said in the soft voice he had when he was angriest.

The Stalker laughed and raised his hands. Dr. Timberi let out a tortured groan, and a golden tiger jumped out of the air and pounced on the Stalker. They rolled into the sand, and Dr. Timberi collapsed again, unconscious.

Melanie looked up and saw a dozen black clouds racing across the horizon toward them.

"Guys," she said, "I think we need to get out of here really fast."

# CHAPTER 33.

# BEHIND THE CURTAIN

CONNER LOOKED AT THE CLOUDS MELANIE had noticed. He mostly felt numb. The Darkness of the Shadow Box had faded a little, but his soul still felt dim and grimy, as if he were no longer swimming in a sewer but still had muck and filth all over. He felt distant and vague, separated from everyone else by a fog of shame and guilt. He had a hard time caring about much of anything. However, his mind told him that being recaptured by Darkhands was not a good thing. "Yeah, good call. They're probably Darkhand versions of the Magi comets. Where do we go?"

"The Otherwhere," Lexa said.

"Are you sure that's a good idea?" Melanie hesitated. "The voices there didn't seem very friendly last time."

"What do you want to deal with, grumpy voices or *those things*?" Lexa pointed to the clouds swirling closer and closer. "Conner, reach into Dr. Timberi's shirt and find the keys around his neck."

"Why me?"

"Because you're a boy, and we're not, so it's less awkward! Hurry! You can be weird about it later."

Conner reached inside the collar of Dr. Timberi's shirt—*Awk-ward!*—and found the chain hanging around his neck. He pulled it out and grabbed the keys. "Which one?"

"I don't know!" Lexa shouted. "Try them all. Hurry!"

Conner found this difficult since he didn't know exactly what he was trying to do. One by one, he held keys up and turned them. Nothing happened. Finally, the third key lit up, and he felt some resistance, like a key in a real lock. The air in front of them shimmered and opened like a curtain, which was good because the black clouds were only about twenty yards away.

Conner's superstrength gift proved useful. He grabbed Dr. Timberi under the arms and carried him through the opening. Lexa and Melanie jumped in after them. Conner tossed the key to Lexa, and she twisted it in the air. Silver curtains flew shut, and the desert disappeared.

Conner looked around. They stood in a strange corridor with four arches: one was gold, one was silver, one was pearl, and the one they'd come through was wood.

As soon as the curtains closed behind them, the gold archway lit up, and a deep rumble filled the space.

"Who is there?" Words floated through the rumble like trees in a flash flood.

"I'm Alexandra Louise Dell." Lexa curtsied. "This is Melanie Stephens, and my brother, Conner Brent Dell. This is Morgan Timberi. He's a member of the Sodality. We seek passage through these domains." Conner had to admit that Lexa actually sounded like she knew what she was saying. *She can talk her way out of anything*, he thought.

They heard another wordless rumbling, and the voice returned. "We recognize Morgan Timberi. But why does he not speak? Have you stolen his key?" "Please." Lexa curtsied again. "We were attacked, and he's hurt. We need to get him back to the Sanctuary.

Blinding, burning, white-hot Light shot out of the arch and roared around each one of them. Every bad, unkind, insensitive, and stupid thing Conner had ever done jumped out of his memory and flashed in his mind. And since he was a thirteen-year-old boy, he had a lot to remember.

Most of all, he remembered the Shadow Box and what he'd done. Him. Not the Stalker. Him. Conner Dell. Mr. Stanley's words echoed in his mind. "You're a Darkhand now." The memories burned like hot coals in his brain, making him feel guilty and dirty. His heart weighed a thousand pounds, and the sorrow and guilt hurt him physically, flaring back up to inferno levels. Meanwhile, the Light burned brighter and hotter until he felt like a roast chicken in the supermarket deli.

Just before he moved past medium-rare, the Light faded and the heaviness inside of him lifted. The voices behind the curtains roared again.

"We know you, Conner Dell. We welcome you back. You have done well. You and your companions may pass through our realm. However, you may not pass into a Sanctuary. You have none of the required keys and only those with keys may go there or take others. That is a law that cannot be broken. Instead, we will allow you to travel to another place within your world, a place of your choosing."

Then, in Conner's mind, he heard another voice. It was the voice he'd heard earlier in the tunnel. *Do not be troubled. What happened in the Shadow Box was not your fault. And it was not real.*

*You know what happened?* Even though he stood in shame, it was a relief that someone—something?—else knew and he wasn't alone.

*Yes. And you must move beyond it. Do not let your memories extend the torment and break your spirit in a way your enemies failed to do.*

Light washed over and through him. The guilt parted enough to let a few rays of peace shine through.

Lexa interrupted the conversation. *Conner, what do the voices mean that they know you and you've done well? You weren't here with us when we came through earlier.*

Conner knew their praise would bug Lexa. He hesitated. *It's a long story.*

*Tell me!*

*Uh, Lexa, can we talk later? Like, maybe after we're not in mortal danger?*

*Fine. Whatever,* Lexa said. *Where should we go?*

*How about the school?* Melanie suggested. *Remember the day the Stalker attacked and the teachers said the school was warded?*

*Okay, that sounds good. Let's go.* Conner sighed, glad to have the subject changed.

"Please, can we go to our school?" Lexa curtsied again.

"Yes," the voice rumbled. "Pass through the arch on

your right and walk down the corridor. When the portion of the Shroud on your right glows, you will know you have reached your destination. Touch nothing except the portion that glows or you will be destroyed."

"Thank you." Lexa curtsied again.

Conner lifted Dr. Timberi over his shoulders and staggered.

*Are you okay, Conner?* Melanie asked.

*Yeah, I think. I'm a little tired. This Light-enhanced strength comes and goes, and he's a pretty big guy.*

Lexa and Melanie went to help, each of them taking a leg.

They walked under the pearl-colored arch on the right and started down a long corridor lined on both sides with silver curtains as far as Conner could see. It was exactly like the corridor that Mr. Stanley's tunnel had cut across.

*Did you guys feel like that Light was going to burn you up?* Melanie asked.

*Yeah,* Lexa thought. *And did you guys, um, remember, like, dumb things you've done?*

*Yes,* Melanie answered.

*Yeah.* Conner felt relieved that it wasn't just him.

*Conner, what were the voices talking about? How do they know you and what have you done well?* Lexa wasn't going to let go of that one. He took a deep breath.

Conner felt his soul clench. *A bunch of stuff happened at the Darkhands' base. I don't want to talk about it.* A patch of curtain on the right started to shimmer and glow, which was good since it distracted Lexa. Melanie stood next to him, which made his soul clench tighter. He felt so dirty next to Melanie.

They walked through the curtains and entered a truly strange place. They hovered on the street by the school, but the world was black-and-white, and they couldn't touch or feel anything, as if they were only halfway in their own dimension. The school was in front of them, completely surrounded by a thick bubble of Light with no obvious way to get inside.

Dr. Timberi groaned something that sounded a little bit like "courtyard."

"Wait! Remember what the teachers said about gates the day the Stalker came? They said he was at the courtyard gate!" Melanie said.

A car turned the corner and drove right through Conner, but he didn't feel anything. He also noticed that Dr. Timberi had become completely weightless, which was helpful.

They floated around the school and came to the courtyard. At the top of the courtyard stairs, a huge fountain of rainbow-colored Light burned brightly in the compass star carved into the concrete. It blocked a small opening in the bubble.

"How do we open it?" Melanie asked.

Lexa waved her arms and yelled, "Open Sesame!"

Nothing happened.

Dr. Timberi groaned again. "Sigil."

Lexa sent her dolphin swimming through. The fountain flashed, then faded, and they floated through the empty opening.

Passing through the gate returned them to the normal world and seemed to help Dr. Timberi. He opened his eyes and smiled. "Well done, dear ones! You have been so brave and resourceful. You'll be exceptional Magi." He pulled himself up onto his feet, then swayed and almost fell. Conner and Lexa grabbed him. "Thank you. I'm so sorry. Could you please help me into the cafeteria? I need some water. And then, if I could just sit down for a few moments . . ."

They walked across the courtyard and into the cafeteria, where they helped Dr. Timberi sit down at the closest table.

"Do you want cold water?" Melanie asked.

"Yes, please. As cold as possible." His voice sounded weak. "I feel rather feverish. I'm sorry to be so much trouble."

They walked into the big freezer to get ice. Since this was a school kitchen, there were no ice trays like people had at home. All they found were a dozens of boxes of frozen, individual pizzas.

"There's a regular fridge up in the faculty lounge. Maybe there's ice up there," Melanie said.

"I'll come with you," Lexa replied.

They ran upstairs, and Conner went back to check on Dr. Timberi.

"The girls went to get some ice. Are you okay?"

"Yes, Conner, thank you," he wheezed. "I didn't expect that blast of Darkness, so I wasn't shielded, and it hit me at close range. Physically I still feel weak, but thankfully, the spiritual and emotional effects are fading. That's where the Darkness affects you the most, you know—the body, to some extent, but mainly the spirit. Terrible, terrible stuff. Like poison in your soul." He grimaced like he'd just chugged rancid Dr. Pepper.

*Yeah, I know a little bit about that,* Conner thought. *Should I tell him? It might be nice to get it off—*

"Tsk, tsk, tsk."

Conner looked up and froze. His heart fell into his stomach and then to his knees, which shook like dashboard bobble-head dolls.

The Stalker stood in the doorway of the cafeteria.

# ·CHAPTER 34·

# FIERY, FLYING PIZZAS

THE STALKER LAUGHED. "YOU LEFT THE gateway wide open. You'd better watch that. You never know what might sneak in." He looked at Conner. "Didn't your mommy ever tell you to shut the door behind you?" His face wrenched into a picture of hatred, and his voice flared into a shriek. "My mommy didn't teach me anything, because she couldn't!" He snarled at Dr. Timberi, and his sharp teeth made him look like a rabid wolf. "She was gone! And my—"

"You'll leave right now." Dr. Timberi's voice cut the Stalker off, his tone sharp. His face looked pale, but his lips and jaw were set. "Leave and do not come back."

The Stalker flexed his fingers, and a shadow knife appeared in them. Rage twisted his face. He slashed down with the knife, slicing a vicious cut in the air. Dr. Timberi flinched and fell backward as a jagged line of blackness opened up where he had been sitting.

He pulled himself up and staggered again, faint and

dizzy. He caught himself on the edge of the table, then flicked his baton. A whiplash of bright Light appeared and snapped back at the Stalker. The lash twisted around the blade of the shadow knife and then crackled. The knife began to glow.

The Stalker yelped and dropped it. He flicked his wrist and a new knife appeared in his hand. He grabbed the blade and threw it at Dr. Timberi. He repeated this until the air was thick with black blades slicing through the air.

Dr. Timberi hummed "Comedy Tonight" and waved his baton back and forth. Each time his baton flicked, one of the knives lit up, glowed, then vanished. The Stalker threw them faster and faster, but Dr. Timberi flicked his baton faster and faster until his whole right arm became a blur.

Dr. Timberi seemed to be keeping up with the Stalker, but his face had gone completely white, and his wheezes competed with his panting, making him sound worse.

He held up his left hand and shoved it out hard. A big jet of Light shot out, like water from a fire hose. The Stalker jumped out of the way as the Light slammed into the spot where he had been standing.

The Stalker did a full ninja-roll and jumped back onto his feet. He shouted strange words, and gusts of wind rushed through the room, whipping his long, greasy hair. A swirl of darkness appeared at his feet, growing bigger and faster each time it rotated. It circled higher and higher around him until he was covered by a swirling tornado of Darkness. Before he completely disappeared, he pointed at Conner and stabbed the air. Dark wisps appeared and twisted around Conner, eating through his skin down into his spirit. Darkness and depression pummeled him, burning like acid on his soul. He couldn't fight back because he didn't want to. He didn't care anymore. Everything from the Shadow Box came back.

Dr. Timberi yelled, and a shimmering golden swan flew at Conner. It tore at the wisps, and Conner felt a flash of pain, like someone pulling a scab off. The depression faded as the dark wisps fell to the floor. The darkness writhed back toward him, but the swan swooped down and tore it to pieces.

"Conner, hide!"

Conner ran into the kitchen to take cover but peeked out of the doorway. *I can't just leave him alone.*

Dr. Timberi blurred into his golden comet. He shot forward and crashed into the tornado, detonating a major boom that sounded like New Year's Eve crashing into the Fourth of July. For a few seconds, the comet and the tornado locked together, spinning and spewing sparks and smoke. Then the tornado broke away and jumped from table to table with the comet right behind it. Each time one of them landed, sparks flew and the air trembled.

The tornado got blurry and then vanished completely. Dr. Timberi reappeared, hunched over and panting. He held his baton out in front of him and looked around the room, moving his head and eyes constantly.

A shadow flickered behind the lunch counter. All the silverware in the cafeteria rattled and clanked, glowing with Darkness. The utensils floated out of their containers and hovered in the air for a fraction of a second. Then they shot toward Dr. Timberi. He waved his baton, and a stack of lunch trays flashed with Light and jumped up to intercept the incoming flatware.

The knives and forks slammed into the trays, blades

and prongs piercing the plastic. The spoons pounded massive dents in the trays before falling to the floor. Each time a new wave of utensils came, the trays moved to block them from Dr. Timberi.

Dr. Timberi's voice got soft and sad. "Please, please. Stop this before it is too late."

Behind the counter, the Stalker's breath rattled in his heaving chest, and he looked gray instead of black. Conner remembered the Stalker's recent wrestling match with the illuminated tiger and hoped he was weak too.

Melanie and Lexa walked in. "We found some bottled water in the—"

The Stalker's head snapped up when he heard the girls. He grinned and muttered something. A huge clanking noise rang out from the kitchen behind Conner. His instincts yelled at him to drop, and he hit the floor as all the sharp kitchen knives shot through his personal airspace. They came so fast that they were nothing more than blurs. They rushed over him, aiming for Melanie and Lexa.

Surprised, Lexa froze for a second, which was all it took for the knives to get over to her and Melanie.

"No!" Dr. Timberi stopped sending bursts of light at the Stalker and turned toward the girls. His hands flew in front of him like he was weaving something. The second— that split second—the knives got to Lexa and Melanie, a glimmer of Light flashed in front of them. The knives hit this shield, bounced off, and fell to the floor.

As soon as they fell down, the knives jumped back up and flew at them again and again. Dr. Timberi kept weaving and reinforcing the Light shield in front of them, but that meant his back was turned to the Stalker.

The Stalker flicked his wrist and sent five shadow knives toward Dr. Timberi. From the corner of his eye, Dr. Timberi saw the knives hurtling toward him. For half of a heartbeat, Lexa thought Dr. Timberi would turn around and fight or protect himself. Instead, Dr. Timberi looked at Lexa and Melanie. He clenched his jaw and stood up a little straighter.

"I love you," he croaked. "I'm sorry."

Lexa heard Conner scream as the knives buried themselves in Dr. Timberi's back with five sickening thuds.

Dr. Timberi's eyes bulged. He gasped and shuddered, then fell to the ground. Since they were shadow knives, there was no blood. The wounds were inside, not outside. There was nothing Lexa could do.

From the place the knives hit him, dark veins snaked out all over Dr. Timberi's body, like drops of black dye in a glass of water.

The Stalker cackled, and the knives attacking Lexa and Melanie clattered to the ground. The Stalker was gray and bent. His breath sounded like a dying rattlesnake, but his laugh sparkled with evil.

"Now, for you three." He staggered toward Conner, but his steps were slow, and he stumbled. He managed to stand up but had to support himself on the tables. He flicked his wrist, and a long knife appeared in his hand—a real one, not the shadow kind. He stroked the knife and smiled like he had just heard a joke. Black fire flared in front of all the doors and windows. "Please don't leave. I don't want this to end too soon." He laughed and tossed the knife to his left hand and flicked his wrist again. Another knife appeared.

As the Stalker staggered toward him, Conner ran and stood in front of Melanie. He grabbed a large soup ladle that had flown out and tossed some salad tongs and a wire whisk to Lexa and Melanie.

The Stalker laughed. "Whisks and spoons will not help you very much. You'll die slowly, of course. You've made my life difficult lately." He smirked at Dr. Timberi's body. "And he will hear your screams while the Darkness eats his soul."

Lexa raised her hands to send a sigil, but the Stalker yelled something, and a black column wrapped around her. Similar columns appeared around Conner and Melanie.

"Sigil traps are great fun, aren't they?" The Stalker snickered. "So simple, but effective. Did anyone tell you about them? How about sigil torture? Now that is a fascinating game."

On the floor, Dr. Timberi groaned. His skin, hair, and clothes were completely gray and covered with wriggling, black streaks. His face looked like a mosh pit of fright, pain, and despair.

He screamed, his face blazing with agony. He gritted his teeth, trembling and perspiring.

Then, in a croaky, quivering voice, he started singing "Some Enchanted Evening," squeezing it out of his throat like the last bit of toothpaste in a tube.

*What is he doing?* Conner shouted in his head. *Darkness is eating his soul, the Stalker's about to turn us into sushi, and he's singing songs from* South Pacific.

*South Pacific!* The words echoed in Lexa's brain, igniting a flash of memory.

It all rushed back. Her dream. The lunchroom. Dr. Timberi singing. And what was she doing?

And then she knew. The memory of her dream sparked a powerful theeling. Lexa laughed out loud because she knew what to do. It seemed crazy, but it couldn't hurt. And she knew it would work.

She jumped up on a table and started to reach out with the Light.

*Lexa, we can't do Lightcraft in these traps,* Melanie said.

*I think they only stop the Light* inside *of us,* Lexa thought, *not the Light* around *us. Anyway, I have a theeling.*

Lexa imagined the frozen pizzas in the freezer. She closed her eyes, trying to ignore the fact that the Stalker was getting closer and closer. She reached out and connected each pizza to the Light, picturing them glowing brighter and brighter until they burst into brilliant Light, as if they were on fire. The big freezer door slammed open, and glowing, individual frozen pizzas shot out, whirling through the air like rabid UFOs.

She found she could guide the pizzas by waving the wire whisk. She yelled and sent the first batch of glowing pizzas at the Stalker, who threw up his arms to protect himself. The pizzas fell to the ground.

Conner and Melanie ran over and jumped on the table, waving their kitchen tools too.

*Good thinking, Lex! We're using the pizzas as a delivery system for Light.* Melanie laughed in her thoughts.

Conner tried to push past the Darkness and let another ray of Light in through the clouds, but the Shadow Box memories and the guilt they brought were like a chain that locked his gateway. He concentrated as hard as he could. Still nothing.

His soul strained to feel the Light. He felt himself get dizzy and faint, feeling hot and feverish.

*Are you okay?* Melanie grabbed his hand.

The chains around his gateway shattered. Warmth and Light rushed through him like a flash flood.

"Pepperoni or cheese?" Conner waved his ladle, and more pizzas burst out. The Stalker managed to stop some of them with blasts of Darkness, but Conner flicked the ladle, and they came even faster. Melanie clicked her salad tongs, and another batch flew out of the freezer.

It was like an explosion in a radioactive pizza factory as fiery pizzas flew, slamming bursts of Light into the Stalker while he shrieked and snarled.

*I don't think he likes pizza*, Conner thought.

The combined Light from a few dozen more pizzas brought the Stalker to his knees. More pizzas crashed into him, and he collapsed. The sigil traps vanished, and the flames by the exits disappeared.

Lexa ran over to Dr. Timberi, followed by Conner and Melanie. Dr. Timberi had stopped singing, and his body shook and shuddered.

"Guys, what do we do?" Lexa shouted.

Melanie pointed her salad tongs in the air, and her pink unicorn appeared.

"Go get Madame Cumberland and Mrs. Grant—all of them," she yelled. "Hurry!"

The unicorn galloped a few yards and disappeared.

"I have an idea," Melanie said.

"What?" Conner asked.

"What if we shoot our sigils at him? They hurt Darkhands, so maybe they'll help him."

"Or kill him," Lexa hesitated. "He looks pretty bad."

"If we don't do something, he's dead anyway," Conner said.

They called up the Light, and their sigils leaped at Dr. Timberi, hitting him at the same time with a blinding flash. He screamed and shook. Then his body went silent and still.

Conner was sure they had killed him. He started to cry, and Melanie joined him.

"Guys, look!" Lexa squeaked.

A glow appeared in Dr. Timberi's chest and spread outward, pushing the darkness away.

"It's working!" Melanie yelled.

They wiped their tears away and shot sigils at Dr. Timberi like machine guns. Each sigil pushed more of the gray away, and he grew brighter and brighter.

Dr. Timberi's eyes fluttered, and a shadow of a smile flickered on his face. "Well done, dear ones," he whispered. "You saved my life and probably my soul." His eyelids fell down again, and he slipped back into unconsciousness. But this time he looked peaceful.

Everyone let out big sighs of relief. But the relief didn't last too long.

Conner looked over his shoulder.

*Oh, freak, you guys! The Stalker's gone.*

Madame Cumberland and Mrs. Grant arrived and called a special Magi doctor, who took Dr. Timberi to the Sanctuary to rest. They said his soul had been badly wounded, and his body had been through a lot of stress, but they promised he'd recover. Eventually.

The Phalanx beat the Darkhands at the desert lab and freed all the victims, which was good, but Lady Nightwing got away, which was bad. And no one was sure what happened to the Stalker, which was also bad. Spring break ended, which was bad. Life was normal again, which was good. Mostly. It also seemed a little boring.

The night after school started again, Lexa and Conner went to Melanie's to study for a pre-algebra test—a much simpler task now that they could hear each other's thoughts.

"I'm not doing this during the test, though," Melanie said. "Only to help you study. During the test, I'm blocking my thoughts off. So you figure the surface area of a trapezoid by . . . "

After a few hours of working on the surface area of different shapes, Lexa's brain had stopped. Even Melanie couldn't stand it anymore, and she looked up from Mr. Duffy's endless diagrams. "Oh, I forgot! I saw Madame Cumberland today after school. She said Dr. Timberi would be back in the next week or two."

Conner cheered. "I don't like the choir sub very much."

"And we're supposed to have auditions for the fall play pretty soon. Plus, there's a lot of things I still want to know," Lexa added.

"Yeah," Conner said. "Have you noticed how every time we ask a question lately, everyone's too busy? At least when he was busy, Dr. Timberi tried to answer our questions."

"Hey, let's make a list of questions to ask when he's back." Melanie pulled out some paper. "How could Madi see Conner shoot a sigil at the Blacks?"

"I want to know how come we didn't see a miasma around the Blacks," Lexa added.

"How did Pilaf see me break Geoffrey's lacrosse stick?" Conner jumped in.

"What were the Darkhands going to do with all those kids who Kindled?" Melanie made another note.

"Mel, if you don't want to join the Magi, why do you care about this?" Lexa asked.

"Well . . ." Melanie paused. "I'm still not completely sure. But I guess if there are bad people out there, I want to protect myself."

"Yeah, Melanie!" Conner gave her a high five. Lexa noticed it lasted longer than most high fives.

Melanie saw Lexa staring and pulled her hand away, blushing darker than her hair. "Okay." She looked down at her paper. "Other questions?"

Suddenly, Lexa had a question for both Conner and Melanie, but that could wait. "I want to know more about what Adumbrators do," she said. "And when we start our training again."

Conner looked thoughtful, like he had a really deep question. "I want to know . . . how long it took to clean up all those pizzas."

Hn 5-6 13
V.G.

# About the Author

**B**RADEN BELL LIVES WITH HIS FAMILY ON a quiet, wooded lot in Tennessee. He teaches music and theatre at a small private school and enjoys reading, gardening, and long walks with the dog. Braden loves interacting with readers. You can contact him at www.bradenbell.com.